The First Paget Brothe

A Scandal in Scarborough

Stuart Fortey

Copyright © 2016 Stuart Fortey

All rights reserved, including the right to reproduce this book, or portions thereof, in any form. No part of this text may be reproduced, transmitted, downloaded, decompiled, reverse engineered or stored in any form, or introduced into any information storage and retrieval system in any form or by any means, whether electronic or mechanical, without the express written permission of the author.

ISBN: 978-1-326-50971-2

PublishNation
www.publishnation.co.uk

for Sue,
with whom I have spent
many crime-free hours
in Scarborough

1

Arrival

The whole business began with a short article in the *Scarborough Daily Post* that caught my brother's attention:

> MAN VANISHES
> There was a strange occurrence at the People's
> Palace and Aquarium yesterday afternoon, when
> a young man apparently vanished into thin air.
> His fiancée, Miss Julia Meakins, said Thomas
> White went into the attraction in order to have
> his photograph taken and never came out again.
> A search was made, but to no avail. 'He would
> never leave me,' said Miss Meakins. 'I can't
> think what can have happened.'

After reading it out, Walter flung the newspaper down beside his chair, wrapped his arms tightly round his knees and, rocking slowly, stared out at the sea beyond the open window.

'A simple enough matter,' I remarked.

'No,' he said, 'there's more to this than meets the eye.'

'Surely not. The fellow thought better of the engagement and did a bunk.'

'His fiancée is of a different opinion.'

'Or he fell into a tank of exotic fish and was eaten alive. Very rapidly.'

'Sidney, you are not taking this seriously enough.'

'I'm taking it as seriously as it deserves. It's a piece of tittle-tattle in a local paper.'

Walter gave me a pitying look. 'I will consider the matter and come up with a solution.'

And he continued to stare out to sea, waiting for a thought to strike him like a lightning bolt, propelling him into action.

Behind us, Bert, the valet allocated to us by the hotel – an invisibly efficient presence with a fashionably pointed beard – was finishing hanging up our clothes. 'Do the gentlemen require anything else?'

'Not for the moment, thank you,' I said.

'You have only to ring.' He pointed to the bell-pull, and silently withdrew.

Walter stared out to sea, oblivious.

I am still not sure whether I did the right thing in taking my brother to Scarborough that time. The scene with the newspaper that I have just described occurred in room 185 of the Grand Hotel, on the morning of Tuesday the 4th of July, 1899. A day like any other, yet one which had to begin in room 185 – such was Walter's opinion, at any rate; an opinion so vehemently held that I felt it wise not to resist. The previous occupants of the room, although surprised at being asked to vacate it late the previous night, were more than happy to do so once a generous financial inducement had been agreed; so on that matter my conscience was at rest. They were, however, offered no explanation for their removal other than that it was my brother's whim. Had they known the true reason they might have thought him not fanciful but mad.

The true reason was this. Our guidebook to Scarborough and District, which Walter had read from cover to cover during our long train journey from King's Cross, informed us that the Grand Hotel, opened in 1867, is a representation in yellow brick of a calendar year. There are twelve storeys for the twelve months. Spread over these storeys are 365 rooms. The seasons are echoed in the four towers at the corners of the building, and the fifty-two chimneys remind us of how many weeks there are in a year.

Damn its numbers! Nothing could have been more certain of

focusing Walter's mathematical mind and pulling him under its spell. As soon as he had devoured these details, he determined on staying at the Grand, even though we were expected elsewhere. Nothing could shake his resolve. And with the logic that so often ruled him, he insisted on taking the room which would correspond to our first full day in Scarborough: floor seven, number 185, since the 4th of July is the 185th day of the year. Thank God we did not arrive on February the 28th in a leap year, for I do not know what the outcome might have been!

He was staring out to sea. The sea – that is why I brought him to Scarborough; to let the sea work its soothing magic on his restless soul. Many was the time we had sat together elsewhere, high on some rocky outcrop, gazing at the endless motion of the waves rising and falling quite independently of man's control. In that acknowledgment of powerlessness we had often found solace, a release from striving. Yet now it was precisely that powerlessness which was worrying me, for Walter's mind was beginning to toss about again, this way and that, like flotsam on a changing tide.

My hope – a vain one, it seemed – was that leaving London behind would also be to leave behind all the confusions and obsessions that had originated there. Many of Walter's friends and acquaintances had commented on his looks in a way that had clearly disturbed him. He had believed them when they claimed he was someone else entirely. And he had begun to act in an unpredictable manner. Only a few weeks before, he had been taken into custody after causing a public disturbance in a most spectacular fashion. He had erupted into a society wedding being held in Chelsea Old Church, insisting that the ceremony be halted on the grounds that the bride was already married to a man sitting in a pew just a few feet behind her. That this man had turned out to be her husband-to-be's valet made matters considerably more distressing. Walter had been saved from the wrath of the wedding guests by the timely intervention of a passing policeman, and saved from the full force of the law by my promise to keep him under strict surveillance so as to prevent any recurrence of his extravagant behaviour.

Fortunately, I believe I was the only person to recognize the source of his delusion: a magazine story in which the fictional bride was indeed discovered to be at risk of bigamy. As this story was one in which I had had a hand, I felt I was just as much to blame as Walter, if not more so.

He shifted his position, closed his eyes. He dropped his arms onto his chest and stretched out his legs. Turning to the next sheet of my sketch pad, I laid down in pencil the lines of his willowy yet angular figure. Walter remained in this relaxed pose for several minutes, just long enough for me to capture its essentials, before he jumped up, his eyes gleaming with excitement.

'We must visit Miss Meakins,' he said.

'Who?'

'The fiancée of the vanished man.'

With a practised swing of the arm he snatched up his deerstalker from the table, jammed it on his head and strode towards the door and the corridor beyond. If you did not know any better you would have sworn that walking towards the lift on floor seven of the Scarborough Grand was none other than Sherlock Holmes!

I was out of room 185 in a flash, but only in time to catch a glimpse of deerstalker before the lift doors clicked shut. I raced down the stairs, taking them two at a time, to the sixth floor, then down again to the fifth, then again and ever downwards. I was not going quickly enough. I would lose sight of him. But the lift must have descended very slowly, for I arrived in the foyer just as the doors were opening to let out a top-hatted gentleman in a morning suit. I nodded to him and waited for Walter to emerge. He did not. I peered into the lift, saw it was empty and immediately cursed my stupidity. He had done this so often before, and still I allowed myself to be duped.

I hurried to the library, into which I had seen the man in the top hat disappear. The room, lined from floor to ceiling with bookcases, had a cluster of armchairs at its centre. In one of these, Walter sat reading a book. The top hat was perched on one of his knees.

I said: 'The Master of Disguise.'

He acknowledged the compliment with a nod.

'You must learn to look properly,' he said. 'Had you looked at the face and not the clothes, you would have recognized me.'

'How did you do it?'

He jumped up, snapped his book to and laid it on his chair.

'I was able to fool you by the simple method of depositing a bag containing this morning suit and top hat in the lift some time before. Now I'd better retrieve my tweed suit and deerstalker from the same place before someone takes a fancy to it. I won't be long.'

While he was gone I glanced through the book he had chosen, and was dismayed to discover it was a cheap novel of the most sensational kind.

He returned remarkably quickly. 'A good book that,' he said.

'Really?' I tossed it aside.

'Let's be going.'

'Where to?'

'I've told you. To interview Miss Meakins.'

'Yes, but where will you find her?'

'Here.'

'Here?'

'When I read out the newspaper article I omitted a crucial piece of information – the lady's place of residence. Fortunately for us, she is staying in this hotel. Come, let's find her room.'

He shot out of the library as if his life depended on it and made his way to the reception desk. By the time I had caught up with him he was already receiving the information he required in exchange for a few well-chosen coins.

'Miss Meakins is staying in room 281,' said the receptionist, 'together with another lady, somewhat older.'

'Chaperoned to death, eh?' said Walter.

'I wouldn't know, sir.'

'Come, Sidney. Room 281 – so 10th floor, I think.'

Walter sprinted for the lift. I took the stairs, one at a time.

Before I go any further I must lay bare the details of how and why my brother, from time to time, becomes — to all intents and purposes — the Great Detective. There are probably by now very few readers who are not aware of at least some of the facts, although many distortions of them have put my involvement in a more unfavourable light than it deserves. Here, then, is the truth of the matter. If, in the final analysis, I am thought to be blameworthy, I accept the blame; but I believe I am entitled to a fair hearing, in proper consideration of all the evidence.

My brother and I are artists. Or, to be precise, we are illustrators and occasional painters, our chief occupation being the drawing of pictures for magazines and books. You may have seen Walter's illustrations in a recent edition of *Robinson Crusoe*, while my paintings in last year's Royal Academy exhibition received a good deal of favourable comment. I am three years older than Walter, and so have that little bit more experience. He denies the importance of this, claiming that his innate artistry gives his work the advantage over mine. Be that as it may, my income, compared to his, is a fair indication of my success.

No doubt you will have heard of the Sherlock Holmes stories. Indeed, you may have read some in the *Strand* magazine. If so, the initials SP, visible at the edge of each illustration, will have caught your eye. They are my initials, on my illustrations. SP for Sidney Paget. In other words, I am responsible for the physical appearance of Sherlock Holmes. I like to think, and the publishers certainly think, that my work has contributed to the popularity of each issue. So far, twenty-four episodes of *The Adventures of Sherlock Holmes*, all with my illustrations, have appeared in the *Strand*, and although Mr Doyle claims to have lost interest in his detective, and has expressed his lack of interest by sending him to his death at the Reichenbach Falls, yet I am confident that popular demand will soon bring forth further adventures which have hitherto lain dusty and forgotten at the bottom of Dr Watson's battered dispatch-box.

It is the unusual manner in which I came to be commissioned as illustrator that is the nub of the matter. Mr George Newnes, publisher of the *Strand*, has informed me that it happened in the following way. The editor, Mr Herbert Greenhough Smith, had been impressed by Walter's pictures of the Gordon Relief Expedition that had appeared in the *Illustrated London News*, and had decided to offer him the Sherlock Holmes commission. Unfortunately, he could not recall my brother's Christian name. A colleague of his, having heard of me but not of Walter, insisted that the name Sidney should be the one to precede Paget. Accordingly, Mr Smith's letter was sent to me, I supplied two sample drawings as requested, and the job was mine. Only some months later did the editor discover his error, by which time he was more than satisfied with my contributions. Quite properly he did not inform my brother, but the same propriety was not observed by a member of staff in the *Strand* offices who promptly told Walter of the mix-up. He was livid. He berated me for stealing his commission. Naturally I pleaded ignorance, and pointed out that I could hardly stop illustrating the stories now that they had begun to be published. In any case, I did not regard myself as at fault. I had been offered the work and was carrying it out to my employer's satisfaction. What must have galled Walter in particular, although he did not say so, was that he was posing as model for my drawings of Sherlock Holmes. This must have seemed like deliberate mockery. His face will be forever associated in the public imagination with the face of Sherlock Holmes – whereas I, not he, will be credited with its creation.

One of my skills is the ability to produce a very faithful likeness of the person sitting for me. The unfortunate result, in my brother's case, is that he is frequently recognized wherever he goes. Only the other week, a chamber concert at which we arrived late was brought to a halt as one spectator after another rose to exclaim: 'Look! There's Sherlock Holmes!' And if he wears his deerstalker – the very one he wore when modelling for the *Strand* illustrations – why, then pandemonium ensues as crowds gather round him, shouting and jostling.

Why he should wear his deerstalker and thereby encourage

public disorder he has never properly explained. I used to be almost certain that he does it out of a wish to embarrass me, but he swears that is not so. I have requested him not to wear it when in crowded places. He seems to ignore me. I feel helpless, and a little humiliated.

2

Two Ladies

Walter rapped on the door to room 281. After a moment it opened to reveal a large middle-aged woman in a green dress, wearing a string of pearls and a scowl.

'Yes?'

Walter said: 'We would like a word with Miss Julia Meakins.'

'She is not in.' The door began to close. Walter kept it open with his foot.

'We have come to help her trace her missing fiancé.'

'She is not in, I tell you.'

From somewhere behind her came a voice: 'It's all right, Euphemia. I will speak to the gentleman.'

'There are two of them.'

'Then I will speak to them both.'

Euphemia sniffed and pulled the door wide open. We entered a spacious and well-appointed room, clearly the sitting room of a suite, with high, heavily curtained windows. The blinds had been lowered on this remarkably sunny day, so that the features of the young lady reclining on the couch were at first indistinct.

'Do you bring me good news?' She wiped her eyes with a lace-edged handkerchief.

'We bring no news at all,' Walter said, 'but we hope to do so after we have heard your account of what took place.'

'I'm afraid there's nothing much to tell.'

'It will all be of value.'

Once my eyes had grown accustomed to the shadows I could see that Miss Meakins was a singularly good-looking woman, well dressed and well aware of her attractions and their effect. Meeting her in other circumstances I might have called her coquettish. She fixed her attention on Walter.

'Are you from the police?' Walter shook his head. She stared at him intently. 'You look rather familiar.' This although he had, of course, removed his deerstalker upon entering the room.

He said: 'I am a private detective.'

'I see. And this gentleman ...?' She glanced in my direction.

'Is my brother Sidney. Rather a slow fellow, but sometimes quite useful.'

I inclined my head but said nothing. I had learned from bitter experience that thwarting Walter in word or deed while he was in Great Detective mode served only to prolong the agony.

'We have informed the police,' Miss Meakins said, 'but they don't appear to be making much progress.'

Euphemia spoke. 'You had better go, sir. We are not enough in funds to engage the services of a private detective.'

'My services,' Walter said, 'are free. The case interests me.'

'You are generous,' Miss Meakins said.

Euphemia would not be persuaded. 'They are just like the rest of them.'

'The rest of whom?' I asked.

'Men always come running,' Euphemia said, 'as soon as they read that one's fiancé has disappeared.'

'Then,' said Walter, 'you are fortunate that yours has not.'

Euphemia was about to huff and puff in reply when Miss Meakins laughed gaily. 'Gentlemen, this is my maiden aunt Euphemia Fitt. She is not in the market for marriage.' Miss Fitt gravitated to the far end of the room, where she sank onto a chair and into silence.

'Now,' said Miss Meakins, 'I will tell you all I can, Mr ...?'

'Paget. Walter Paget.'

'Mr Paget, in the hope that you will be able to shed some light where others have failed.' She twisted her handkerchief round her hand and began.

'Yesterday was a lovely day, just like today. In the morning

Thomas – that is, Mr White, my fiancé – and I went for a walk along the seafront on South Bay. We passed below the hotel and came to the People's Palace and Aquarium. I don't know if you know it?'

Here Walter's thorough perusal of the travel guide and his excellent memory came to his aid. 'I know *of* it. "Twelve hours continuous entertainment for sixpence" is its slogan, I believe.'

'That's right. Although why anyone would want to be indoors for twelve hours in Scarborough is a mystery to me.'

'To me too. But please carry on.'

'Thomas said he wanted to have his photograph taken, so that I should be able to look at it and see him, so to speak, in his absence. There is a photographer's inside the People's Palace.'

'McNair's,' Walter said, recalling the advertisement at the back of the guide.

'Yes, I think that's the name. I wanted to go in with Thomas, but he wouldn't hear of it. Too expensive, he said, and anyway he wanted the photograph to be a surprise. So I waited at the entrance. He said he wouldn't be long. I waited for a full hour, getting more and more worried, then I paid my sixpence and went in, looking about me all the time to see if I could spot him anywhere. But I couldn't.'

'Was it very busy inside?'

'No, not at all. The fine weather kept most people out of doors.'

'Then what did you do?'

'I found the photographer's and inquired whether a Thomas White had recently been photographed. I was told that he had, and that the photograph would be ready for collection in the morning.'

'That's today.'

'Yes. But as to Thomas's whereabouts the photographer had no idea. So I went out and found a policeman and told him what had happened. He organized a search of the Palace, but Thomas was nowhere.'

At this reminder of her fiancé's disappearance Miss Meakins sobbed into her handkerchief.

Walter said: 'Be assured, I will do all I can to find your fiancé. Do you have a photograph of him?'

'No. That was why he was having one taken.'

'Quite. I thank you for your time, Miss Meakins.' He bowed, then nodded to Miss Fitt. 'Madam.'

'Thank you,' I said.

'All the thanks will be on my side,' said Miss Meakins, 'if you can find Thomas.'

'I have hopes,' was Walter's parting shot. 'High hopes.'

Outside, in the corridor, I turned on him. 'What do you mean, you have hopes? You have no idea where the man is, and no means of finding out. You're giving the lady *false* hopes, that's what you're doing.'

'As usual, Sidney, you are underestimating me. I work by intuition. I find it is the best way.'

'Your intuition has brought you nothing but trouble. I don't want to have to rescue you again.'

'I can look after myself.'

'It's the general public I'm looking after, not you. It wouldn't be so bad if you'd ever solved a case.'

'There's always a first time.'

'Not necessarily.'

'I'm shocked, but not surprised, by how little faith you have in your younger brother.'

We had been walking down the stairs, without thinking where we were going, and had come to the entrance of the hotel, emerging into the brightness of St Nicholas Cliff Garden, which dazzled us momentarily with its beds of bright red geraniums.

'I really think it's time we visited Lancelot,' I said. 'He's been expecting us since yesterday.'

'Send him another note to say we've been further delayed.'

'But we haven't been further delayed.'

'I have. I'm working on a case.'

'I'm going to see him,' I said. 'Now.'

'And I'm going to make inquiries at the People's Palace and Aquarium.'

'You're wasting your time. The man's done a bunk.'

'We'll see who's right,' said Walter, smiling and putting on his deerstalker. He walked off towards the steps down to the seafront, and within a matter of seconds he was surrounded by inquisitive passers-by buzzing like bees round a honey pot. And the buzzing all sounded the same: 'Sherlock', it went. 'Sherlock, Sherlock, Sherlock Holmes.'

I walked in the opposite direction, through the centre of Scarborough, without going down to the beach, until I came to St Mary's church in the east of the town. It was here, in Church Stairs Street – one of the steep, narrow lanes that descend from the castle – that my friend and fellow artist Lancelot Pemberlow had his residence. His ambition, which was great where his art was concerned, was content in matters of lodging with the rental of a terrace cottage, consisting of an upstairs studio with living quarters below.

He had never exhibited in Scarborough, considering its citizens philistines. Every so often he would take the train to London, one of his smaller paintings under his arm, and there berate the gallery owners for their poor taste before returning, painting unsold. I was never certain what he lived on, for even when I got to know him in London many years previously he very rarely exhibited and even more rarely made an attempt to sell any of his works. The art journals considered him far too avant-garde, which delighted him.

He greeted me with the flamboyance I had come to expect of him. He was wearing a smock and a battered straw hat, and had at least a month's growth of beard, somehow coloured red. I might not have recognized him, were it not for his delicate hands and sonorous voice, which could belong to nobody else.

'Where's Walter?' Lancelot asked.

'Off on a case,' I said.

'Wasn't this little trip supposed to cure him of all that?'

'I can only do my best.'

He led the way up the stairs to a sort of small lumber-room.

'I do apologize for not turning up yesterday,' I said. 'I hope I haven't put you to too much trouble.'

'None at all.' He gestured to a mattress in the corner. 'That's your bed, if and when you do decide to take up my offer of accommodation.'

Silently vowing to remain at the Grand after all, I changed the subject. 'Why the beard?' I asked. He had always been clean-shaven, like Walter and myself, in all the years I had known him. 'Are you following a trend?'

'Following a trend?' said Lancelot. 'You know me better than that, I think. No, I'm trying to get inside the mind of Vincent Van Gogh.'

'The Dutch fellow who went mad and shot himself?'

'That's right.'

'*His* paintings didn't sell either.'

'No, poor man. He was much misunderstood. But what use of colour! Masterly! I want to look at the world through his eyes for a while.'

'Then go to the South of France like he did. That's where you'll get your colour.'

'Oh no, I like it too much here in Scarborough. But it's amazing how much it helps to dress and look like him.'

'And has it helped your sense of colour?'

'Come and see.' He took me into the adjoining studio, a space filled with natural light that streamed in through glass panes in the roof.

'My God!' I couldn't help saying. At the far end of the studio, taking up all available space, stood a vast canvas bursting with Mediterranean vibrancy. Thick swirls of vermilion, cadmium orange and yellow ochre created a sun-blasted expanse of sand, while in the foreground a starkly solid mass of grey represented a platform of rock or an altar.

'It's not finished, of course,' Lancelot said. 'I've still got to put in two figures.'

'What's the subject?'

'Endymion and Selene.'

'Ah yes, let me see. The moon goddess Selene falls in love with Endymion and condemns him to everlasting sleep and eternal youth so she may kiss him every night.'

'Well done! There's nothing like a good classical education.'

'So I presume Endymion lies on the flat rock there while Selene hovers, moon-like, above him.'

'Almost. I'm giving it a modern twist, though.'

'I wouldn't expect anything less from a genuine Pemberlow.'

Lancelot let out one of his rich chuckles. 'I must get hold of a couple of models soon, while the muse is still on me. Although it might prove a bit tricky here in Scarborough.'

'Why?'

'They'll have to pose naked. A bit too much for some of the citizens.' He eyed me strangely. 'I don't suppose you'd fancy –'

'You suppose right,' I said. 'I'm far too busy with Walter.'

'You're probably a touch too old anyway.'

This deserved a critical riposte. 'But you've got it all wrong. Endymion slept in a cave. And Selene came at night.'

'My Endymion sleeps outdoors in the blazing sun. Artistic licence.'

'Artistic licentiousness, more like.'

Lancelot roared and slapped me on the back. 'Talking of which, Sidney, let's have a drink.' He moved to a small cabinet, on which there stood a decanter and several glasses.

Not wishing to be impolite, yet eager to get back and discover if Walter had created any mayhem in my absence, I allowed Lancelot to pour me a small glass of port on the understanding that one glass was my limit. We might spend a whole evening drinking when in London (if my wife Edith was visiting her cousin), but now that I had paid my respects to Lancelot I did not want to leave my brother to his own devices for longer than could be avoided. I told Lancelot as much.

'I understand perfectly, my dear fellow. Black sheep of the family and all that.'

'Not quite,' I said, sipping my port. 'In fact, I'm not sure how far Walter might be playing a trick on me.'

'How do you mean, a trick?'

'I don't know whether he is deliberately playing at being Sherlock Holmes or whether what happened with the *Strand* commission has caused some sort of mental disturbance in him.'

'Is he aware of what he's doing?'

'Oh yes. He says he gets carried away and can't stop himself. But that doesn't really decide it one way or the other.'

Lancelot closed his eyes, drank some port and sighed. 'What did the poet say? Great wits to madness nearly are allied.'

'I don't know about great wits,' I said, finding his quotation remarkably unhelpful. 'I suppose as long as Walter doesn't become embroiled in investigating a real crime, thereby putting himself and others in danger, there's no harm. The trouble is that he sees crimes in everyday occurrences and is being continually set off like some hare. And I have to sweep up after him.'

'Perhaps he *is* getting his own back for the Sherlock Holmes illustrations.'

'I don't know.' My gaze drifted back to the half-finished *Endymion and Selene*. 'Is it a commission?' I asked.

'What do you think?'

'Do you at least have a buyer in prospect?'

'No. All done for my own pleasure.'

'Then what do you live on?'

'Look behind you.'

I turned and, for the first time since I had entered the studio, found myself facing the wall half-hidden by the open door, which Lancelot now closed. Supported on an easel was a large oil painting with perhaps a hundred figures crowded into it. The style was conventional; one might even have said old-fashioned.

'Did you do this?'

'I am doing it, yes,' said Lancelot. 'It's not finished either.'

'It's nothing like a Pemberlow.'

'No, it's a Parker.'

'A Parker?'

'My pseudonym when I'm turning out stuff like this to keep the pot boiling. It would ruin my reputation as an avant-garde artist if it got out that it was I who had painted it. I trust I can rely upon your discretion.'

'Of course,' I said. 'What does it represent?'

'Well, the building at the back is the Spa –'

'I can see that.'

'And the gent in the centre there with the pointed beard and funny hat is Prince Rupert of Denmark. Last year he was the guest of the Earl of Londesborough at his home in the Crescent and visited the Spa with his wife, Princess Sophia, who's next to him.'

'So he's commissioned this portrait?'

'Oh no. I shall probably donate it to the Town Hall when it's finished.'

'Then how on earth do you make money from it?'

'By selling faces.'

'What?'

'The people crowding round the Prince – look at their faces.'

I did. 'Well, some of them have got faces,' I said, 'but others have just a bare patch of canvas where their face should be.'

'Exactly. Those with faces have paid me a fairly handsome sum for the privilege of appearing in the picture next to royalty, even royalty of the foreign kind. Those without faces are still for sale.'

'You mean people pay you money, come and sit for you –'

'No, no. A colleague of mine, a photographer, takes a picture of them and I work from that.'

'Who is this photographer? Or does he too have a reputation to maintain?'

'His name is McNair. He has a studio in the People's Palace.'

'Yes, I've heard of him.'

'Then, if you're interested – I mean if you want to be immortalized in this picture – you only have to visit him and –'

This was too much. Reminding Lancelot of my duty of care to my brother, I took my leave and hastened back to the Grand.

On the way I stopped at a little shop and bought half a dozen picture postcards. I had promised Edith I would write every few days to let her know how Walter and I were spending our holiday. Already I had decided what to tell her: 'weather sunny', 'having a wonderful time', 'wish you were here'. These would cover all eventualities as well as a multitude of sins.

3

An Impostor

In room 185 I found Walter standing immobile at the window, staring seawards again. He had not reacted when I entered, but that meant nothing, or rather it could have meant one of several things: enjoyment of perfect serenity, endurance of inner turmoil, or immersion in the Slough of Despond.

'Well,' I said, 'how did you get on at the People's Palace and Aquarium?'

He did not change his position or show by any gesture that he had heard me, let alone understood what I had said. I repeated my question. After a while he turned and looked at me from under heavy lids as though waking from a deep sleep.

'The People's what?' he asked.

'The People's Palace. You were going to make inquiries.'

'Oh, that,' he said in tones of the deepest misery. 'The case is over. There is no case. There never was a case.'

'What did you find out from the photographer?'

'Nothing. Absolutely nothing. That is, I found out that Thomas White, Miss Meakins's fiancé, had his photograph taken and didn't come back to collect it.'

'Why should he bother, if he's done a runner?'

'Why indeed?' Walter reached inside his jacket and brought out a photograph. 'He's a shifty-looking blighter, don't you think?'

I took the photograph from him. On the back the name Thomas White was scribbled in pencil. On the other side a grinning young man with dark hair and moustache and bright eyes challenged me to return his gaze. He looked a dubious fellow indeed.

I asked: 'Where did you get this?'

'From McNair, the photographer, of course.'
'But why didn't the police take it from him?'
'Because, as I had rightly reasoned, Mr McNair had told them the session had failed for technical reasons and that no photograph of Mr White was available.'
'Why should he do that?'
'So he could deliver the photograph to any relative or acquaintance or anyone at all who would be willing to pay good money for it. That person happened to be me. But there is not even the scent of a clue as to Mr White's whereabouts, and no reason to believe a crime has been committed, and therefore ...'

I resisted the temptation to gloat. Throwing himself down on his bed, Walter proceeded to stare at the ceiling.

'Shall I throw this away?' I asked.
'What?'
'The photograph.'
'Good heavens, no. I shall make a present of it to Miss Meakins. She may like to have it as a reminder of happy times.'
'Or of the rogue who deserted her.'
'Let us see which.' Walter sprang up from the bed, snatched the photograph from my hand and marched from the room. I followed.

Although I was relieved by his apparent determination to abandon his hunt for Mr White, I was nevertheless worried that his interest might have been directed into a different, but equally intense, channel. I have mentioned the occasion when Walter interrupted a marriage ceremony. It transpired that he was motivated to do so, or so he claimed, by a sudden burning passion he had felt for the bride, whom he had first set eyes on only a few minutes before. Now, in the Grand Hotel in Scarborough, I was fearful lest the charms of Miss Julia Meakins had had a similar effect on him, and now that there was no fiancé to stand in his way ...

The words of Miss Fitt echoed in my ears as I stumbled after Walter: 'Men always come running when one's fiancé has disappeared.'

Miss Fitt opened the door to us with the bad grace to which she had already subjected us. 'Oh,' she said, 'it's you again.'

'Do you have any news?' cried Miss Meakins. 'Please come in.'

We entered. The lady was walking up and down. Walter immediately took hold of her hand. 'I fear you have been crying,' he said, at which she burst into a tearful confession. 'I cannot help myself. I love Thomas so much. Have you found him?'

In response, Walter looked at the floor. Miss Meakins withdrew her hand and resumed her lamentation. I felt something needed to be said, so I said it. 'Your fiancé seems to have vanished of his own free will.'

'No!' Her voice was steely.

I persevered. 'There is no evidence of kidnap or any other crime having been committed.'

My explanations were met with silence. Walter held out the photograph. 'This is the picture he wanted you to have.' She took it, dried her tears with the handkerchief Mitt Fitt had slipped her, and studied the intended token of love, now become a reminder of what might have been.

'What's this?' she cried. 'This is not Thomas.'

'Not your fiancé?' Walter was immediately by her side. 'But it must be. Look – on the other side – his name.'

'Yes, his name. But the man in the photograph is not Thomas. He looks very much like him – Thomas also has swept-back hair and a moustache, and I'd swear that was his tie, but Thomas is blond and would never grin like that.'

'Ha! I knew there was more to this case than meets the eye. With your permission, Miss Meakins.' Walter took the photograph from her and put it in his inside pocket.

'Call me Julia, please.'

'Julia ...,' he began, before becoming lost for words. He soon recovered. 'I will find your fiancé. I swear I will.'

'Thank you, Mr Paget. You are very kind.'

'You are very stupid,' I said, as soon as Miss Fitt had closed the door behind us. 'You still have no proof that any crime has taken place. For all you know, Mr McNair got a couple of photographs mixed up. Perhaps Thomas White's picture is in a drawer in his studio with this other chap's name on it.'

'Oh no,' said Walter. 'You'll see. There are dark deeds here. Dark deeds, dark deeds.' And he continued to repeat the words all the way back to room 185.

We sent down for a couple of seltzers, and a few minutes later Bert brought them in on a tray. By that time I had already begun to have words with Walter.

'Why can't you leave this business alone? We're supposed to be in Scarborough to relax.'

'My dear Sidney, I was about to drop the case, but this latest development is sensational.'

'A muddle at the photographer's, that's all.'

'Impossible.' Sitting with legs crossed, Walter sipped contentedly at his seltzer.

'Can't you stop being Sherlock Holmes?' I said.

'I'm not Sherlock Holmes.'

'You're acting like him.'

'I haven't become him simply because you draw me as him.'

I ignored the gibe and continued with the sketch I had just started: Sherlock Holmes relaxing with a glass of something. The more of these off-the-cuff sketches I could do, the less I would need to bother my brother with the formal modelling sessions which annoyed him so much.

Walter continued: 'I find my mind is excited by enigmas and puzzles which I then want to solve. I can't help it. When the investigative urge is on me there really is nothing else I can do.'

'Then why do you wear that deerstalker, if not to be provocative?'

He smiled. 'Because I think it suits me.'

By now I was getting rather rattled. 'And how are you going to hunt for Mr White when you don't even have a picture of him?'

'We have this picture,' he said, patting his breast, 'which is very like him. But I shall pay another visit to the photographer, Mr McNair. Perhaps he may be able to recall some details about the missing man.'

'I'll come with you,' I said. 'We'll find there's been a mix-up, you mark my words.'

'Ha!' With this childish cry of derision, which Walter had been using far too often for my liking, he sprang to his feet and led the way.

You go down the steps beside the Spa footbridge, and just across the road is the low roof of the People's Palace and Aquarium. It looks far too squat for an attraction that boasts it can accommodate 5,000 visitors at any one time, until you realize it is built underground, with extensive rooms and corridors offering entertainments of many kinds, not only those of an aquatic nature.

It is a different world: a flickering, shadowy world, lit by thousands of gas jets. Everything has been done to provide as great a contrast to everyday Scarborough as possible. You might think yourself in a rajah's palace or a Hindu temple. Everywhere there are pillars and arches, elaborately decorated in the Indian style with colourful, patterned tiles. There are tiles on the floor too, except where Turkey carpets have been laid down.

As you enter the Palace you pass down a wide staircase into a vast dining room, then through a reading room amply supplied with books and newspapers, and on along corridors flanked with fish tanks, until you come to an alligator pond, an aviary, a fernery, a monkey house, a concert hall, a Japanese theatre and innumerable booths and stalls offering services such as phrenology, chiromancy, photography and letter-writing. The *pièce de résistance* is the world's largest tank, holding 75,000 gallons of water. Captain Webb, the celebrated Channel swimmer, once spent sixty hours in the tank – so a plaque informed us – though when Walter and I were there the tank was occupied by two rather bored-looking sharks.

We found Mr McNair standing outside his booth in his shirtsleeves. He was a large man, built on the curved lines of a barrel, with a thick belt to hold in the staves, so to speak, and a short, stout pair of legs to support them. He was shifting from one foot to the other, looking as bored as the sharks. Business was evidently anything but brisk. It was another warm and sunny day, and the visitors to Scarborough had chosen wisely.

His face lit up as we approached, then just as quickly went out again. 'It's you,' he said.

'It is,' Walter said. 'And I'm delighted to meet you again, Mr McNair. May I introduce you to my brother Sidney.'

'How do you do,' I said.

Mr McNair tipped his bowler with all the effort required to flick away a fly.

Walter brought out the photograph of 'Thomas White'. This had an effect. Mr McNair sprang into life as though 3,000 volts had been sent through him by Victor Frankenstein.

'I don't do refunds.'

'I don't want one,' said Walter. 'What I would like is a little more information.'

'Would you?' said Mr McNair, leaving a long pause meant to be filled, as it *was* filled, by Walter's extracting a coin from his pocket and pressing it into the photographer's hand. The venality of the lower classes never ceases to amaze me.

'How can I be of assistance?' Mr McNair had become cooperation itself.

'There appears to have been a mix-up,' Walter said. 'This is not a photograph of Mr White after all.'

Mr McNair's face hardened. 'I don't do mix-ups.'

'Perhaps just this once –'

'Give me that.' He snatched the photograph from Walter, flipped it over and handed it back. 'That's him all right. Thomas White.'

I was not prepared to give up. 'You don't think that perhaps you have another photograph waiting to be collected that –'

'I don't have any waiting to be collected. And I don't do mistakes,' he said.

Walter said: 'Can you tell us anything about the man in the photograph?'

'Only that's what he looked like. Now, if you gentlemen will excuse me, I've work to do.' He disappeared into his booth, eager to set about his non-existent labours.

'There we are then,' said Walter. 'I told you there had been no mix-up.'

'You did. But how did you know?'

'The tie.'

'What do you mean, the tie?'

'If you recall, Miss Meakins said that although the man in the photograph was not her fiancé, she was sure the tie was his. Therefore ...'

Walter left the sentence for me to complete. This was another trick of his that he had started to inflict on me.

'Therefore,' I said, 'someone must have taken his tie, put it on and pretended to be him.'

'Exactly. We'll make a detective of you yet, Sidney.'

'I don't want to be –'

But Walter had moved away, and was striding rapidly down the corridors and back, darting here and there between the stalls and the fish tanks.

'There are goodness knows how many doors here,' he said as he returned.

'I suppose there have to be,' I said. 'For all the people who work here to come and go through.'

'Or for Mr White to be bundled through.'

'Do you think he's been kidnapped?'

'Or killed.'

'Why on earth do you think that?' I said.

'If he's alive, or at least free to go where he chooses, why is someone else pretending to be him?'

'I've no idea. But why would anyone want to kill or kidnap him?'

'That, my dear Sidney, is what we must find out.'

'Do we really need to know?' I said, but I knew the answer already, and it came as sure and as swift as the truest arrow.

'Of course we do. This case is becoming extremely interesting.'

4

Mr Legard

Whether his initial burst of enthusiasm had run its course, or whether the absence of solid clues was making itself felt, Walter began the next day in a subdued mood. We rose late, went down together to the dining room and ate a leisurely breakfast, over which I made various proposals, based on a perusal of our guidebook the evening before, as to how we might spend the day in a relaxing manner. We might stroll to Clarence Gardens and listen to the band, or saunter along the beach, or climb up to the castle …

'You decide,' said Walter, pouring himself half a cup of coffee. 'I don't care one way or another.'

'Well, in that case,' I said, 'I'll choose something to lift your spirits. We'll go up the Revolving Tower on North Cliff.'

Of course, Walter had also read about it in the guidebook. 'I'd rather not,' he said. 'It's just a tower that revolves.'

'The sea views are supposed to be really special. From a height of 135 feet.'

He spread marmalade onto a roll and corrected me: '155 feet. The sea looks the same from any height.'

'At any rate, let's go out and stroll about a bit. The good weather's holding up.'

'I'm not,' said Walter. He took a tiny bite out of his roll and dropped the rest of it onto his plate. I finished my kippers, drained my teacup, wiped my mouth on my serviette and stood up, ready to face the world. Walter heaved himself up with a sigh and followed me into the foyer, down the steps and out into St Nicholas Cliff. He must have been feeling particularly low, for he left his deerstalker where it was, in his pocket.

We descended with the cliff tramway to Foreshore Road, turned right and strolled in the company of other holidaymakers along the edge of South Sands with its serried ranks of bathing machines. Very soon the crowd thickened, as more and more people, keen to display their finest going-out clothes, joined the general toing and froing in front of the Spa.

We stood for a while and watched, as a photographer set up his tripod by the sea wall in anticipation of passing custom. Along the promenade there passed a parade of fashions: gentlemen in boaters mostly, but also sporting the occasional homburg and bowler; gentlemen in light-coloured slacks and close-cut blazers, some tapping the cobbles here and there with their canes as they walked; ladies in tight-waisted outfits of satin or cotton, wearing splendid hats decorated with lace or bows or artificial flowers; and children in sailor suits or little dresses and bonnets wandering, apparently lost, gripping their buckets and spades. Many of the promenaders would walk to one extremity of the Spa building then turn and walk back the way they had come, as far as the other extremity, where they would turn and repeat the procedure again and again. It is certainly a way of getting yourself noticed.

'Look,' I said, giving Walter a nudge. 'There's our Miss Meakins and her lovely aunt.' The two ladies were gliding towards us, Japanese parasols held high above their heads. Miss Meakins was wearing a dazzling white dress which hugged her slim frame, setting off a ruby necklace. I could not help but think what a fine specimen of womanhood she was. Beside her, Miss Fitt, somewhat more corpulent, could not hope to compete, and had made do with a simple blouse and skirt in light shades of blue.

'No doubt Miss Meakins is walking about looking for her fiancé,' said Walter.

I said: 'More likely she's forgotten about him and she's after a new fancy man.'

'Don't be cynical.'

'Look how she's dressed. Making the most of her charms, I'd say.'

'She doesn't have to go around wearing black. Not yet anyway.'

As the Misses Meakins and Fitt passed by they noticed us and

Miss Meakins politely inclined her head in our direction. We reciprocated. As soon as they were out of earshot I said: 'Why are you defending her? For all we know about her she might have been lying when she said it wasn't her fiancé in the photograph.'

'Why should she do that?' said Walter.

'Perhaps she's annoyed he's given her the boot and wants to get him into trouble.'

'Ha!' said Walter, and we fell silent, watching the two ladies turn and promenade back towards us. Suddenly, without a word, Walter shot off away from them. I followed as he turned under the Spa footbridge and up past the People's Palace and Aquarium.

'What's wrong?' I said.

'Nothing, except the sheer tedium of watching society parade about watching itself. In any case, I couldn't see anybody who remotely resembled Thomas White.'

'So *you're* looking for him! But you think he's been killed or kidnapped.'

'One never knows for certain,' he said, turning his back on me as if offended. 'But there –'

I followed his gaze, which was trained on a finely dressed gentleman in morning coat, top hat and gaudy yellow checked waistcoat who was coming down the other side of the road towards the Rotunda. Walter strode across to meet him. What happened next was rather odd. The gentleman raised his hat, smiled at Walter, made a slight bow, then – as if a switch had been thrown – replaced his hat, turned and walked as quickly as he could back the way he had come. My brother's reaction was lightning-fast, and in two seconds he had the man by the arm. I hurried over.

'Unhand me!' the gentleman said.

'What do you think, Sidney?' Walter took out the photograph from his inside pocket. 'Thomas White or not Thomas White?'

I looked at the photograph – which, of course, was not a photograph of Thomas White but of someone pretending to be him – then at the features of the man struggling in Walter's grip, then at the photograph, then at the man ... I could not deny there was a certain similarity with regard to bone structure, eyes and mouth, but the gentleman before me had thick mutton-chop whiskers (and no moustache), grey streaked hair and a distinctive wart above his lip – none of which features was possessed by Mr White's impostor. Whether they were possessed by Mr White himself was impossible to say.

I began: 'I don't think –'

'I do,' said Walter. 'Fetch a policeman.'

'You are impudent, sir!' said his captive.

'Fetch a policeman!'

Knowing from experience that Walter would only relinquish an idea once its inaccuracy had been proved, I dashed back to the Spa Promenade in search of a passing constable. I was in luck. I quickly explained the situation to him, and he accompanied me at a run to the scene of the incident.

Walter had released the man in the yellow checked waistcoat, who was now calmly awaiting our arrival, a piece of paper in his hand. 'My good man,' he said, addressing the policeman, 'this rogue has laid hold of me and detained me, for what reason I know not.'

Walter said: 'For this reason,' and thrust the photograph under the constable's nose. 'This man is the missing man Thomas White. The resemblance is obvious.'

I shuddered as I struggled to imagine how I would explain the details of the case to one who was not familiar with them, but I was in luck again. The police constable I had come across happened to be the same police constable who had assisted Miss Meakins at the time of her fiancé's disappearance in the People's Palace and Aquarium. Consequently, he was able to jump, so to speak, into the thick of it. He looked at the photograph, then at the bewhiskered and top-hatted gentleman.

'This is all nonsense,' the gentleman said. 'My name is Arthur Legard. I am a guest of Lord Londesborough and staying at Londesborough Lodge. This is my invitation.' He held out the piece of paper. The policeman took it, glanced at it and handed it to me. I looked at it and handed it to Walter.

'A forgery!' he cried.

The policeman retrieved the invitation and returned it to Mr Legard. 'I think,' he said to Walter, 'you ought to be moving along.'

'You are failing in your duty, constable,' Walter said.

'Perhaps I'm failing in my duty by not arresting you, certainly. Now move along.'

'Thank you,' said Mr Legard.

'My pleasure, sir.' The policeman tipped his helmet and waited as the gentleman removed himself from Walter's vicinity and walked away up the hill.

'Come on,' I said to Walter, taking him by the arm. He looked crushed, as though all the world were against him. 'Let's go back.' And we moved off towards the Spa.

A wave of sympathy for my brother swept over me. I could only guess at the desperation that had driven him to accost Mr Legard – the desperation to find Thomas White and to demonstrate thereby his natural intelligence. Unfortunately, the result of striving unsuccessfully to reach a goal can so often be, as it is with Walter, a steep descent into a depressive mood. The thought did flit across my mind that he was trying to make me look ridiculous with his antics, but I really am not as cynical as Walter would have me. The truth was that he had become unhealthily obsessed with the 'case'.

'I'm sure that was Thomas White,' he said. 'Did you see how he turned away as soon as he recognized me?'

'I did. But Thomas White has never seen you, he doesn't know who you are, so he can't have recognized you.'

'No. That's right.' His mood took another dive. 'Then why did he turn away?'

I had no answer. Indeed there were several questions to which I had no answer, including who was the man in the photograph taken at McNair's and what had happened to Thomas White? I steered Walter back to the sea front.

'Where is she?' he said, once we had arrived outside the Spa.

I did not need to ask the question, but I did: 'Who?'

'Miss Meakins, of course.' He spoke in a tortured voice that might have belonged to a knight returning to his lady without the dragon's head.

I scrutinized the milling mass of promenaders. Miss Fitt was still parading back and forth with a smile fixed somewhat painfully on her face. Her companion was no longer at her side.

'There she is,' Walter said. 'Talking to that man by the lamp post.'

The man was sporting a boater instead of a battered straw hat, but he still had his red beard. Miss Meakins was twirling her parasol and laughing.

'Could *he* be Thomas White?' Walter asked, half in hope and half in anguish.

'No,' I said. 'That's Lancelot. Surely you recognize him.'

'Not when he looks like that, I don't. Why has he got all that hair on his face?'

I explained about Van Gogh. What I could not explain was why Lancelot was conversing with Miss Meakins. Were they acquainted? Why, after all, should they not be? Miss Meakins was only visiting Scarborough, it was true, but perhaps they had met during a previous visit. Then again, Lancelot might have simply decided, in that way that certain artists have, to exchange a few words with a pretty passer-by. Miss Meakins inclined her head and moved on. Lancelot smiled and made his way towards the South Cliff tramway that would take him back up to the Esplanade. It seemed to have been an innocuous encounter.

'There's something fishy there,' Walter said.

'Why?'

'Her fiancé's disappeared and she's laughing.'

'Let her laugh. Let her enjoy life.'

'She was despondent yesterday. Prostrate.'

'She may still be. Deep down.'

'There's something not right anyhow.'

We directed our steps northwards, away from the crowd beside the Spa and towards the harbour, the castle and the wide, peaceful bay beyond. We had not gone far when we heard a high squawking voice and soon we came on a group of people, mainly children, gathered around a Punch and Judy booth. The story was well underway. The baby was being thrown back and forth between Punch and Judy until, once Judy had left, Punch threw it out of the booth completely. The crowd howled disapproval. Judy returned and, learning of Punch's negligence, sent for the policeman. Punch took up his slapstick and beat the policeman about the head. Walter's laughter rang out so loud that the children turned to look at him. Almost instinctively, I imagine, he whipped out his deerstalker and crammed it on his head.

I dragged him away.

On returning from our walk, which after the Punch and Judy embarrassment was mercifully free of incident, we found the Misses Meakins and Fitt taking tea in the Grand. In reply to Walter's inquiry Miss Meakins said they would be delighted if we would join them, and we seated ourselves at their table. Miss Fitt seemed somewhat less than delighted, and so, I must confess, was I. I had been hoping the whole missing fiancé business would start to wither on the vine. I attempted to keep the conversation on the straight and narrow.

'I trust you enjoyed your walk,' I said.

'Indeed we did,' said Miss Meakins. 'I trust you enjoyed yours.'

Before I could reply, Walter butted in. 'I am still looking for Mr White,' he said. 'All endeavours are being made.'

'You are most kind.'

I felt I had to inject a little reality into the situation. 'Although it's quite likely that he has been kidnapped or even done away with.'

Walter snapped: 'Sidney!', and Miss Meakins burst into tears.

I said: 'It's only what you said yourself.'

'The truth never hurt anyone' – this from Miss Fitt, to whom I was beginning to warm. A simple soul, full of common sense. Her words seemed to have an effect on her niece, who stopped snivelling almost at once.

A silence set in, during which tea was drunk and cakes were eaten. Then, in order to satisfy my curiosity, I asked Miss Meakins: 'How long have you known Lancelot?'

'Lancelot?'

'Yes.'

'You mean King Arthur's knight?'

'No, I mean Lancelot Pemberlow, the local artist.'

There was a short pause before she said: 'I don't know anyone of that name.'

'You were talking to him this morning,' I said. 'Outside the Spa.'

'Was I?'

'Fellow with a beard and a boater.'

'Oh, that gentleman. Yes. I didn't know his name.'

'You'd do well,' Miss Fitt said, 'not to know it.'

'Please don't interfere, aunt. I'm quite capable of looking after myself.'

Her aunt snorted.

Walter said: 'Are you able to tell us, Miss Meakins, what you discussed with Mr Pemberlow?'

'I am afraid it is confidential.'

'I understand.'

Walter may have understood, but I did not. Why should he be helping this young woman look for her fiancé if she was not prepared to take him fully into her confidence? Then again, her conversation with Lancelot probably had nothing whatsoever to do with her fiancé, dead or alive. Walter pursued another line of inquiry.

'How long was Mr White staying in Scarborough for?'

'A fortnight,' said Miss Meakins, 'like ourselves.'

'And whereabouts was he staying?' he asked.

Miss Meakins looked down at her teacup, and I thought at first she had not heard the question. But then she raised her head abruptly and fixed her eyes on Walter. 'I've no idea.'

Miss Fitt said: 'Nonsense. He was staying here. In the Grand.'

'Aunt!'

'It ought never to have been allowed.' And Miss Fitt took a resolute bite out of her Eccles cake, as if to imply that there was nothing more to be said on the matter.

Miss Meakins had taken refuge once more in the contemplation of her teacup. After a while she spoke: 'His room was not on the same floor as mine, naturally.'

'Naturally,' I said.

'In fact, I've no idea whereabouts in the hotel he was staying.'

I glanced at Miss Fitt. Her eyes were open as wide as they would go.

5

A Corpse

'Well?' I said, as soon as Walter had come back into our room and closed the door behind him.

'According to the receptionist, there hasn't been a Mr White staying here recently.'

'Then Miss Meakins is lying.'

'Possibly. But in the circumstances I wouldn't expect Mr White to stay here under his own name, would you? In such close proximity to his fiancée.'

'I suppose not.'

'I got a glimpse of the register. Mr White was probably in room 320.'

'How do you know?'

'That room was taken by a Mr Smith. The imagination of the ordinary man is rather limited. You or I might choose a name such as Fortescue or Robertson, but –'

'Yes, yes,' I broke in, 'so what do you propose to do?'

'I think you mean what do *we* propose to do, Sidney. I can't carry on without your assistance.' He gave me one of those helpless-younger-brother looks that he has been giving me, on and off, all his life. He knew I could not resist. This time, however, I tried as hard as I could to do so – only to realize that I too had got sucked into the 'case'. Everything in my nature told me there would be straightforward explanations for the minor mysteries which we had uncovered, but Walter's enthusiasm was infectious and I could do nothing but go along with it, for the time being at least.

'Very well,' I said. 'What do you want me to do?'

'Distract the receptionist in some way.'

'Why?'

'So I can borrow the key to room 320 from the board behind him.'

'What do you expect to find in room 320? Thomas White's body?'

'Who knows? Come along. No time like the present.'

He opened the door and waved me through into the corridor.

I said, 'How am I supposed to distract him?'

'I leave that to your fertile imagination.'

We went down in the lift. During that brief descent I worked out what I would do.

The receptionist bestowed his formal smile on us. Walter dropped back a little as I approached the reception desk and put my plan into action.

I had remembered that in one of the early Sherlock Holmes stories (which I had been asked to illustrate) Holmes fell to the ground, feigning injury, in order to gain entrance to some house or other – for who would not rush to help a suffering fellow human and bring him inside? My situation was very different, and I was not disguised as a clergyman as Holmes was, but the principle was the same.

I opened my mouth as if to speak to the receptionist, then collapsed on the floor in what I hoped looked like a fainting fit. I think it did, because he dashed round the desk and helped me up into a sitting position. He asked if I was all right, and upon my reply that perhaps the heat was to blame but that a glass of water would cure things, he nodded and disappeared. The next moment, Walter was bending over me.

'Very good, Sidney. I hope you didn't hurt yourself. It was most convincing.'

'I do feel somewhat numb in my nether regions,' I said, much to Walter's amusement.

The receptionist returned. The glass of water miraculously revived me, and amid a profusion of thanks and expressions of concern Walter and I slipped back into the lift.

'Eleventh floor,' Walter said, holding up the key.

Room 320 was musty and dingy. It was located on the sunny side of the hotel, but the curtains were closed so that only a fraction of light filtered in. The usual items of furniture were present: bed, wardrobe, dressing table, chair, bedside table – all unremarkable as far as I could see.

Walter had made straight for the bed. He knelt down and felt underneath it. After a moment he pulled out a small brown suitcase, which he flung on the bed. He opened it. It was empty.

'No Mr Smith here,' Walter said. Emblazoned in gold inside the lid in a somewhat flowery script were the initials TW.

He shot open the drawers of the dressing table, and flicked them shut again.

'What about the wardrobe?' I suggested.

There was a long mirror fixed to the outside of the wardrobe door, and Walter swung sideways and into himself as he opened it. Inside was a suspended row of suits, jackets and trousers. Shirts, underwear, socks and ties were carefully stowed on shelves down the left-hand side.

Walter was rifling through the hanging garments. 'Rather a lot of clothes here for one man,' he said.

'Some men are as vain as women when it comes to fashion.' He seemed not to hear my remark, which was understandable considering his own excessive devotion to matters sartorial. He carried on searching through the wardrobe.

'Aha!' He pulled out a waistcoat on a hanger. 'Where,' he said, 'have we seen this before?'

I hesitated.

'Mr Legard,' Walter said. 'The man I seized hold of this morning.'

'It certainly looks similar.' The waistcoat was bright yellow and bore a large check design.

'It's exactly the same. My artist's eye doesn't mistake things like that.'

'You forget that I too have an artist's eye,' I said. 'And I would only go so far as to say it *might* be the same one.' The truth was, I did not want to inflame my brother's excitement. It was the same waistcoat all right. Unless, that is, two men in a small area of Scarborough had identical waistcoats made from the same unusual cloth. Not beyond the bounds of reason, but not a possibility I could honestly entertain.

Walter said: 'Things are getting a trifle complicated, don't you think?'

'On the contrary,' I said, 'that waistcoat simplifies things. If it's the same one, it shows that Thomas White was dressed up as Mr Legard.'

'It shows nothing of the kind, Sidney. You fail, as usual, to grasp some important facts.'

He did not enlighten me – at least not straight away. He never does. It is his little way of proving that his intelligence is at least a match for mine. All it proves, of course, is that he lacks confidence in his own deductions, or that he delights in annoying me.

Walter replaced the waistcoat on the rail and closed the wardrobe door. Then he subjected the room to a rapid but thorough search, during which he looked behind the curtains and on top of the wardrobe. 'There's nothing else here of any interest,' he said. 'Let's get the key back to where it belongs.'

I could not very well pretend to faint again. In my confused mind I turned over possible courses of action as we went down in the lift. Just before the doors opened on the ground floor inspiration struck. I would ask a question about a book in the library, thereby enticing the receptionist away from his desk. That should do it.

And indeed it did.

The next morning found us sauntering along the beach, indulging at last in a little seaside recuperation. After breakfast I had asked our valet, Bert, if he knew of any pleasant walks in the vicinity, and he had unhesitatingly recommended a walk along the coast. This sounded like just the thing, so we changed into our most casual outfits and set off. At Scalby Mills, which is at the northernmost tip of North Bay, we took a beer each at a table outside the refreshment room before continuing along the cliff-top path that begins at that point.

The path rises and dips, dodging behind hedges of fragrant gorse before boldly skirting the cliff edge once more. We walked at a stroll, looking about us, observing and naming as much of nature as we felt competent to name: a lapwing swooping over the fields to our left, a peacock butterfly resting, opening and closing its wings, a clump of celandine ... We ate our lunch, which we had bought at the refreshment room, sitting on a rock overlooking a wide cove. Puffins and gannets stood in niches in the cliff face opposite like so many medieval saints ranged on the west front of a cathedral. They too were eating, and feeding their young. Walter and I sat in silence. I felt a deep peace, which I had not known since we had come to Scarborough, fill my soul. I stared at the sea, and the sea began to work its magic.

Then Walter spoke. Evidently his thoughts had been elsewhere. 'The clothes,' he said.

'What?'

'The clothes in the wardrobe in room 320.'

'Oh, those clothes.'

'Including the yellow checked waistcoat of our friend Mr Legard. They can't belong to Thomas White.'

'So you said. Why not?'

He waved away my question impatiently. 'I'm still thinking.'

While he thought I returned my attention to the sea, waiting for its gentle undulations to soothe my mind. I had had more than enough of men dressed in someone else's clothes, or men dressed in their own clothes but not being who we thought they might be, or having clothes that could not be their own, or ... My mind was a whirl of clothes and men's faces, some bearded, some moustachioed, some clean-shaven; some with whiskers, some with warts.

'What does it all mean?' I asked.

'Do you mean life? Or this particular case?'

'I think this case is enough to be going on with.'

There – I too had now called it a case. For how could I deny there was something suspicious and possibly criminal going on? This meant that my duty was now to keep an eye on Walter's bull-at-a-gate investigative style and to minimise any potentially damaging effects it might have on innocent bystanders. In other words, I had no option but to investigate the case myself and thereby anticipate my brother's every next move.

Walter stood up. When engaged in intense concentration he becomes restless, as if his thoughts were plaguing him like midges. Now he began to pace back and forth along the cliff top as he summed up for my benefit what we had seen and heard over the past few days.

'The facts are as follows. A certain Thomas White, who was staying at the Grand Hotel, has disappeared. So, either he has disappeared of his own accord or he has been kidnapped or he has been killed. Do you agree with me so far?'

There was the danger – as there always is with Walter when he is in one of his Sherlock Holmes moods – that this was a trick question, designed to make me look foolish as he explained how the summary he had given could not possibly square with the truth. Nevertheless I felt fairly confident as I agreed with him.

'Good. The next fact we know is that someone looking very much like him had his photograph taken, while claiming to be Mr White.'

'That's right.'

'Which strongly suggests that Mr White did not vanish of his own accord and that he was indeed subjected to some sort of foul play.'

'I suppose so,' I said. 'But surely it's also possible that he willingly disappeared and is, for whatever reason, participating in some bizarre plot, which I don't understand, in which someone has dressed up like him.'

'Excellent, Sidney. Never discount the bizarre.'

'In which case, Mr Legard was not Thomas White but was Mr Legard, or someone calling himself Mr Legard, pretending to be

Thomas White dressed up as Mr Legard. Wait a minute – does that make sense?'

'Perfectly.'

'The problem is we don't know if Thomas White is party to his own disappearance or not. So we don't know if he's roaming free, held against his will, or dead.'

'No.'

'He could have lost his memory,' I suggested.

'If so, I think he would have turned up by now – either seeking help at a police station or found wandering the streets in a confused state of mind.'

Walter sighed, whereupon the birds flying to and from the cliff set up a fearful screeching which, to my ears, had the ring of mocking laughter about it.

I said, 'Are we then back where we started and none the wiser?'

'Fortunately, I think not. Several clues have come to light which will prove to be useful, I have no doubt.'

'Which clues?'

'I can't say yet. We need more pieces of the puzzle to fit onto the ones we already have. It is rather frustrating but at the same time quite enthralling.' And indeed, his expression was not one of downcast misery, as I might have expected, but one of eager anticipation.

Our lunch finished, we walked on along the cliff path. The day was still extremely hot, although the occasional breeze from the sea brought some relief. We had agreed to walk as far as the village of Cloughton and then to return by train, and once we have agreed something it takes more than weather to undermine our determination. With only a boater each to protect our faces against the sun, we pressed on, happy at least that we had brought our lightweight slacks and jackets with us to Scarborough.

After another hour or so of slow and silent rambling, we hit upon a stony path leading down to a cove. According to our guidebook, which I had brought with me, this was Cloughton Wyke. We descended to it in the hope of shade, but soon discovered that the sun was beating mercilessly on every surface of cliff, rocks and pebbles. We rested for a while before deciding it was time to seek the shelter of a railway carriage leaving Cloughton station for Scarborough. We had started to scramble back up the path when we heard what I can only describe – at the risk of sounding like a penny dreadful – as a blood-curdling scream. Walter flew back down to the beach and stood listening …

After a moment there was another scream, just as loud, just as desperate, which seemed to come from somewhere beyond the headland forming the northern end of the cove. I raced after Walter as he sped to investigate. The rocks at the foot of the cliff were wet and slippery, and so uneven that we made slow progress, but eventually, after a good deal of slithering and tripping and cursing, we rounded the headland and emerged onto a small area of shingle beach. Then we stopped or, rather, were stopped in our tracks.

The first thing that struck me when I saw the man's body was how artistically he was posed: in the manner of a mythological painting, with a well-positioned leg hiding the genitals. The second thing was the knife with the ivory handle, thrust deep into his ribs.

He was lying on his back, completely naked, his head turned away and his left leg drawn up as if he were about to lever himself off the platform of rock that was his deathbed. His hair was blond and his skin pale, except where the blood had stained it dark.

Once we had recovered our composure, Walter approached the body with an eagerness I found a little disconcerting. As for me, I felt something nagging away at the back of my mind, as if I were trying to tell myself something but could not quite grasp what it might be.

Walter had gone round behind the rock. He took out the photograph as I joined him. The twisted expression on the poor man's face told of the agony he must have endured. But the similarity was definitely there this time.

'So now we know what has happened to Thomas White.'

I could not argue with his conclusion. Here then, undeniably, was proof that my brother was right when he declared he had a nose for crime. This was hardly reassuring. It meant I would have to keep an even closer eye on his movements. It would never do to be confronted by a scene like this every day of the week. And, of course, it left Walter – and me – open to other dangers.

'What if the killer is still here?' I said. 'Watching us and ... and ...'

'You need have no fear on that count,' Walter said. 'We are in no danger.'

'How do you know?'

'Trust me.'

It shows how far I had come along the path of acceptance that I actually did what he asked. I trusted him.

'The police must be informed,' he continued. 'Do you think you could go to the railway station at Cloughton and send a message?'

'And you?'

'I'll remain here to keep guard, so to speak.'

Something in my expression must have betrayed my suspicion that he had something else in mind, though exactly what I had no idea.

'I am merely being practical,' he said, and then, seeing that I still hesitated, 'I promise you I won't disturb the scene of the crime. The only alteration I'll make is this.' Whereupon he removed his jacket and draped it over the man's nether regions. 'Decency demands it.'

I nodded in agreement, then turned and started back over the rocks.

6

Enter Inspector Brasher

My message, delivered at Cloughton station, eventually brought two constables cycling up from Scarborough to investigate. They dismounted at the entrance to the station yard and secured their bicycles to the railings. I recognized the larger of the policemen: he was the one who had responded both to the disappearance at the People's Palace and to the Legard incident. When he saw me his face registered, in a matter of seconds, surprise, then suspicion, then dismay, and finally a sort of sad resignation.

'Making a habit of it, are we, sir?' he asked.

'Are we?' I said. 'A habit of what?'

He sniffed. 'I'm Constable Brightman. This is Constable Rudge.'

Constable Rudge was young, slim and very pale, as if the sun had neglected to shine on him. By contrast, the buttons on his jacket gleamed like tiny stars. Constable Brightman was so corpulent that I feared he would burst out of his uniform at any moment. He was perspiring profusely, and wiping his face, which was red, with his coat sleeves.

'If you'd be so good as to lead the way,' he said.

We had almost descended the path to the beach when my brother appeared round the headland. He waved. 'Good afternoon, Constable!'

'Is it, sir?' said Constable Brightman.

'I think so. A very special afternoon. After all, you don't get many murders here in Scarborough, do you?'

'Thankfully not. I'm Constable Brightman. This is Constable Rudge. Now, gentlemen, if you would conduct us to the scene of the crime ...'

Constable Brightman's shock upon seeing the murdered man appeared to be as great as mine, and was eloquent testimony to the fact that murder was indeed not an everyday occurrence on the Yorkshire coast. He was speechless for some little time before his duty got the better of him.

'Stay here and keep watch, Rudge.'

'Sir.'

'If you two gentlemen will come with me, I'll take statements off you at the station – the railway station, I mean.'

'Certainly. I'll bring this if you don't mind,' said Walter, pulling his jacket off the corpse.

'Rudge! Jacket!'

Rudge took off his jacket with the gleaming buttons and laid it where Walter's had been.

'Don't touch anything.'

'Sir.'

We sat with Constable Brightman over tea and biscuits in the little station buffet. He scratched away diligently with his pencil on his pad, but in truth there was not much to tell. His disappointment was clear, as was his lack of enthusiasm for our theory that the dead man was the Thomas White about whom he had already heard so much – too much, if I read his expression correctly. The photograph made as little impression on him as it had done the last time it was flourished under his nose. After ascertaining that we would be resident at the Grand for another ten days or so, he bade us goodbye and cycled back to Scarborough.

Luckily, Walter and I had only a minute or two to wait for a train.

'All quite fascinating,' Walter said, when we had sunk exhausted into our seats and were rattling along steadily.

'I have to agree,' I said.

'Far too fascinating a case to turn over completely to these country bumpkins.'

'What do you mean?'

'I mean,' Walter said, 'that I was a little less than forthcoming about ... this.' And, reaching inside his shirt behind the waistband of his slacks, he pulled out a piece of crumpled fabric, which, once he had shaken it out and held it up, revealed itself to be a man's navy blue bathing costume, of a kind that is to be found almost everywhere.

'Good heavens,' I said, 'where did you find that?'

'Among the rocks at the base of the platform the dead man was lying on.'

'You told me you wouldn't disturb the scene of the crime,' I said.

'So I did. It was wrong of me to take it, but I couldn't resist.' He turned over the hem at the top and held it out to me. 'What do you make of this?'

'It's a name label,' I said, taking the garment and peering at it. 'Very faint. Probably faded through lots of swimming.'

'No doubt. What name can you read?'

'H ... no, let me see ... A ... A. Barnes, is it?'

'Yes, I agree. A. Barnes.'

I looked up at him and my hands began to tremble.

'I see you're as bothered as I am.'

'Well yes,' I said, 'because ...'

'Yes?'

'If this says A. Barnes, what has happened to T. White?'

'Exactly. What indeed?'

Our doubts were groundless. The next morning the dead man was identified as Thomas White by the Misses Meakins and Fitt. Meeting them outside the Grand on their way back from their unpleasant task, we expressed our commiseration. They thanked us and were about to move on when Walter said: 'Could I have the pleasure of a walk with you this afternoon, Julia?'

She looked at him, offended. 'Alone, you mean?'

'Yes,' said Walter, tossing a smile in the direction of an unsmiling Miss Fitt.

'Mr Paget,' Miss Meakins said, 'I am in mourning.'

'Carry on as before is what I say, and you'll be as right as rain in no time.'

'Do you have no sense of decency?' she said.

'Of course I do,' Walter said, 'but I thought I was due a reward, and a walk would be – '

'A reward?' Miss Meakins's attractive features became distorted into a grotesque mask as she spat out the words again: 'A reward?'

'For finding your fiancé. I said I would, and I did.'

I dragged Walter away before he could do any more harm. Miss Meakins was dissolving in tears, and availing herself of Miss Fitt's handkerchief. Miss Fitt herself seemed, like Cerberus, to be eager to inflict a nasty wound on my wayward brother.

I started in on him again. 'What on earth are you thinking of?'

'How to solve the case.'

'It seems to me you were propositioning a distraught young lady with indecent haste.'

'That shows how little you know me, Sidney. I intended, on my walk with her, to sound Miss Meakins out with regard to Thomas White.'

'Really?'

'Really.'

'And that's all?'

'That's all. I've realized we know hardly anything about the murdered man – where he came from, what he did for a living, what his financial circumstances were, and so on. We didn't need to know all that when it was simply a case of someone gone missing, but now it's a case of murder one can never have too much background information.'

'Well, you'll have to get it some other way.'

'Oh, I shall,' he said with a certainty I found quite worrying.

'Or leave it to the police,' I suggested.

The knock on our door that afternoon was expected, but it surprised me by its hesitancy and quietness. Walter was, as usual, relaxing in one of his languourous poses, so it fell to me to admit our guest. I put to one side the postcard I was writing to Edith and opened the door.

The man standing in the corridor smiled broadly, cradling his bowler in the crook of his left arm. He was wearing a light brown three-piece which had seen better days. His shoes were badly scuffed. His tie was askew. I had expected him to make a better impression.

'Good afternoon,' he said. 'Inspector Brasher.'

'Good afternoon, Inspector,' I said. 'Do come in.'

When Constable Brightman had called the day before to inform us that the celebrated Brasher of Scotland Yard was being brought in to take over the case of Thomas White, I had felt a thrill run through me. Brasher was almost a myth, a name much repeated but rarely made flesh. His cases made headlines. He was reputed to be a match for the cleverest and deadliest of criminals. This was hard to square with the diminutive character who now shuffled into our room, fidgeting and twitching like someone who had recently risen from a bed of fleas. The Scarborough Police, in its wisdom, had decided that this case of murder, with no obvious culprit or motive, was too difficult for the likes of Brightman and Rudge, but I had my doubts whether Brasher, by the look of him, would fare any better.

Walter leapt up. 'Do be seated, Inspector.'

'Thank you kindly.' Brasher lowered himself into the vacated armchair with a little grunt of relief, while Walter sprawled out on his bed. I sat down on the corner of the other bed and waited for the inspector to speak. He placed his bowler carefully on the arm of the chair and patted its crown as if to tell it to stay put. Then, after a few moments spent looking first at one of us, then at the other, then back again, he began.

'I understand you're brothers,' he said.

'Correct,' I said. 'I am Sidney Paget, and this is my brother Walter. We are artists.'

'Artists! Well, well.'

'I illustrate the Sherlock Holmes stories in the *Strand*.'

'And I,' said Walter, 'am illustrated in them.'

'Indeed?' the inspector said. 'I've no time for reading detective stories. Not when there's so much real crime about.'

I felt as if I had somehow been rebuked for offending him, whereas the response I had expected should have been quite the opposite. I studied Inspector Brasher more closely. He was sitting in an attitude of complete relaxation, as if he were paying a social call on two old friends, instead of interviewing two witnesses to a crime. His legs were crossed, and the upper leg was jiggling lightly up and down. His fingers were intertwined and his hands laid upon his chest. His roughly shaven, ruddy face was expressionless.

He continued: 'Which of you found the body?'

'We both did,' Walter said.

'Both of you?'

'Yes,' I said, 'we came upon the scene in the course of a walk along the coast.'

Walter added: 'After hearing screams.'

'That's right,' I said. 'After hearing screams.'

'Screams? How many screams?'

'Three,' I said.

'Two,' said Walter.

'Shall we agree on two and a half?' said Brasher without the glimmer of a smile.

'It was two,' I said.

'You're sure?'

'Yes.'

'How far apart were they?'

I let Walter answer. 'About ten seconds, no more.'

'A man's voice?'

'I should think so,' I said, somewhat irritated by the inspector's reaction to my miscounting of the screams. 'Wouldn't you scream if you'd just had a knife stuck into you?'

Brasher sat stony-faced and silent, as Walter said: 'Very probably you would. But it could have been a woman's voice all the same.'

'How could it?' I asked.

'But it wasn't. You're right: it was a man's voice.'

Brasher must have found all of this as puzzling as I did, but he showed no sign of it. 'So, you were walking together along the beach when you heard a scream, then another scream a short while after.'

'Excellent, Inspector,' said my brother. 'You've got it in a nutshell.'

'So, what did you do?'

'We naturally went to investigate,' Walter said. 'We made our way with some difficulty round the headland and were confronted with the shocking spectacle of a man lying on a rock with a knife through his heart.'

'Can you tell me what position he was lying in?'

'I can do better than that, Inspector – I can show you.' Walter took out his pocket sketchbook, turned to a page and handed it to Brasher. 'I did it as a sort of *aide-mémoire*.'

'You didn't tell me you'd done that,' I said.

'Didn't I? It was a way of passing the time until you turned up with the two slops.'

Brasher appeared unperturbed by Walter's use of 'slop'; all his attention was focused on the sketchbook. I stood up and, moving round behind him as though just wanting to stretch my legs, I cast a glance over his shoulder before sitting down again. Walter had done a very creditable sketch of the dead man: his left leg raised and bent at the knee; the knife perfectly perpendicular; the head turned away. Had the inspector seen fit to ask, I would have had no hesitation in endorsing Walter's representation of the crime scene. Brasher tossed the book back to Walter and began picking tiny bits of fluff off his suit. After a minute or two of this, he spoke.

'Odd, isn't it?'

'Is it?' I asked.

'Very odd.'

'What is?'

'That the victim should be completely naked.'

'Oh, I don't know,' said Walter. 'Spot of sunbathing, probably. The weather's been splendid.'

The inspector said, 'How many people get killed while they're sunbathing?'

'I don't know,' said Walter. 'How many?'

'None, as far as I know.' Brasher smoothed out his de-fluffed waistcoat.

'There's always a first time,' I put in.

'People usually wear a bathing costume on the beach, I'd have thought.'

'Most,' said Walter. 'Not all. Scarborough's a conservative town, but Thomas White wasn't from Scarborough. At least I don't think he was. *Autres pays, autres mœurs.*'

I thought for a moment Brasher was going to ask what the devil that meant, but no – instead he asked the tricky question: 'You didn't find a bathing costume, did you?' There was a pause before Walter replied truthfully: 'I wasn't looking for one', which was really no reply at all, but it seemed to satisfy the inspector.

Seeing the famous Brasher of the Yard slouched in front of me, fiddling with his clothes and his mind apparently elsewhere, set me thinking. That he had successfully investigated the most difficult cases was undeniable. That he was as far from exhibiting the intellectual brilliance and physical energy of Sherlock Holmes as it was possible to be was equally evident. Were the two facts related? Did he deliberately present to the world an impression of lazy indifference the better to catch the guilty off guard? Who would imagine that this crumpled mess of a man could have one of the sharpest minds in the country? Or was I seeing the truth, and were his successes as a detective down to the hard work of his colleagues, or even to sheer luck?

The mystery encompassed his name: always Inspector Brasher, with never a mention in the newspapers or the court reports of his Christian name. Of course, it is the same with Inspector Lestrade, whom Sherlock Holmes often runs up against. In none of the twenty-four adventures that have appeared so far has Mr Doyle mentioned Lestrade's full name. I have often wondered if this makes him less of a fully formed character and thus leads to my infrequent and rather unexceptional illustrations of him.

I gazed at Brasher and fell to musing on possible names. He looked a little like a Henry and quite definitely like a Bernard, but not at all like an Algernon. I was continuing happily in this vein when the subject of my deliberations heaved himself out of the chair and picked up his bowler.

'I'll bid you gentlemen good day,' he said. 'Thank you for sparing me your time.'

Walter rose and opened the door. 'Glad to have been of assistance.'

'Assistance?' Brasher said. 'Ah yes, assistance.' And with that enigmatic thrust he departed.

Walter closed the door and resumed his place in the armchair. 'Well, what did you make of him, Sidney?'

'I don't rightly know,' I said. 'Either he is very deep or very superficial.'

'Yes, I think we can say that.' He held out his open sketchbook. 'What do you think?'

'Very good.'

Indeed it was: a striking, if exaggerated, sketch of Brasher of the Yard, emphasizing his large face, which peeped out from a mass of crumpled suit.

'Thank you,' said Walter. 'If you ever need an illustration of a villain who is a match for Sherlock Holmes, I think you could do a lot worse than to use this. Please feel free. I won't charge.'

I ignored this gibe. I had heard so many similar ones over the years that I was immune to them.

'What did you mean,' I said, 'about the screams?'

'Ah, the screams.'

'How could they have possibly come from a woman? The person murdered was a man.'

'Definitely. But it wasn't the murdered man who screamed.'

'What? How do you know?'

'We found the body very soon after we heard the screams, did we not?'

'Yes.'

'How soon?'

'Half a minute, perhaps, at the most.'

'And yet there was no movement from the dying man, and the blood was no longer flowing, was it?'

'No. No, you're right.'

'Which indicates that he had been murdered some time before.'

'Then who screamed?'

'The killer, of course. Who could, in theory, be a woman. But the screams were not high-pitched enough. It was a man who screamed, pretending to be the man he had killed a little while before.'

'But why?'

Walter smiled, no doubt amused at my slowness. 'Because he wanted us to find the body.'

'What?'

'I can think of no other reason.'

'Why should he want us to find the body?'

'I don't know. Not yet. But that's how I knew we were in no danger from the killer as we looked at the murdered man.'

'And now? Are we in danger now?'

'Who knows?'

7

Endymion and Selene

I spent that evening turning over in my mind all that had happened, seeking clarity but finding none. For his part, Walter had announced his intention to pursue some activity on his own, and no amount of questioning could get him to reveal its nature. 'I'll tell you all about it when I get back,' he said. 'And please don't follow me.'

I sat in our room awaiting his return, staring seawards, attempting to clear my mind and then to build up, piece by piece, a mental image constructed from the evidence. What had happened was fairly straightforward. Thomas White had gone missing and had, after a couple of days, been found murdered several miles along the beach. What I found harder to explain to myself and to fit into an overall pattern were the odd things that had occurred during those two days. Why had someone had his photograph taken while claiming to be Thomas White? Why had Mr Legard taken fright when he saw Walter? What was the meaning behind all the clothes in room 320? Why had Thomas White taken off his bathing costume before being murdered, and why did it bear the name Barnes?

On top of this, niggling away ever since our discovery of the body, was a conviction that something was staring me in the face and I was being too stupid to see it. I gazed at the sea, my old comforter, and waited for an answer. The tide was going out. Thin lines of silvery foam travelled one way, then back again, glittering in the moonlight. How often had that picturesque effect been used by artists? Atkinson Grimshaw had worked it to death. I had used it myself on a number of occasions ... Of course! The moon!

I was out of the chair in an instant and pacing round it with excitement. The moon! Selene! *Endymion and Selene*: Lancelot's painting. A man lying on a platform of rock, naked in Lancelot's version, or so he said. What did this mean? Was Lancelot in some way involved in the death of Thomas White? Or was it sheer coincidence? There was only one way to find out. I would tell Walter when he returned, and the next morning we would go to see Lancelot. When I sat down again my mind was so relieved that I must have fallen asleep almost at once.

I was woken by a key turning in a lock. The door opened, but instead of Walter a heavily bearded man came in. He was wearing an elegant cape over a suit of broad pinstripe and a top hat. I stared at him, hardly knowing if I was in actual fact awake or still dreaming.

'Good evening, Sidney,' the man said. 'Or perhaps I should say good morning.'

'What time is it?'

'Just after two.'

Walter tossed his hat on his bed, shrugged off his cape and proceeded, with the aid of the dressing table mirror, to remove his moustache and beard.

'Who are you supposed to be?' I asked.

'Lord Dibblesdale.'

'And where have you been, Your Lordship?'

'You weren't worried, were you?'

'Of course not. I just hope you didn't do anything silly.'

'So do I. But I'm pretty certain no one saw through my disguise.' He picked off tiny patches of hair that were still clinging to his chin. 'It's one of my best.'

'Why did you need a disguise? What have you been up to?' Walter smiled but said nothing. 'You said you'd tell me.'

'I have been,' he said, 'to a soirée.'

'A soirée? Where?'

'At Londesborough Lodge.'

'Lord Londesborough's residence?'

He nodded. 'It's behind the Rotunda, just over the way from the People's Palace and Aquarium.'

'I know where it is. But how did you get in?'

'I simply walked in confidently and, when approached by one of the flunkeys, announced that I was an intimate of Mr Legard. So, you see, meeting the pompous fellow has proved to be useful after all.'

'Did you see him there?'

'Yes, but I'm sure he didn't recognize me this time.'

'He didn't recognize you the first time.'

'Oh, he did.'

'But he can't have done. He didn't know you from Adam.'

'All the same ...'

'Well, at least we know now that he's not Thomas White pretending to be someone else, as you thought he was, since Thomas White is dead.'

'True.'

'Did you speak to him?'

'Briefly. We talked about my lily.'

'Your what?'

'The lily I was carrying.'

I thought my brother had finally taken leave of his senses. I decided to humour him.

'Ah, that lily. Where is it now?'

'I gave it to him.'

'This may seem a ridiculous question, but why were you carrying a lily?'

'For precisely that reason.'

'What?'

'If you recall, Sidney, the lily is a flower much beloved of Oscar Wilde. So much so that he went parading down Piccadilly with it, and caused quite a stir.'

And look where it got him, I wanted to say. Wilde had come out of prison a few years ago a total wreck and had immediately left the country. But then the significance of Walter's words dawned on me.

I said: 'Do you mean? ... Good heavens, you don't mean ...'

'Quite right. It was an all-male soirée.'

'Ye gods!'

'But extremely discreet.'

'Did you ... I mean, are you ... have they ...?'

'I have come to no harm, nor am I likely to. I had a hunch that Londesborough Lodge might be a gathering place for those, shall we say, of a certain persuasion, and I was right. It all ties up, you see.'

'Ties up with what?'

'With Thomas White being naked.'

'Oh no,' I said. 'Surely not.'

'Why not?'

'On the beach?'

'A secluded cove. Only himself and the murderer. Both are naked, having cast off their bathing costumes, which are both of that common navy blue type. They have their fun. Then the murderer strikes. Picks up his bathing costume – or rather what he thinks is his bathing costume ...'

'But is actually Thomas White's.'

'Correct.'

'So the killer is Mr Barnes.'

'Or someone calling himself Mr Barnes.'

By now I was striding about the room while Walter, tired after the evening's exertions, was lying on his bed, hands behind his head.

'I've got some new information as well,' I said.

Walter sat up. 'Then let me hear it.'

I explained to Walter about the painting I had seen at Lancelot's: the beach, the platform of rock, Lancelot's intention to depict Endymion and Selene in the nude. He had to admit it seemed something more than coincidence. We agreed to pay Lancelot a visit in the morning.

'And later in the day,' Walter said, 'there is a fancy-dress soirée at Londesborough Lodge.'

'Are you going?'

'I am.'

'Do be careful.'

'And you're coming with me. Don't worry: I've got a wonderful costume for you.'

I was so tired I slept soundly the rest of that night, but shortly before I woke I had a disturbing dream. I was in the People's Palace and Aquarium at some sort of social gathering in which all the other guests were men. They were all beautifully dressed. I was the only one there who was completely naked, though no one seemed to mind or even to notice. A man in a navy blue bathing costume was swimming in the large tank. Each of the guests found a partner, and the couples began to dance, even though there was no music to dance to. Suddenly Walter appeared and came towards me. He too was naked, apart from a top hat. He grabbed my arm and started to shake me ...

He was dragging me out of bed. It was only seven o'clock. I could see in his eyes that glint of enthusiasm he had always had as a child whenever an adventure beckoned. As soon as I was dressed he hauled me down to a hasty breakfast, then out into another warm morning.

My brother's spirits were soaring. At his suggestion we went the long way to Lancelot's, descending to the promenade then strolling along to the harbour, from where we climbed up Castlegate to the neighbourhood of Lancelot's studio. All the way Walter could not help but chatter about the case, about how it was all coming together, about some great mystery or other that was at the bottom of it. As far as I was concerned, I simply wanted the murderer to be found and punished. I could not deny that there was something intriguing in the air, but I was more than willing to forgo the delights and dangers we were bound to encounter.

'Shouldn't we leave things to Inspector Brasher?' I said. 'Now the police are involved we don't need to be.'

'Do you really think that nincompoop will be able to solve a tricky affair such as this?'

'He doesn't make a good impression, it's true, but he has a huge reputation.'

'Reputation be damned. The man's obviously a fool. He's bored with the case already – we saw that when he questioned us yesterday. Whereas we, Sidney, we are fired up. We shall succeed where others fail.'

'We shall ruin our health, more like. We came to Scarborough for rest and recuperation, and here we are, getting excited and charging about like a couple of schoolboys.'

'Yes, you're right. It's making me feel young again.'

'I want you to feel *well*.'

'I appreciate your concern, Sidney, but it is precisely this mental stimulation that is making me feel well.' And, without once breaking step, he took his deerstalker from his pocket and positioned it carefully on his head.

We looked down at the mattress, dusty and stained with drink and sweat.

Lancelot had abandoned Vincent Van Gogh. He now had a dark moustache and goatee and was dressed in simple Renaissance-style blouse and leggings. A sword hung at his side, impeding his movement whenever he changed direction.

He said: 'You're both very welcome to stay. Not as luxurious as the Grand, of course, but it won't cost you a penny.'

'Thank you,' I said, as Walter flashed me a look of disbelief. 'It's kind of you.'

'It's what friends are for. Now, is this a social visit, to be marked with a glass of something? Or does it have some deeper meaning?'

'Oh, it's deep, extremely deep,' said Walter. 'In fact so deep that I'll let Sidney explain. But we could have a glass of something while he's doing it, couldn't we?'

Lancelot laughed, opened the door to his studio and disappeared inside. There was a brief clattering as his legs fought with his sword. 'Port all right, I hope? Come on through.'

The studio looked exactly as it had done a few days before, but with one exception, and this exception was so big, so blatant, so full of significance that I could not stop myself from crying out.

'What's the matter?' said Lancelot. 'Don't you want a port?'

'The painting,' I said.

'Yes, a masterpiece, don't you think? It's nearly finished.'

Walter merely said, 'Good heavens' and lapsed into silence. We stood there, gaping, for some time, until Lancelot woke us from our daze by pressing glasses of port into our hands.

'I just have to find a Selene, but I think you'll agree my Endymion has turned out rather well.'

Where before there had been a platform of rock amidst the fiery colours of a Mediterranean coast, there was now a platform of rock supporting a man lying on his back, completely naked, his left leg drawn up to preserve his modesty. He was young, his hair blond, his skin pale, except where the blood had stained it dark. There was a knife with an ivory handle thrust into his ribs. Unlike his counterpart at Cloughton Wyke, his face was turned towards the viewer, fully visible.

'I don't believe it,' I finally managed to say.

'Thank you,' Lancelot said. 'I did give of my best.'

Walter looked at me. 'Are you thinking what I'm thinking?'

'I think so,' I said. 'But it can't be.'

Walter produced the photograph of the fake Thomas White and handed it to Lancelot. 'Was that the man who modelled for Endymion?'

Lancelot put down his glass, pushed his sword into a comfortable position and studied the photograph for some time, looking now and then at the painted face on the canvas beside him.

'It looks a bit like him, I grant you, but my model didn't have a moustache.'

'Well,' said Walter, 'a moustache can easily be shaved off.' Taking back the photograph, he asked Lancelot, 'What was the name of your model?'

'Now that I don't know. He didn't give his name. Said it was on account of the explicit nature of the painting.'

'You paid him?' I asked.

'Oh yes.'

Walter said, 'Where did you find him?'

'Well, unfortunately I don't have a brother like you I can call on when I need help with modelling. You're very lucky, Sidney.'

I thought to myself, you're very lucky, Lancelot, that I don't biff you one for that remark. 'That's debatable,' I said, 'but it's neither here nor there at present.' Then, steering him away from that particular can of worms, I repeated Walter's question: 'Where did you find him?'

'Not among the fine citizenry of Scarborough, you can be sure of that. The airs and graces these people give themselves! A bit of artistic posing is beneath them, though they're happy enough to have classical nudes on their dining room walls. Hypocrites! No, I turned to an acquaintance of mine, Old Simon, who is a useful link to the underside, shall we say, of Scarborough life.'

'The underside of Scarborough life?' I said. 'Is there one?'

'There's a underside to every society, and it's no bad thing. It's where you'll find a lot of real living goes on, away from the superficiality and artificiality of modern life.' Lancelot stood in the middle of his studio and opened his arms wide. 'It's the difference between Selene and Endymion and the poseurs of Scarborough Spa.'

His left hand directed our gaze towards the canvas on the wall behind the door. There were still lots of faces waiting to be painted in and thereby immortalized by the artist known as Parker. Each of the available spaces was attached to a beautifully detailed set of fashionable clothes, guaranteed to elevate the sitter in the viewer's estimation. I had already mentioned to my brother this mercenary side of Lancelot, and he now treated it with the disdain it deserved.

'You seem quite happy to take advantage of the poseurs of Scarborough Spa.'

'It's because I have no choice. When the buying public takes no interest in truly great art ...' And with a flourish of his right hand he re-directed our attention to the agonies of Endymion.

Walter said, 'Did Old Simon find a model for you?'

'He did. He rarely fails me. He is in touch with all sorts of people only too glad to earn a few pennies through honest work felt by so many to be beyond the pale. Often it is simple modelling as a fisherman or blacksmith or other sentimental figure for one of my Parker paintings. Sometimes he's known who to contact if I'm in desperate need of a rare pigment, say – that sort of thing. This is the first time I've asked him to get me a nude model. He knew exactly where to look.'

'And where was that?' Walter asked.

'I've no idea. Old Simon likes to keep his contacts to himself. It's how he makes his living, after all.'

'I see.'

'Where does he live?' I said.

'I don't know that either. I always meet him in the Beehive Inn on Sandside, down by the harbour.'

I nodded, storing that piece of information away for future use. Meanwhile Walter was contemplating Endymion.

'Tell me, Lancelot,' he said, 'when did you paint him into the picture?'

'Let's see now. It was after you came to see me the other day, Sidney, that's obvious. In fact, it was the day after. Old Simon got me this fellow straight away and I did him as Endymion in the afternoon.'

Walter turned to me. 'When did you visit Lancelot?'

'Tuesday,' I said. 'The day after we arrived.'

'Which means Endymion was painted on Wednesday. When did we find the body?'

'Thursday.'

'So ... the murderer was copying the picture.'

He looked hard at Lancelot, who stared back.

'I don't understand,' he said. 'What's this about a murder?'

'Haven't you read the report in the *Daily Post*?' I asked.

'No. I don't read the papers.'

Walter explained how we had discovered Thomas White's corpse, and how the scene matched in almost every detail the painting in front of us.

'But that's impossible!' Lancelot said.

'Whose idea was it to portray Endymion with a knife in him?'

Walter asked.

Lancelot said: 'Mine, of course. It's the modern twist I was telling Sidney about. Instead of Selene condemning Endymion to everlasting sleep, she stabs him to death, which is a sort of everlasting sleep.'

'He won't keep his youthful looks though, will he?' I said. 'His corpse will decompose.'

'Precisely. That's Selene's mistake. That's the irony of it. I was thinking of adding a shaft of moonlight hitting the handle of the knife, but it's perhaps too melodramatic, especially in the blazing sun. What do you think?'

Walter cut through the artistic chatter. 'So you painted the model who sat for you –'

'He lay for me, actually.'

'You painted him as he held a dagger on his breast?'

'That's right.'

'And how do you account,' Walter said, 'for the fact that the murder scene resembles your painting so closely?'

'I can't. All I know – and I hope you know, my friends – is that I didn't kill him.'

There was an uneasy moment of silence as we looked at each other. We *were* friends, after all, weren't we? Or did we not know each other as well as we imagined we did?

'If I did kill him,' Lancelot went on, 'why would I draw attention to myself by imitating my painting?'

'That's a good point,' I said.

'A clever form of double bluff, perhaps,' said Walter.

Lancelot laughed. 'Too clever for me.'

'Yes, I think you're right,' said Walter somewhat unkindly. 'The only other possibility is that your model fellow, or someone he's talked to, is to blame. He decided to kill Thomas White in the same manner you want Selene to kill Endymion.'

'But why?' said Lancelot.

'That we shall endeavour to find out.' Walter handed his empty glass to Lancelot. 'Thanks for your hospitality. We'll be in touch.'

'There's a bed here for you whenever you want it.'

'By the way,' I said, giving him my glass, 'why are you dressed like that?'

'It's for my next painting, which is going to represent – in a modern way naturally – a brawl in a pub. So I'm trying to get into a dark mood by being Caravaggio.'

'Caravaggio? Didn't he murder someone?'

'That's disputed by several authorities,' said Lancelot, hurrying on. 'I've only got another day to go, thank goodness. This sword is giving me no end of trouble.' And, on cue, he stumbled over it as he led us downstairs.

'One last thing,' Walter said. 'Do you have the knife you used in the modelling session for Endymion?'

'Of course.'

'May I see it?'

With a sigh, Lancelot stomped back up the stairs to his studio. We heard him banging about and cursing for several minutes before he returned.

'I can't find it. It's gone.'

I said: 'The man who modelled for you must have taken it.'

'I suppose so,' said Lancelot.

'That's one possibility,' said Walter.

Lancelot's face clouded over. 'The other possibility being what?'

Walter smiled by way of reply. Lancelot put his hand on his sword and half drew it out of his belt.

'Who do you think you are?' he said. 'Sherlock Holmes?'

It was too late: the words had been spoken. Walter took out his deerstalker once more and jammed it on his head. What's more, he produced a calabash pipe I had never seen before and began to flourish it as he walked away.

'Mad!' cried Lancelot before slamming the door.

8

Ale and Cakes

That afternoon, after Walter and I had taken lunch at the Grand, I decided to strike out on my own. The sooner someone solved the case, I told myself, the sooner we could salvage the little that remained of our holiday, and I saw no reason why that someone should not be me. It was true that my brother had a sharp eye and a lively brain, but what practising artist worth his salt does not? I see things just as well as he does, if not better. I consider myself no slouch in matters of the intellect. In short, I was certain I could give him a run for his money. And there was an added incentive: if I could indeed clear up the murder before Walter did, it it might bring him down to earth and put an end to any further Sherlock Holmes escapades.

When I produce an illustration for a story, I always read that story before I commit to paper a single pencil stroke. If I am not completely satisfied that I understand the context into which the illustration is to be introduced, I make enquiries of the author or publisher. In other words, before anything of a creative nature can be born, I need to be thoroughly conversant with the world in which it will see the light of day. This rule has always stood me in good stead, and I fancied it would do so again.

Having read all twenty-four Sherlock Holmes adventures for which I provided the illustrations, I knew that Holmes's first action when starting out on a case was to turn to his scrapbooks and directories for information regarding the individuals involved. In the same way, I felt in need of information about both the murdered man and the suspected murderer: about Thomas White and the man, probably named Barnes, who sat for Lancelot's painting. I could make inquiries about the former with Miss Meakins or Miss

Fitt during one of our inevitable meetings in the days ahead; about the latter I would have to question Old Simon, an altogether trickier task since I was unknown to him and he to me. I decided to grasp the bull by the horns. Accordingly, while Walter sat in our room turning over the facts of the case, I found myself down at the harbour, outside the Beehive Inn, the reputed haunt of Old Simon.

It had a makeshift look about it. The narrow front door had been let into the lower half of a bay window, on top of which a wooden board leant against the wall. It bore the following inscription:

BEEHIVE INN
Within this hive we are all alive
Good ale will make you funny
If you are dry as you pass by
Step in and taste our honey

Relieved I had had the foresight to wear my least elegant clothes – although I feared even these might make me stand out like a dressmaker's dummy in a second-hand clothes shop – I climbed the four steep steps into the hive. The buzzing of voices stopped as I entered.

I looked about me, from one face to the next. All were staring back with alarm in their eyes, as if I were some strange creature from another world. It was as though time were standing still while they considered if I was an acceptable addition to their company or not. Apparently I was, for after a few seconds they resumed their activity as abruptly as they had interrupted it. The barmaid finished filling a glass, the elderly man in the corner wiped his mouth on the sleeve of his shabby suit, and the couples who made up the rest of the clientele banged their drinks down on the tables and returned to their conversations and their petting.

It was, without a doubt, the smallest public bar I had ever been in – about half the size of our room at the Grand. The sun flooded in through the windows, brightening the dust dancing in the air. Indeed, there was a dusty feel to everything. A good washing-down would revive the place.

The barmaid tossed her head, flipping her dark curls out of her eyes. 'Got the right one, have you?'

'The right what?' I asked.

'Right pub.'

'Oh yes. The Beehive.'

She came from behind the bar, put the glass of beer down on a table and wiped her hands on her apron.

'Only we don't get many of your type in here.'

'Oh?' I said. 'And what type's that?'

A laugh erupted from one of the tables behind me.

'Take no notice, love.' The barmaid ran her eyes up and down my person and smiled. 'I suppose you'd like a taste of my honey.'

'Pardon me?'

Again, a burst of laughter.

'What're you having?'

'I see. Mild, please.'

'Pint?'

I am not a drinker of large quantities. On the occasions when I have frequented a public house in London, usually in the company of Walter or Lancelot or another of the artistic fraternity with whom I am acquainted (my wife, very naturally and properly, staying at home), I have always consumed whisky or sherry. A pint seems such a lot to drink.

'A pint, of course,' I said.

That settled matters. I became just another customer, neither to be stared at or laughed at. The barmaid set about pulling my pint.

I said: 'I wonder if you can help me.'

'I wonder,' she said. She leaned back, and her bosom rose. 'Fire away.'

'I'm looking for a friend of a friend.'

'Are you really?' she said in the tones of one who has heard it all before.

'Yes, really.'

She placed the glass, filled to the brim, in front of me.

'Old Simon's over there, as usual,' she said, glancing towards the man in the corner.

'How do you know I'm looking for him?'

'Well, aren't you? That's tuppence.'

I paid and took my glass, spilling some of the contents. As I made my way over to Old Simon, I dripped beer, first from one side of the glass, then from the other.

'May I join you?' I said.

Old Simon raised his head and looked at me with all the interest an aged turtle might show towards a visitor at the zoo. He had thick white hair and a greying beard and moustache. One hand firmly gripped his glass; with the other he motioned to me to sit down next to him.

For the next few minutes we both sat staring silently in front of us. A comment about the hot weather drifted into my head but remained unspoken. How should I start? I could hardly talk about the murder. Old Simon might not have heard about it, and then I would have to explain things at length. That might put him on his guard if he were in some way mixed up in it. I needed to be circumspect. I had a feeling that everyone in the pub had half an ear cocked, eager to overhear my business. This was the first time I had conducted an investigation, although I was familiar with many through my collaboration with Mr Doyle. I asked myself what Sherlock Holmes would do in my situation, then realized I was in danger of acting like Walter – all I needed was a deerstalker. I decided to stick to simple facts.

'I'm a friend of Mr Pemberlow,' I said.

I thought Old Simon had not heard me, for his only response was to pick up his glass and drink from it.

'Mr Pemberlow,' I said.

Old Simon grunted. 'I heard you.'

He wiped his mouth on his sleeve. I could see this was going to be a slow interrogation. He stroked his beard. He took another sip of beer. After another minute or so he spoke.

'Don't know no Pemberlow.'

'I think you do,' I said. 'Lancelot. The painter.'

'Oh yes, I know Lancelot.'

Good, I thought. That's that established. Perhaps now we can get to the nub of the matter.

'He came to see you the other day.'

'Did he?'

A further silence. Things were not going well.

'He did.' Here I was, answering my own questions. This was the wrong way about.

'He came to ask you to find a model for him.'

'Might have done.' This seemed some sort of progress. With any luck I would soon extract a definite answer from him.

He said: 'Model of what?'

'No,' I said, 'a person. A model for a picture he's painting.'

'Ah.'

'A picture of Endymion and Selene.' As soon as I had uttered the words, I knew I should not have done.

'End what?'

'It doesn't matter. You found him someone to model for him.'

'I did.'

Success! Euphoria mounted within me, as if someone had given me the key to life. At this rate, I thought, I will have solved the crime before Walter has had time to smoke a single pipe of shag.

'Can you remember the man's name?'

'What man?'

'The one who you found to model for Lancelot.'

'Oh, that one.' He paused, took a drink, wiped his mouth. I could see he was searching his memory. There was a sudden silence in the pub.

'Didn't give a name,' he said. The hum of conversation started up again.

'Do you know where he came from at least?'

'No.'

And that, it seemed, was that. Old Simon clammed up for good, opening his mouth again only to pour in more beer.

I said, 'It's been nice talking to you,' got up and left the wretched place, pursued by the barmaid's shouted reminder that I had only drunk a tiny fraction of my honey and was there anything wrong with it?

Outside I moved into the sun as quickly as I could, shaking off the gloom and dust of the Beehive. People were coming and going out here; life was proceeding normally. I was about to set off along Foreshore Road back to the hotel when the barmaid's voice again sounded behind me.

'Wait!'

She came running out of the pub, her hair and bosom bouncing and her apron flying.

'I'm sorry,' I said, 'I'm not a big drinker.'

'That don't matter,' she said, panting a little. 'What you was saying to Old Simon ...'

'Yes?'

'He don't say nothing for nothing.'

'Pardon me?'

'You should have given him something. Then he'd have told you.'

Here we were again: everything had its price for a certain type of person.

'In that case,' I said, my spirits sinking, 'I'll try him again.'

'Or you could try me,' she said.

I was not sure of her meaning, and suspected some lascivious motive. But looking into her eyes, which were clear and honest, I saw I had nothing to fear.

'I can tell you what you want to know,' she said. 'For a small consideration.'

I had got the message by now. I reached into my pocket and dropped a shilling into her outstretched hand.

'The model for his artist friend ...'

'Yes?'

'He came from the usual place, I'm sure.'

'And where's that?'

'Old Simon gets all his people from Londesborough Lodge. That's well known.'

'Is it?'

'To them as know.' And with a flash of her eyes she turned on her heel and flew back into the hive.

Once more I shuddered at the mercenary nature so blatantly on display. Had I been asked to provide similar information I would have done so only too readily and without expectation of recompense. Nevertheless, I set off with some uplift in my heart, for I had secured an important piece of information and felt proud of having done so, although in truth I had had little influence in the matter.

My luck seemed to be in that day. As I walked past the beach, cluttered with stalls selling oysters, carriages awaiting custom and holidaymakers enjoying their rest, I spied Miss Fitt a little way ahead of me. She had laid a shawl on the sand and was sitting alone, under her parasol, in front of that strange Moorish construction that is the Seawater Baths. In the mid-distance behind her, the Grand rose in imposing majesty. As, it must be said, did Miss Fitt when she saw me coming towards her. I do not think she was trying to escape me; rather she wished to be on the same level when greeting me.

'Please don't get up,' I said.

'I ought to go,' she said. 'They will have finished by now.'

I looked at her properly for the first time, in the full light of day, even if a little obscured by the shadow of the parasol, and I could see that she was not without a certain attraction. She was in no way the equal of her niece, or even of the barmaid who had just touched me for a bob, but she had a gentleness around her eyes which hinted at a feminine delicacy of soul, and her lips were small and shapely, quite out of keeping with the rest of her large frame.

I asked: 'Who will have finished?'

She regarded me as though I were an imbecile.

'My niece and your brother. Who else?'

'But Walter said he was going to sit and think things over.'

'Ha!'

'I assure you, Miss Fitt, I have no idea to what you are referring.

And I must tell you I am not my brother's keeper, in the same way you are not your niece's.'

She must have recognized the truth of what I said, for she softened on the instant.

'Please do not misunderstand me, Mr Paget. Far be it from me to restrict the pleasures that come so naturally to the young. However, I made a promise to my sister, on her deathbed ...'

'I understand entirely,' I said.

'So that when your brother suggested going for a walk with my niece, and when she – unlike the previous time – agreed, and when they both insisted, most vehemently, that they did not desire my company ... well, I feel that I have failed.'

She turned her face away, dabbing at her eyes with a handkerchief. 'I dragged myself down here, where I thought I could be alone with my shame and misery.'

'You poor woman,' I said. This was perhaps a mistake: she let out a sorrowful howl and collapsed on the sand in a flurry of tears and chiffon. I was nonplussed. For what seemed like an eternity I hesitated. But the thought that Walter would have known how to act, and would in all probability have acted already, spurred me on to personal sacrifice.

Bending down, I said: 'Allow me to escort you back to the hotel.' I held out my hand, which she took at once.

'I do apologize,' she said. 'I don't know what came over me.' She got to her feet, brushing the sand from her skirt and raising her parasol, which flapped on one side like a bird's broken wing where she had fallen on it.

'Perhaps it can be mended. There must be an umbrella shop in Scarborough.'

'It doesn't matter,' she said. 'Broken parasols are of no consequence.' She sighed. 'Unlike broken hearts.'

I had not expected this. I had thought her defences impenetrable, but no: a crack had appeared and a personal tragedy had forced its way out. But to whose broken heart was she referring? Her own? Her niece's? Someone else's? Judging by the heaviness of her sigh, I deduced it was a long-lost love of her own that was at the root of her distress.

I knew that on the way to the Grand there was a little tea shop which had a reputation for excellent sandwiches and cakes. To my suggestion that we stop off there and restore ourselves Miss Fitt agreed wholeheartedly. We set off up the beach, her arm in mine, for all the world as if we were a courting couple out for a day at the seaside.

We took a table for two as far away as possible from the window of Tilly's Tea Room, well out of the gaze of curious passers-by. I had the impression, gleaned from numerous simpering noises and glances of interest, that Miss Fitt was reliving some dalliance from her past. I hoped that was all she was doing; I did not want to be the innocent cause of another broken heart to add to her collection. The thought of my wife seeing me there and misinterpreting my intentions troubled me, even though I knew she was safely in London. Would she have believed I was taking tea with this lady solely in order to extract information from her? Did I believe it myself? Or were Miss Fitt's smiles and gentle gestures, in spite of her overall plainness, having an effect on me? Perhaps, I told myself, I had misjudged Walter and he was wooing Miss Meakins – if that is what he *was* doing – solely in order to learn some facts about the case. I could do worse than copy him, I thought, thereby keeping my emotions under strict control.

Until then Miss Fitt and I had chit-chatted about the weather, about the pleasures of Scarborough, about the choice of cake to have with our tea. Now I steered the conversation into a more relevant channel.

'Is Miss Meakins very much upset by what has happened to Mr White?'

'What a question!' said Miss Fitt. 'She is prostrate. Wouldn't you be if you had been going to marry him?'

She realized the impropriety of her question too late.

'Oh, I didn't mean –'

'It's quite all right,' I said. 'I understand what you mean. I was not going to marry Mr White – why, I hardly knew him –'

She had the kindness to smile at my little jest.

'But had I been going to marry him and he was then murdered – yes, I think I should be exceedingly upset.'

'Then there is your answer.'

'I ask the question because of what you said earlier – that Miss Meakins had insisted on taking a walk, unchaperoned, with my brother. It does seem rather irregular.'

'It is extremely irregular, Mr Paget. But Julia is somewhat headstrong. She will have her way. And since she is paying for our holiday ...'

'Quite.'

'But I can assure you she was very attached to Thomas – Mr White.'

'I'm glad to know it. Do you know how they first met?'

'Oh yes. I was there.'

A waitress brought our tea – Darjeeling for Miss Fitt, Assam for me – and a three-tiered stand bearing rock cakes, macaroons and iced fancies. I poured and handed Miss Fitt her cup and saucer. I thought for one moment that the arrival of the tea and cakes had distracted her to the point that she had lost the thread of what she was saying, or even that she had decided to say no more about the first meeting between her niece and Mr White, but she was simply pausing for breath and a macaroon before launching into her tale.

'They met,' she said, 'in Blackpool, many years ago. Julia and I were on holiday there. One day we were strolling along the promenade when a young man leading a dog came from the other direction and lifted his boater to us. We acknowledged him with a nod and moved on. The next thing we knew, his dog – one of those yappy little things, a chihuahua – was barking round Julia's heels and altogether giving her quite a fright. The young man eventually regained control of the beast and apologized profusely, as was only right. Julia said there was no harm done. He said the dog, called Rascal, was really a sweet, affectionate creature (how many times have I heard that!). He encouraged Julia to bend down and stroke Rascal, which she did. The dog had become adorable, of course, and she made a great fuss of him. For the rest of that day Thomas White – that was his name – was our constant companion, and a very interesting and witty one at that. Well, it turned out that he was staying in Blackpool for a week, as we were. We saw each other every day. By the end of the week he and Julia had grown very close – to the extent that he asked if he might be allowed to write to her.'

'That was very proper of him.'

'Oh, he observed all the social niceties, I'll give him that. He wrote, giving an address in Norwich for Julia to reply to. We thought this strange, since he'd told us he came from London. Anyway, Julia replied, and shortly afterwards she received another letter from him, this time giving an address in Reading. This seemed very odd indeed, until he informed us, after sending five or six more letters to us from different locations, that he had to move about the country a great deal on account of his business, which he declined to talk about, saying it would bore us, being of a dry commercial nature. After the correspondence had continued for about nine months, he inquired of Julia where she might be spending her summer holiday that year and whether she might be disposed to his joining her there. Well, Julia had nothing against it, for she had decided he was a very agreeable and amusing young man, as indeed he was, but I had my reservations about his rather vague background and I counselled caution. Julia would have none of it. She invited Mr White to join us in Brighton. They stayed in separate hotels – that goes without saying.'

'Of course.'

'After that, for the next five years or so, the same thing was repeated. Julia and Mr White met up on holiday, each year at a different place: Folkestone, Torquay, Skegness, Ramsgate and now Scarborough. So there you have it, Mr Paget. An unusual courtship, I think you'll agree, but a successful one. In Ramsgate Julia accepted his proposal of marriage.'

During this admirably detailed account Miss Fitt had been

fiddling with a rock cake, and now, having reached the end, she rewarded herself by putting it to its intended use.

I considered what she had told me. Thomas White's peregrinations did strike me as unusual, yet I could not imagine what advantage there might be in not telling the truth about them. Miss Meakins's letters were sent to those places he mentioned and he obviously received them there and replied to them. Perhaps he was, as he had hinted, a simple travelling salesman, but pride had not permitted him to admit as much.

I asked: 'Did he speak with an accent?'

'Not that I'm aware of.'

'And did he have any relatives?'

'He didn't mention any. Not to me anyway.'

'Perhaps the police will be able to dig out some more information about him.'

'Perhaps.'

I finished my tea and wondered whether I should have an iced fancy or not. I have to watch my diet: the smallest irregularity can upset my stomach. I put it down to an artistic sensitivity; Walter puts it down to nerves. Miss Fitt had no such scruples. Her side of the cake stand resembled nothing so much as a battlefield – devastation amongst the crumbs.

'What did the police tell you,' I asked, 'about Thomas White's murder?'

'Inspector Brasher said he'd been killed on the beach just north of Scarborough. With a knife. Dreadful.'

'Was that all?'

'Isn't it enough? Poor Julia went into hysterics.'

'He didn't, for example, say what Mr White was wearing when he was killed?'

'No. Why? Is it important?'

'It might be.'

I lapsed into silence, leaving her curiosity hanging. After a moment she transferred it to her tea and seemed perfectly satisfied.

I don't know if it was because I insisted on paying for the tea and cakes, but all the way back up to the hotel she would not abandon the subject of broken hearts and the mending of the same. This time it was quite clear she was referring to her own ordeal in this regard. A sergeant-major with a controlling mother was brought up from the dim and distant past and his weaknesses and iniquities were dwelt upon. She painted me as a saint by comparison. I could only think that Miss Fitt had not had a wide experience of life if that were her conclusion. I slipped into the conversation, as naturally as I was able, a mention or two of my wife, but in no way succeeded in putting a halt to the romantic flow of words. It occurred to me that Miss Fitt was herself in need of a chaperone. Praying that a good night's sleep away from the debilitating heat of the sun would cure her of this warmth of expression, I bowed my head and submitted to her blandishments, as we laboured ever upwards.

9

The Birth of Reginald Smithers

The postcard showed a group of finely dressed promenaders outside the Spa. I addressed it to Edith and, in the space provided for correspondence, wrote simply: 'Aren't I in good company? But wish you were here too!'

Walter lay back on his bed as if to demonstrate the ease with which he went about everything. 'I thought it unnecessary and unbecoming,' he said, 'to chase after Old Simon in some seedy public house, so I simply betook myself to Londesborough Lodge – in my guise as Lord Dibblesdale – and asked if Old Simon had been there today looking for a model. I received a reply in the negative, which told me, of course, that he *had* been there on a previous day.'

'But how did you know he got his model from Londesborough Lodge?'

'I didn't, but from what I saw there yesterday, which is what you'll see there yourself tonight, it seemed a reasonable guess. And I was right.'

He was, damn him! Whereas I had wasted fourteen pence and a good hour buzzing around the Beehive.

'I suppose,' he continued, 'you spent some time with Euphemia.'
'You mean Miss Fitt.'
'I thought she might put herself in your way.'
'She did nothing of the kind.'
'You wouldn't notice, of course. She has a soft spot for you.'
'I doubt it.'
'Julia's opinion, not mine.'
'Julia?'
'Yes, Julia. I found out all about Thomas White from her.'

'So did I, from Miss Fitt.'

'But I got it straight from the horse's mouth.'

'A very poorly chosen metaphor, if I may say so.'

'You may. Anyone with less equine features I cannot imagine.'

What I really found hard to stomach was not so much Walter's inappropriate use of language as his ability to get information without having to fork out on tea and cakes. My 'interrogation' of Miss Fitt in Tilly's Tea Room had set me back a fair whack, which together with the money I had spent at the Beehive had made for rather an expensive day.

'You said you were going to sit quietly and cogitate.'

'And so I did. I pulled the chair up to the window and contemplated the waves in their timeless cycle. After a while I entered into a state of perfect peace.'

Knowing Walter as I do, I found that hard to believe.

'But then,' he continued, 'I heard voices outside. I opened the window, thrust my head out and was just able to see, beyond the edge of the bow window on my right, two small boys go running and laughing towards the sea, then back up the beach until the hotel hid them from view, then down to the sea again, in and out of my field of vision.'

His words brought back to me – as strong as it had ever been – the memory of two boys playing on the sands at Cromer. The long row of painted beach huts. The pier, solidly staking its claim to be in the sea. The forlorn donkeys waiting in a line. Walter stamping on my sandcastle because he could not build a better one. Me chasing him, both of us laughing, into the water. Out too far. The laughter stopping. Walter flailing, me holding him up, pulling him back onto the sand, gasping for air. This was the time I saved my brother's life. Walter cannot remember it. He says that if it did happen, which he doubts, he had not been in difficulties and it was another instance of my interference in his life.

For me to see all this in my mind's eye took, as ever, no more than a few seconds. Walter still lay on the bed, staring at the ceiling.

He said: 'I don't know what it was, Sidney, but the moment I heard those boys laughing something stirred within me, something very deep. I became restless. I felt the need to go out into the daylight, to engage with life. And I thought I might as well do it in pleasant company. I found Miss Meakins and Miss Fitt taking tea in the hotel tea room and asked Miss Meakins if she would like to come for a walk with me, my intention being, of course, to ask her some probing questions about the case.'

'Are you sure those were your intentions?'

'I'm positive. But in any case, there can be nothing wrong with escorting a lady whose fiancé is deceased.'

'Very recently deceased.'

'She agreed to come for a walk, thus releasing her aunt for an afternoon of leisure. I mentioned that you had gone down to the harbour. I dare say she took up a position to intercept you.'

'You didn't know where I'd gone.'

'Where else would you go? I saw your eyes light up when Lancelot mentioned Old Simon and the Beehive Inn.'

'All right,' I said, 'that's quite enough about me. What did you find out from Miss Meakins?'

'Anything and everything you could want to know about Thomas White.'

'Really?'

'Which is next to nothing.'

My relief was great. 'That's exactly how much I found out from Miss Fitt,' I said.

'That her fiancé and she would meet every year in a different seaside resort?'

'Yes.'

'That he would write to her from different addresses, moving around the country?'

'Yes.'

'That they met in Brighton while he was walking his dog?'

'No.'

'No?'

'I was told they met in Blackpool.'

'Not Brighton?'

'No.'

Walter leapt up from the bed. 'That's an important discrepancy, don't you think?'

'Hardly,' I said. 'One of them simply remembered it wrongly. I can't see it matter two hoots where they first met.'

'No, that doesn't matter at all.'

'I wish you'd make up your mind. Perhaps none of this matters, not to us anyway. Perhaps we should just let the police do their job.'

'Oh, but they won't. That Brasher didn't look up to the task, did he?'

'Appearances can be deceptive.'

'Don't I know it!' He began to pace about the room. 'I'm sure it was her!'

'Who?'

'Julia,' he said. 'Miss Meakins. In the picture.'

'What picture?'

'Good heavens, Sidney, how can you be so obtuse? The picture Lancelot is painting. All those people parading in front of the Spa, some of them still with a blank piece of canvas for a face.'

'Oh, that. What has that got to do with Miss Meakins?'

'Didn't you see?'

'What?'

'When we were there, at Lancelot's, didn't you see her face, as plain as anything, staring out at you?'

'No.'

'Right next to the fellow in the middle with the pointed beard and funny hat.'

'Prince Rupert of Denmark.'

'Really? Well, I asked her about it. She claimed it wasn't her, that it must be someone else.'

'Don't you believe her?'

'No. Oh, I don't know.'

'I suppose all she would have had to do,' I said, 'is to go to our friend McNair and have her photograph taken.'

'Perhaps that was what Lancelot was suggesting to her when we saw them talking together the other day by the Spa.'

'Possibly. But even if she did have her face painted into the picture, it doesn't implicate her in the murder, does it?'

'I don't know,' he said, 'I really don't know.'

He threw himself down in the armchair. Several minutes passed, during which he sat staring at the carpet, his brow furrowing.

'No,' he eventually said, 'I can't make head nor tail of it.' He sighed. 'Not yet anyway.'

'You need to rest,' I said.

'You're right.' I could hardly believe my ears. But then he continued: 'And what better way to rest than to relax at a soirée? Remember we're going to Londesborough Lodge in two hours or so. Perhaps you'd like to try on your costume.'

Before I could say anything to stop him, he had darted to the wardrobe and pulled out a dark suit of clothes.

'What's that?' I asked.

'What do you think?'

'It looks like ...'

'Yes?'

'A valet's uniform.'

'That's exactly what it is. I borrowed it from Bert – a most obliging fellow.'

'You want me to go to the soirée dressed as a valet? Your valet?'

'I'm Lord Dibblesdale. Of course I'd have a valet. Don't worry, I've got a moustache and beard for you. You'll be completely unrecognizable.'

'That's what I'm afraid of.'

What could I do? There was no time to make alternative arrangements, and in any case where would I go to find a costume? At least as a valet I would not be expected to say a lot, which would come as a relief. I had spent much of the day talking to two women, whereas normally I spend most of the week talking to no one, book illustrating being a solitary occupation by and large. On top of that I had no idea what sort of questions I should be asking at

Londesborough Lodge, let alone of whom I should be asking them. Walter, I imagined, had probably prepared enough questions to keep us going all evening.

I tried on the valet's uniform while Walter busied himself with preparing my facial hair.

'What's the point of all this?' I asked. 'Why are we going incognito to Londesborough Lodge?'

'Because of a hunch I have.'

'A hunch? Am I making a fool of myself all because of a hunch of yours?'

'Several threads of our little mystery join at Londesborough Lodge – Old Simon, the model for Endymion, Mr Legard –'

'Mr Legard? You do harp on about him. I don't think the poor chap has anything to do with anything.'

'We shall see. Now sit down at the dressing table.'

I sat down. Walter applied some sticky substance to my chin and around my lips.

'I'm hoping,' he continued, 'that we can learn something tonight that will explain the mess we've got ourselves into.'

I looked at myself in amazement. I was a different person. I now had a trim brown beard and moustache, a perfect match for my hair colour.

'We haven't got ourselves into a mess,' I said, 'but I've a feeling we're going to.'

'All the components of a solution are there. I just can't fit them together into a satisfactory whole.'

I said: 'Neither can I.'

This was enough of an encouragement for Walter. During the next hour or so he set out the facts as he understood them, stopping now and then for my interruptions, in which I agreed or disagreed with his interpretation. By the time we had finished, my beard felt like it had always been part of my face, and we had established that the facts of the case were as follows.

Miss Meakins and her aunt met up for a holiday with Thomas White, as they had done for many years. Mr White went to have his photograph taken but – for whatever reason – another man pretended to be him and Mr White vanished, either of his own free will or he was kidnapped. His room at the Grand was filled with clothes. We found his body on a beach just north of Scarborough. He had been stabbed, probably with the same knife that Lancelot had used as a prop while painting a picture remarkably similar in appearance to the scene of the crime. The man he had found to model for this picture had been procured for him by Old Simon – uncommunicative frequenter of the Beehive Inn – from Londesborough Lodge, residence of the Earl of Londesborough.

That was it. Not much to work with, but surely enough to enable us to make a few deductions, if deductions could be made, or guesses, if they could not.

'Out of all those facts,' said Walter, 'do any strike you as extraordinary?'

'That Thomas White should be stabbed to death in exactly the same way as Lancelot's Endymion.'

'Bizarre, I'll grant you, but hardly extraordinary, considering it was probably Lancelot's model who went on to commit the murder with Lancelot's knife. I was thinking more of facts that don't make a lot of sense when looked at together with the other facts.'

'Such as?'

'Thomas White's room being filled with far too many clothes for a short holiday in Scarborough.'

'How do you make sense of that?'

'Looking at it logically, which I think we ought to do ...'

He paused and looked at me. I was annoyed by his superior tone, and would normally have said so, but my curiosity got the better of me.

'Yes, yes,' I said. 'Go on.'

'Logically, there could be any one of three explanations. First, it might not have been his room. Second, they might not have been his clothes. Or third, he might not have been here for a short holiday.'

'Well, the room was taken in the name of Smith, so perhaps it wasn't his.'

'What about the suitcase under the bed with the initials TW?'

'Oh yes, I'd forgotten about that.'

'A good job I haven't. So that rules out the first explanation. And he was quite clearly here for a fortnight's holiday, because Miss Meakins told us so. Therefore, we are left with the second explanation: they are not his clothes. And indeed the labels in the suits are those of Scarborough tailors, whereas Mr White was not here long enough to have suits made for him.'

'I didn't see any labels.'

'You didn't look. But I did. Do you agree with my reasoning?'

'Not entirely,' I said. 'Suppose he borrowed them or hired them.'

'For what purpose?'

'To disguise himself. The check waistcoat we found strongly suggests he disguised himself as Mr Legard.'

'But why would he want to disguise himself? And remember that Legard recognized me. Thomas White, on the other hand, had never set eyes on me.'

'Then who was Legard?'

'Who indeed? Now the second extraordinary fact, more remarkable than the clothes in room 320, is the following.' He paused for effect. '*We* found Thomas White's body.'

'Why shouldn't we have?'

'Because we were looking for him.'

Walter's grasp of logic is usually very secure, but here he seemed to have loosened his hold.

'What?' I said.

'We were the ones looking for him and we found him ...'

'Yes.'

'During a casual stroll. Something of a coincidence, don't you think?'

'It's possible, surely.'

'But highly improbable. If my reasoning is correct – and I'm inclined to think it is – the murder was committed where it was committed precisely so that we would discover it.'

A thrill of fear ran through me. Walter's suggestion was as frightening as it was intriguing. If he was right, we were being watched and controlled by a murderer.

During his explanations I had seen Walter flitting back and forth behind me as I adjusted my beard in the mirror. Now he stopped, turning towards me. I leant forward and peered upwards to see the full effect: top hat, cape, facial hair, superior smile; in short, Lord Dibblesdale. I glanced at myself then swung round to congratulate him.

'Thank you, Smithers,' he said.

'Smithers?'

'Reginald Smithers. You saw military service in the Zulu War, where you picked up a light leg wound and a Distinguished Conduct Medal at Rorke's Drift. You are handsome but unmarried, and altogether a very faithful servant.'

Have I mentioned that Walter's imagination sometimes runs away with him?

10

A Soirée

In the Crescent, coloured Chinese lanterns were swaying gently between the gateposts, dripping splashes of light onto those arriving for the soirée at Londesborough Lodge. Their excited voices joined forces with those erupting from inside. Music was escaping, too: loud, insistent music for dancing. Thankfully, in my role of Smithers the valet I had the excuse of my leg wound. I decided I would limp. Surely no one would ask a limping man to dance.

Walter and I lingered on a bench in the little park opposite. Before going in, I wanted to know something about the Lodge, and Walter was able to oblige.

Londesborough Lodge is the so-called marine residence of the Earl of Londesborough, who owns several other residences in East Yorkshire, Lincolnshire, the New Forest and, of course, London. He has often played host to royalty, both foreign and British, including the Prince of Wales, who, apart from attending entertainments at the Spa like so many other visitors, particularly likes to shoot game birds on the Earl's inland estate. This much Walter could recall from his perusal of our travel guide. He supplemented it with a few observations he had made himself on his previous visit as Lord Dibblesdale.

'The Earl is away at present and has been away for some time. Nobody seems to know who's in charge of the place in his absence. As soon as you're through the door you'll see that chaos reigns. Everyone is doing whatever he wants, and no one notices or cares. It reminds me of what I've read about the Roman Bacchanalia.'

On this auspicious note we rose and made our way to the Lodge entrance. From an architectural viewpoint, the building is an uninspired, vaguely neo-Greek, two-storeyed chunk of yellow sandstone, surrounded by gardens which, according to Walter, extend behind the house right down to where we had met Mr Legard, near the entrance to the People's Palace and Aquarium.

I asked Walter: 'Won't we need an invitation?'

'I think not. I gave the servant on the door such a large tip last time it'd be churlish of him not to let us in.'

'Let's hope he's on the door tonight.'

Luckily for us, he was. Walter gave him another tip and he touched his cap. We did seem to be spending rather a lot of money which we had originally put aside for holiday amusements. As I fingered my itchy beard, I wondered whether the evening ahead was going to be one of them.

A corridor soon led into a large ballroom. Walter's description had been no exaggeration. Almost every inch of the floor was occupied. There must have been hundreds of men there. Some were playing cards at tables (strip poker was the game, judging by their semi-clothed state); some were standing smoking or drinking, watching what was going on around them; some were huddled in pairs against the thick red velvet curtains that hung on every wall or were sprawled together on the occasional sofa (I declined to observe what they were engaged in). But most were dancing. To witness two men dancing, one assuming the woman's hold and the other the man's, especially if both have beards, is to think a mirror has somehow got into the act, so peculiar does it seem at first. There were so many couples dancing, however, that I quickly became used to it.

The music was being played fortissimo by a small orchestra tucked onto a podium halfway down the wall on the right. Overhead gleamed the biggest candelabra I have ever seen. It was swaying rather precariously in response to the dancers' efforts, its host of wavering candles sending a warm wash of light over those below, who were too interested in their partners to pay it any attention. The candelabra, which was made of brass, came to a sharp point in the centre. This was shifting about uneasily, like the arrow of an archer wanting to be sure of his target.

We stood near the entrance and looked round the room. I did not expect to recognize anyone, but was surprised, very surprised, to see Old Simon sitting at a table on his own, dressed in his shabby suit and bent over a glass of spirits. I pointed him out to Walter, who merely nodded.

I was continuing my survey of the guests when I felt a tap on my shoulder. A man with curly blond hair and rouge on his cheeks had come up behind me. Considering his appearance, I was startled by the depth of his voice. 'Would you like to dance?'

I had my answer ready. 'Sorry, I can't.'

'Can't? Or won't?'

'Can't.' I walked up and down for a while, limping as hard as I was able.

'How cute!' the man exclaimed.

'Perhaps,' I said, 'but I can't dance.'

He giggled and moved away, keeping his eyes on me until an alternative partner crossed his line of vision.

'You're very popular,' said Walter.

'If I send out a distress signal — a scream or something — you will come and rescue me, won't you?'

He laughed. 'Of course I will.'

'You might need rescuing yourself.' I had seen them coming before Walter had: a small posse of over-elegant gents with flowers in their buttonholes and pouts on their lips. They surrounded Walter as a gang of ruffians might, although men less like ruffians it would be hard to imagine.

'Lord Dibblesdale, how are you?'

'Lovely to see you again.'

'No lily tonight? Has it wilted?'

'Come and dance, Your Lordship.'

The group, with Walter hapless in their midst, drifted off towards the dance floor. I was left alone, and immediately began to feel vulnerable.

I practised my limp.

'How did you manage that then? Fall over and hurt yourself on the coastal path?'

The speaker of these words had placed himself directly in front of me so I could not avoid him. I halted mid-limp. He was dressed in spotless evening dress, which flummoxed me for a moment, but there was no getting away from it: it was Inspector Brasher. If there had been a small part of me that believed my disguise was impenetrable, it abandoned that belief now.

'No,' I said, 'just a bit of cramp.'

'I didn't expect to see you gentlemen here tonight.'

'And I didn't expect to see you.'

He was clearly not at ease in his clothes. Every now and then he would give a little wriggle, as if to improve the fit.

'Oh, I have to get about, ask questions and the rest of it. That's the only reason I'm here.'

'Walter and myself as well.'

His eyes opened wide. 'Now why should you two be asking questions? This murder is a police investigation. I acknowledge you and your brother found the body, but that's where your involvement in the case begins and ends.'

'Oh, quite,' I blustered. 'We're asking questions of a different sort.'

'What sort would that be?'

'Artistic questions.'

'Artistic?'

'Yes, we've been commissioned to do some illustrations for a book, and ... we've posed ourselves various artistic questions ... to do with colour and shape and so forth ... and we've come here ... where there's so much life going on ... looking for answers.'

'Must be a very strange book.'

'It is.'

The inspector lowered his gaze to his waistcoat, where his hands scurried about, evidently searching for a piece of fluff to pick off. Finding none, he looked puzzled for a moment before returning his attention to me. He grunted, and with that appeared to signal his satisfaction with my explanation. No doubt he made generous allowance for the fact that we belonged to that peculiar section of society labelled 'artists'.

'Of course,' he said, unwilling to let me off the hook totally, 'I may need to speak to you and your brother again. To clear up a few facts and so on.'

'We are ready to help at any time. Is the investigation going well?'

'You can't expect me to comment in detail –'

'No, no.'

'– but it is progressing. Yes, I think we can say it is progressing. I am here tonight because my inquiries are pointing in the direction of a particular person –'

'How interesting.'

'– whom I cannot name –'

'Heaven forbid.'

He smiled, pleased to be the keeper of such a secret. 'If you come across any further information relevant to the case you'll be sure to let me know, I trust?'

'Of course,' I said. It was then I remembered Lancelot's painting and its similarity to the murder scene. Lancelot was a friend, but I had my duty to do. Anyway, I was sure he had nothing to do with the crime. Brasher listened with his head cocked on one side as I told the tale of Endymion and Selene.

'Very interesting,' he said. 'I shall pay the gentleman a visit. Another artist, you say?'

'Yes.'

He grunted again and asked for Lancelot's address, which I gave him. Then he stood examining me in silence for a few moments, and I fell to thinking again what his Christian name might be. His hangdog look and flabby cheeks reminded me of a St Bernard, so perhaps he *was* a Bernard. Or would Bertram be nearer the mark? Or was that too upper-class for Brasher? He moved towards the door.

'Must get something to drink,' he said. 'Thirsty business.'

I mused that perhaps I should have told him more, but reasoned that he would find everything out for himself if he visited Lancelot. I could have told him about the model, and about Old Simon, who was sitting over there –

Only he wasn't; not any longer. The chair was empty, as was the glass he had left on the table. He was nowhere to be seen, so I concluded that, like Brasher, he had gone in search of further refreshment.

Walter was still in the midst of his admirers. I had some anxiety on his behalf; I knew he was strong enough physically to fend off any unwanted advances, but I could not vouch for his psychological resilience. I wondered what he was hoping to achieve by mixing with such characters. And then the most remarkable thing happened.

The group of gentlemen around my brother quickly dispersed and a space opened up in the centre of the dance floor. Into that space whirled Walter, dancing with Mr Legard! There could be no doubt that it was he: the yellow check waistcoat proclaimed his identity, as did the wart above his lip. They were doing a very passable Viennese waltz, with (I was pleased to note) Walter taking the man's part. Round and round they spun, and with each revolution they increased the area in which they were dancing, until all the other guests were standing on the margins of the floor, watching in delight as the pair waltzed faster and faster.

Faster still they went, the candelabra above them swaying and shuddering in sympathy with their movements. The thing appeared to have a life of its own. And as if to prove the truth of this, when Walter and Mr Legard were directly underneath it the candelabra broke loose from its fitting and hung in the air for what seemed like a good few seconds, as if supported by some invisible force, before crashing down on the pair below.

Pandemonium ensued. The circle of watching gentlemen widened as they instinctively sought safety, then, as soon as the candelabra had come to rest, they rushed back in to help the dancers. A cloud of dust obscured the scene for a while, but it quickly began to clear, revealing Walter and Mr Legard seated on the floor, on opposite sides of the heap of bent metal, as though they had decided to sit and watch how closely they had come to mishap. The point of the candelabra had embedded itself in the floor, and the whole construction had tipped over onto its side. A few of the candles had somehow survived and burnt defiantly for a moment or two before dying.

The two men were soon back on their feet. Some of the guests dusted them down in rather too enthusiastic a manner, but the important thing was that neither of them appeared any the worse for the experience they had had, at least not as far as broken bones were concerned. I forgot my limp and pushed my way through to Walter.

'Well, Sidney,' he said, with a distinct cheeriness in his voice, 'that was a near miss.'

'Are you all right?'

'Perfectly. How was my waltz?'

I refused to treat the incident with the levity my brother obviously accorded it. 'You could have been killed.'

'Do you think so?'

'Or seriously hurt.'

'It was close, I'll give you that, but I was in no danger.'

'How can you say that?'

'I'll explain later. For the present, let's go back to the Grand. It's well past my bedtime.'

The ballroom was still frantic with men rushing about, coughing, talking in high, amazed voices. I could not see Mr Legard anywhere. Perhaps he was receiving care at the hands of his admirers in some nearby nook. Inspector Brasher I could make out at the far end of the room. He was calmly removing pieces of plaster from his jacket.

As we made for the exit we were assailed by queries: 'Are you hurt, Your Lordship?', 'How on earth did that happen?', 'Are you coming back?' and similar questions to which we had no intention of supplying answers. I abandoned the pretence of limping. I had decided never to be Reginald Smithers again.

Emerging into the cool air of the Crescent, we inhaled deeply; in my case as much to remove the atmosphere of the Lodge from my soul as to remove impurities from my lungs. The short walk back to our hotel we accomplished in near silence. We were both exhausted, and Walter insisted there would be time enough the next day for analysis and explanation.

As soon as we had closed the door to our room, Walter collapsed onto his bed without making the slightest attempt to take off either his coat or his disguise. I was about to follow his example when my gaze fell upon a rectangle of white on the carpet, just visible in the slit of light creeping in from the corridor. I bent down and picked it up. It was a note. I went over to the table by my bed and lit the candle there. I read the following:

> *If you value your life and well-being, leave this business well alone, and let the police do their work. Accidents can be made to happen.*
> A WELL-WISHER

After that, I was awake for the rest of the night.

11

A Funeral

As soon as Lord Dibblesdale had woken and, casting off his lordliness, turned into my brother once more, I showed him the note which had been the cause of my nocturnal ruminations.

'Yes,' he said, 'we're getting into dangerous waters. The close shave I had with the candelabra was no accident.'

'How do you know?'

'Something else came down from the ceiling as well – a length of rope that had been holding the candelabra up, and which had been cut through by someone, presumably in the attic space above.'

'Then they were trying to harm you.'

'No, not yet. They were trying to warn me off. Mr Legard asked me to dance, then pushed me from underneath the candelabra at precisely the right moment. It had all been carefully co-ordinated to give me a fright.'

'Well, I hope it has.'

'On the contrary, it has made me all the more eager to follow this case to its conclusion.'

'You're impossible. As your elder brother I have a responsibility to you. I've saved you before, and now I –'

'You haven't saved me before.'

Walter's pride was rising to his defence again. I knew there was no point in arguing with him. The image of him flailing in the sea at Cromer quickly faded.

'Anyway,' I said, 'the note was for me.'

He turned over the slip of paper. 'I think not.'

'Can I have a look?' He passed it to me. Written on the outside were the words: 'For Mr Paget'.

'There, you see,' I said, before stopping myself mid-sentence. For a while a silence hung between us like a thick, heavy curtain.

'You've done it again,' Walter said, and that was all he said, or needed to say.

I changed tack. 'Who is it from, do you think?'

'A well-wisher, or so they claim. Someone who is involved in this business but does not wish to see us harmed.'

'Since we don't know who's involved and who's not involved, that doesn't get us very far, does it?'

Walter said: 'Let's look at it from the opposite angle. Who might wish us well and who might not?'

'Brasher wouldn't. He told me last night we should keep our noses out of the investigation.'

'Euphemia might.'

'What?'

'Euphemia has a soft spot for you.'

'So you keep saying. Do you think she's mixed up in the murder?'

'I've no idea. And neither have you.'

'For that matter,' I countered, 'it might be Miss Meakins who is concerned for your welfare.'

'I hope it is.'

'But that would make her an accomplice.'

Walter reflected on this, his face becoming darker and darker. 'Let's have breakfast,' he said at last. 'We've a long day ahead of us.'

Shortly before ten o'clock we stepped out of the Grand and set off for St Mary's church. Walter had reminded me that it was the day of Thomas White's funeral. As we walked, we wondered who else would be there. The Misses Meakins and Fitt, certainly. Inspector Brasher possibly. And others too; of this Walter was sure. He had a theory, picked up in all probability from some cheap detective story or other, that a criminal always follows their crime through to the very end. They would be standing and watching the burial of their victim.

'Perhaps Mr Legard will be there,' I said. 'He seems to have taken a fancy to you.'

'Fortunately I haven't taken a fancy to him. But I was able to study him at close quarters while we were waltzing, and I can say there is something about his features that disturbs me.'

'Yes, it's that great wart over his lip.'

'It's not that. It's what I felt the moment I first saw him. It's his resemblance to Thomas White.'

'You're surely not suggesting Thomas White might attend his own funeral.'

'Of course not, Sidney. Don't be ridiculous.'

But Arthur Legard *was* there. The weather had taken a turn for the worse, and the morning was overcast, but his waistcoat was visible from some distance as if it were made of gold and the sun were shining. Near him, gathered in a little semi-circle in a corner of the churchyard, stood Miss Meakins, Miss Fitt, Inspector Brasher and Lancelot. I could understand why Brasher was present – no doubt he had a similar theory to Walter's – but what on earth was Lancelot doing there? Regardless of the fact that he was probably wondering why *we* were there, I asked him directly.

'Just happened to wander by, that's the truth of it. Learnt it was that man on the beach you were telling me about. Doesn't seem to have many mourners, poor chap, so I thought I'd make up the numbers.'

'It does you credit,' I said. He was dressed in his studio clothes – light linen smock and dark blue trousers, both bespattered with paint of various colours – which were as much out of place as Legard's careful ostentation.

Brasher had on his usual crumpled suit. The only ones properly dressed for the occasion were the Misses Meakins and Fitt, who had procured black satin dresses discreetly trimmed with tiny blacks tassels. Their faces were half-hidden behind black veils. Walter and I were able to wear the costumes from our disguises of the previous night without standing out too painfully. What a motley set of mourners we were!

Walter exchanged greetings, in the most subtle way, with the ladies. I followed his example. Then we took up positions at the foot of the open grave, with the coffin on our left, and waited for the vicar to arrive and close the circle.

I looked up at Mr Legard, who was gazing over our heads at the town below. He wore his usual expression of bright-eyed self-assurance, as if to say this is just another death, hurry up with it now, there is so much life to be getting on with. Inspector Brasher, standing next to him – or, rather, seeming as though he had been deposited there amongst a heap of clothing – returned my look, adding elements of surprise and disapproval. Miss Meakins had availed herself of Miss Fitt's handkerchief again. The aunt seemed to be bracing herself, physically and mentally, for the ordeal to come. Her arms were gripping one another and her face was rigid.

After a few minutes of silent mutual observation, the vicar came hurrying up, prayer book in hand. He was closely followed by two men, soberly but poorly dressed, with rolled-up shirt sleeves, each carrying a coil of thick rope.

'Man that is born of woman,' intoned the vicar, 'hath but a short time to live, and is full of misery ...'

Well, yes, I thought, Thomas White's life was short enough, but was it so miserable, apart from at the very end? We knew so little about him.

'In the midst of life we are in death ...'

The two assistants ran their ropes under the coffin with the indifferent ease that must come of habitual contact with the dead, and began to take the strain of lifting.

Walter took a step forward. 'May I?' Without waiting for an answer, he grabbed the rope ends from the nearer of the two men and helped to heave the coffin down into its resting place. He returned the rope to the hands of the astonished man, all the time maintaining an expression of utmost solemnity.

Miss Meakins released her handful of soil onto the coffin lid, where it pattered out a brief, muted drum roll. The assistants retrieved their ropes for future use before taking the shovels stuck in the mound of earth and covering Thomas White for the first and, hopefully, the last time.

The vicar said, 'Lord, have mercy upon us,' and those gathered round the grave began to drift off in different directions. Miss Meakins and her aunt immediately started off on the way back to the Grand. Walter hung about in order to have a word or two with Inspector Brasher. I caught up with the vicar as he headed for the church. I had a question to put to him. When he saw me approach he stopped and inclined his head, waiting for me to speak.

'Forgive me if my query is impertinent,' I said, 'but isn't it rather unusual to hold a funeral on a Sunday?'

He looked at me for a few moments but apparently could see no signs of religious zealotry that might express themselves in unexpected and harmful ways, for he prefaced his reply with a smile.

'It is indeed unusual, very unusual. But the fiancée of the deceased particularly requested a Sunday funeral. There would be fewer holidaymakers and passers-by who might intrude upon the ceremony. And the lady insisted there should be no church service, just the burial, and well ... she is such a lovely example of God's beauty in all things that I felt I could not refuse her.'

'And the lady paid for the funeral, did she?'

'Now that is something I am not at liberty to speak about ...'

'I understand.'

'But ...' He nodded his head once, smiled, and passed on into the church.

I tried to look at things from Miss Meakins's point of view. It seems that Thomas White's relatives, assuming he had any, could not be traced; so who, if not Miss Meakins, was to provide a Christian burial for the unfortunate man? In that respect, she was to be commended. And yet ... they were engaged, which betokened a high degree of mutual affection. Could she not have arranged a church service in solemn recognition of their relationship? Perhaps the expense was beyond her means. Or perhaps she did not love him as much as all the weeping into Miss Fitt's handkerchief seemed to suggest. Or was there some other reason? Finding no easy answer, I set possible interpretations aside for future consideration.

Walter was still deep in conversation with the inspector, so I decided to pass the time as I often do: with a spot of drawing. At the eastern end of the churchyard stand ruins of an earlier, larger church – what finer model could an artist desire? My pocket sketchbook, which rarely leaves my person, was soon out and open, and settling myself onto a tree stump behind a high grey headstone I got to work with my pencil, laying down the principal outlines.

I had been pleasantly occupied in this way for several minutes when I heard voices, getting louder as they approached.

'... don't want you doing anything like that again.'

'It was only a bit of fun.'

The first speaker I identified straight away as Lancelot. I peeped round the edge of the headstone, which was large enough to hide me completely from view, to see who the other man was. It was Mr Legard. They continued their exchange unaware of my presence.

'Bit of fun?' This from Lancelot. 'You've got them following you everywhere.'

'I'm following them.'

'And that nonsense with the knife. Are you trying to get me arrested for murder?'

'They can't prove anything.'

'Why are you here today, anyway?'

'Why shouldn't I be?'

'It would have been better if Old Simon had come.'

Legard laughed, whereupon Lancelot turned on his heel with a muttered curse and rapidly walked away in the direction of his studio. Legard wandered back towards Walter and the inspector, interrupted them to bid them farewell, then set off down the hill to the life-giving town.

Too excited by what I had heard (and noted down) to carry on sketching, I put book and pencil away and stood idly among the graves.

His business with the inspector finished, Walter looked around, spotted me immediately, strode up and said: 'Brasher is coming round to see us this afternoon. I suppose we can make an hour or so of our valuable time available to him.'

'Did he say what he wanted?'

'No, but it's quite clear. He kept talking about how odd the whole case seems to him, and what he could be doing if he didn't have to be up here – fishing the rivers of Kent. Angling is his passion, apparently, which doesn't surprise me: I can just see him sitting silently waiting for a bite.'

'It seems to be more or less what he's doing now,' I said.

'Very good, Sidney. Yes, it's obvious he hasn't got any clues to go on, nor a theory worthy of the name. He still thinks a jealous rival in love did away with Mr White.'

'He could be right.'

'He's most certainly wrong.'

'He was looking for someone at the soirée. He wouldn't say who.'

'We'll ask him this afternoon.'

'He won't tell us.'

'He might. If his investigation is going so badly, he'll be grateful for all the help he can get.'

'But he told me to keep out of it.'

'Of course. He has to say that. But if he's getting desperate ...'

I tried to imagine the phlegmatic inspector in a state of desperation, but my mental faculties were not up to the task.

'Why do you think Legard was there?' I asked.

'If he's the killer, he wants to see his victim safely disposed of.'

'And if he's not the killer?'

'Then I don't know. The man is an enigma. We engaged in the usual chit-chat when we were dancing last night, but he wouldn't divulge any personal information at all. For all I know he might be a coal miner living it up for a few weeks by the sea.'

'Hardly.'

'Why was Lancelot there?'

'He said he was just passing, which could be true.'

'Or he could be the killer. Remember the knife.'

'Would you really paint a picture containing a knife you were going to use to murder someone the next day?'

As we approached the Grand, it started to rain; lightly at first, and then the heavens released everything they had been storing up over the previous days. The geraniums trembled and bowed their heads under the onslaught, the sudden liquefaction making them look like a great pool of blood that had dripped from the sky. We pulled our jackets over our heads and ran for the hotel entrance.

'By the way,' I said, as we stood in the foyer shaking ourselves like dogs, 'why did you grab hold of that rope and lower the coffin into the grave?'

'So I could be absolutely certain.'

'Certain of what?'

'That it wasn't an empty coffin.'

'Why should it be empty?'

'It wasn't anyway. I swayed my end a little as I lowered it, and I distinctly felt a pair of feet inside swinging from side to side.'

'Perhaps,' I ventured, 'Inspector Brasher isn't the only one who's desperate.'

12

A Visit from Inspector Brasher

The rain persisted all afternoon. Normally quiet at that time on a Sunday, the hotel quickly filled with temporary guests seeking shelter and refreshment. For our part, we kept Bert busy with frequent requests for drinks to be brought up to our room, as we settled down to await the arrival of Brasher of Scotland Yard. I dug out another postcard, which showed the majestic sweep of North Bay, and jotted down a few words of enthusiasm for the benefit of Edith.

Shortly after three o'clock, bedraggled and downcast, Brasher stood outside our door, hesitating. 'I'm sorry to appear before you like this, gentlemen. I thought I could take advantage of a lull in the rain, but the rain then took advantage of me.' He stroked his damp, creased brown suit again and again, as if to reassure it. Every little patch of wetness seemed to distress him. The crown of his bowler, which he held carefully in front of him, shone where he had been administering his care.

'Come in, Inspector,' said Walter, 'unless you want us to join you in the corridor.'

Brasher grunted. He took his first step into the room as if he were testing the water of an invisible sea. His subsequent steps progressed at a snail's pace, with the inspector continually looking round to check whether, like a snail, he had left a wet trail behind him.

'Please, sit down,' I said, gesturing to the armchair. He seemed alarmed by this invitation; so much so that I felt I had to allay the poor man's anxiety. 'A little rainwater won't damage the chintz,' I said. 'It'll soon dry out.'

Brasher grunted again, and gently lowered himself, with all the slow precision of a statue being set on its plinth, into the chair. Why on earth someone who took so little care over his personal appearance should worry so much about pieces of fluff and drops of water was beyond my comprehension.

Walter, who had watched this performance with a grin on his face, now closed the door and stretched himself out, in his favourite pose, on his bed. I sat on the end of mine, as attentive and alert as my sleepless night permitted. Again I found myself wondering what the inspector's Christian name could be. He was proving to be so exceptionally finicky that the name Nathaniel sprang to mind. Not that all Nathaniels are finicky; just that an uncle of mine undoubtedly was. He wouldn't shave, for example, unless the water he used was at a precise temperature. But that is another story.

Visibly sinking into himself as he relaxed in the chair, Brasher said: 'Thank you for agreeing to see me at such short notice, gentlemen.'

'The pleasure is ours,' said Walter. Another grunt seemed to confirm that it certainly was not the inspector's.

'Before we go any further,' Brasher began, 'would you mind telling me,' and here he looked over at Walter, 'why you had to lower Mr White's coffin this morning? It lent a certain, shall we say, bizarre element to the ceremony.'

'Oh, it was simply that I saw the poor fellow was struggling,' Walter said, 'so I stepped into the breach.'

'That was the reason, was it?'

'That was the reason.'

The inspector glanced in my direction, but I gave him no indication, not by the slightest of facial movements, of my thoughts on the matter. He began to caress his bowler.

He said: 'It was a rum do all round, that funeral.'

I played the innocent. 'In what way?'

'In almost every way. Who was there. Who wasn't. Thomas White seems to have had no relatives or friends to mourn him. None that we can trace, anyway.'

'Didn't Miss Meakins know of any?' asked Walter.

'She gave a very curious account of how she met her fiancé, and how they carried on their relationship.'

'Did they meet at Blackpool or Brighton?'

If Brasher was surprised, he did not show it. 'Yes, one of those two.' He transferred his hand from his bowler to his chin, and began rubbing that instead. 'So, you've been conversing with the two ladies.'

'Yes, we have, Inspector,' Walter said. 'As one does when on holiday.'

'If you don't mind my saying so, you don't appear to me to be on holiday.'

'Don't we?' I said.

'You seem to be interfering in police matters.'

'Heaven forbid!' cried Walter. 'We are assisting as much as we can.'

'Let me remind you that no one has yet been charged with the murder of Thomas White.'

'I'm sure you'll get there in the end, Inspector.'

Brasher glared at Walter. 'What I meant was everyone is still a suspect – present company most definitely not excepted.'

After an uncomfortable silence Brasher continued with his analysis.

'Another rum thing: only the two ladies were dressed for a funeral. Everyone else seemed to be there for some other reason.'

'Yourself included,' said Walter.

'Of course myself included. My reason – and it's a pretty good one, I think – was that I'm conducting a murder inquiry. What was your reason?'

I jumped in before Walter could come up with anything outlandish. 'The offering of moral support to the ladies in their time of sorrow.'

Walter smiled and acknowledged, with a slight gesture of the head, that he was impressed by my readiness of mind. Brasher simply stared at me, without blinking, until I thought he had turned to stone. He offered an explanation.

'You may think, gentlemen, because I am, shall we say, not of an excitable nature, that there is nothing going on in this head of mine.' He spotted a tiny patch of water on his waistcoat and pressed it between his fingers as if he were squashing a fly. 'Let me assure you, on the contrary, that I am putting two and two together and making four.'

'I expect no less,' said Walter, 'from the famous Brasher of the Yard –'

The celebrated man grunted in his usual non-committal way, but an oh-so-slight raising of his shoulders spoke of his pleasure at being mentioned in such terms.

'– but my brother was telling the truth: we are keeping a watchful eye on the welfare of the two ladies.'

Brasher let the point go. 'Yet another rum thing is Thomas White's headstone.'

I said: 'I didn't see any headstone.'

'There isn't one, not yet. It's still being made. But I had a word with the mason, and he told me what the inscription will be.' He reached inside his crumpled jacket and brought out a crumpled sheet of paper, which he flattened out between his hands and passed round.

THOMAS WHITE
Was Photographed upon a Whim,
And Now That's All That's Left of Him.

'No dates?', said Walter.

'No.'

'Well, I can understand there being no birth date, but we all know when he died.'

I asked: 'And this is being paid for by Miss Meakins?'

'Most definitely. All in all,' said Brasher, 'a rather unfeeling commemoration of one's fiancé.'

We had to agree.

'Although perhaps an accurate one,' he continued. 'Miss Meakins tells me you have the photograph.'

'I do,' said Walter. He heaved himself into a sitting position, took the photograph from his pocket and handed it to the inspector. 'But it's certainly not accurate. It's not Mr White, but some impostor.'

'Yes, she did mention that. Could you let me keep it?'

'Of course.'

I was pleased to see the photograph, the cause of so many of Walter's excesses, leave his possession.

'But I've not come here for that,' Brasher said. 'The reason for my visit is this.' He turned over the sheet of paper and passed it to me. Drawn on it was a symbol of some sort: a circle with a plus sign sitting on top of it, with an arrowhead on top of the plus sign. I handed it to Walter, who barely gave it a glance before passing it back to Brasher. 'What does it mean, Inspector?'

'I was hoping one of you two could tell me that.'

'Where did you find this?' I asked.

'On the dead man.'

'You mean in one of his pockets?'

'Sidney,' said Walter, 'he was naked.'

'So he was.'

'It *was* on him,' Brasher said. 'Literally. A tattoo – here, in the palm of his hand.' The forefinger of the inspector's left hand made brief contact with the centre of his right.

'We didn't notice that,' I said.

'No, why should you?'

I glanced across at Walter. He flicked a smile at me. Bearing in mind Walter's removal of the navy blue bathing costume, and now this, I wondered what more he had got up to on the beach while I was fetching the slops, as he called them.

'So you've no idea as to what it means,' Brasher stated rather than asked.

'Afraid not, Inspector,' said Walter.

'I thought it might be some sort of secret society.'

'Like the Freemasons?'

'Something like that. That was why I went to the soireé at Londesborough Lodge last night – the only reason I went – to see if anyone else had it on the palm of his hand.'

'And did they?'

'Not that I could see. Mind you, most of the guests wore gloves.'

'Very fashionable,' said Walter.

'You wore gloves as well.'

'I did. But not now.' Walter held up his hands, palms towards the inspector. 'I come out of it clean-handed.' He laughed at his own wit.

Brasher glowered. 'I'm keeping an open mind,' he said. 'That symbol may be of some vital significance, or it may be some decoration peculiar to the taste of Thomas White, of no relevance to the case whatsoever.'

'True. You don't want to be led on a wild goose chase, do you?' said Walter.

As the inspector lifted himself from the chair, his clothes cascaded downwards, and most of their undulations ebbed away. 'All the clear evidence points so far to his being murdered by the impostor in this photograph' – which he slipped into an inside pocket together with the sheet of paper – 'but for what motive we don't yet know.'

'A love rival?' I suggested.

'It's possible.'

'To steal his money?' This from Walter.

'We don't know that he had any, just as we don't know much about him at all.' The inspector contemplated the carpet, falling into a brief reverie before rousing himself. 'Thank you for your time, gentlemen.' He turned to me. 'I'll now go and see that artist friend of yours – Galahad, I think you said –'

'Lancelot. Lancelot Pemberlow.'

'– to see if *he* can enlighten me.'

He tiptoed across the room as if it were full of puddles he was anxious to avoid. Walter jumped ahead of him and opened the door. Maintaining as little contact with the carpet as possible, swivelling on his heels, Brasher stepped over the threshold.

'Good day, gentlemen.'

'Good day, Inspector,' we chorused.

Once the door was closed, we collapsed on the beds in fits of laughter, just as we used to do as small boys when something one of the servants had said or done struck us as funny. Then we would often laugh until our stomachs hurt. Now, of course, we had serious matters to engage our minds as well.

'Well, what do you think?' said Walter. 'Is Inspector Brasher on the level or is he trying to pull the wool over our eyes, if I may be allowed to mix my metaphors.'

'You may. But what do you mean?'

'When he tells us he thinks the impostor is the killer, do we believe him, or is he trying to deflect us from going after the real killer?'

'So he'll get the credit?'

'So he'll find the culprit before we do.'

'Isn't that likely anyway? He has all the resources of the police force behind him.'

'Ha! What use is that if you can't think logically and arrive at the correct conclusion? No, I think we're ahead of him at the moment and he's playing for time. We must stick to our guns.'

'But we must help him to catch the murderer if we can.'

'Why must we?'

'It's our duty as citizens.'

'Duty be damned. If we can catch him more quickly, and I'm certain we can, then that's what we should be doing. That is how we contribute to society. We engage directly.'

'Or interfere so much that we put ourselves in danger.'

'Well, if you're afraid, Sidney ...'

'I didn't say that. But remember that note slipped under our door. We must be careful.'

'Of course. Careful but clever. And then we triumph.' His eyes gleamed for an instant. 'If I may make a small criticism here – it is not very clever of you to have told Brasher about Lancelot.'

'Why not?'

'He'll only go and ask him lots of questions, and Lancelot might just stupidly admit the knife was his, or he might still have that incriminating painting on display in his studio –'

'I told Brasher about all that.'

Walter was lost for words for a few seconds. 'You did what?'

'I told him about the *Endymion and Selene* painting, and the knife.'

'And the model?'

'No, I don't think so.'

'You don't think so?'

'I'm sure I didn't.'

'And Old Simon?'

'No.'

'You're an absolute fathead, Sidney.'

'I'm only telling the truth.'

'Which is not always what is required. You must learn to read the situation and act accordingly.'

'And you must stop playing the know-it-all detective. You might bring catastrophe on someone, if not on yourself.'

'What nonsense.'

'Not if the killer kills again because you're holding back information. You haven't told the police about the bathing costume you found with the name A. Barnes on it, or the symbol you must have seen on Thomas White's hand when you were alone with his body on the beach –'

'Brasher knows about that.'

'But he doesn't know you were concealing it from him. If he did know, he could infer that you were up to no good.'

'Then he would be wrong. The police must find clues for themselves. I don't see why I should do the work for them.'

'And what did you find out at the soirée last night? Did you meet any men who had that symbol on their hands?'

'I'd rather not say just now.'

'You never want to say. You always want to keep everyone in the dark. I think you're afraid that if you share the information you've gathered, others will solve the crime before you do.'

'Don't be absurd.'

'Then why won't you explain things to me? Tell me what you've found out. I might even be able to help, strange as that may seem to you.'

Walter turned away, as if he wanted to think over what I had said; as if he were perhaps ready to acknowledge at last that he had some need of his elder brother. He turned back almost at once.

'I can't disclose my reasoning until I'm sure it's correct.'

'In other words, you're afraid of failure.'

'Aren't we all?'

'At least I admit failure. I'm ready for others to save me from myself. You're not.'

'I don't need saving.'

'And never have, I suppose.'

'Precisely.'

I heard rain lashing the windows, and the image of the sunny beach at Cromer disappeared. I realized that unless the weather changed abruptly I would be holed up with Walter for a good while yet. I opened my suitcase and took out the book I had brought with me but which I had had no time to read until now. Sitting propped up against the bedhead, I made a great show of being deep in the story of David Copperfield and oblivious of Walter's movements. But I knew that he had done the same. He was lounging on his bed, turned on his side, glancing through one of the illustrated papers he had snatched up at King's Cross ...

Uriah Heep was protesting his 'umbleness for the umpteenth time as I was jolted out of the half-sleep into which I had drifted. Some movement, I thought, in my peripheral field of vision had woken me, and this movement turned out to be Walter, standing by the open door, dressed for going out, adjusting his cravat.

I said: 'Where are you going?'

His hand reached for the doorknob. 'For a walk. The sun's out again.'

It was. A corridor of brightness had laid itself across the room, ending in the illumination of Walter in his casual best and, ominously, with his deerstalker in his hand. The window panes, streaked but dry, glowed. It took only a matter of seconds for me to notice these changes, but that was all Walter needed to slip out and close the door with a resolute click.

So that was the game now. Each man for himself. Very well. If Walter would not see reason, I would have to make him. If he would not behave like a decent, upstanding citizen, I would show him, by example, the error of his ways. I would be ruthless in the exercise of my mental faculties, but fair. Any clues I came across I would communicate to him, and to Inspector Brasher, at the first opportunity. You might call it sharing intelligence, in both senses of the word.

I had no sooner formulated this grand moral law than I realized I had just broken it. Had I not overheard Lancelot and Mr Legard exchanging facts about the case which incriminated them, indeed which seemed to hold the key to the mystery? And had I reported these facts either to Walter or to the inspector? No. A warm shiver of shame ran up and down my body before I overcame it with the following explanation.

I had obviously acted intuitively. Without being fully aware of it, I knew that if I had disclosed to Walter what I had overheard, he would have rushed off and got himself, and perhaps me, and possibly goodness knows how many other people, murdered. Therefore, I had reserved the information, so to speak, for later reflection. What I eventually learnt I would reveal at some point in the future – at a time of my choosing, when I could be sure that Walter would not need to follow it up since its implications had already become clear. This assumed a great deal about my ability to elucidate clues, but it was, I admit, the only explanation which could justify my silence. As to why I had not told Brasher ... well, it had simply slipped my mind. I would tell him everything I knew the next time we met.

13

A Modern Caravaggio

I woke the next day with my conscience considerably soothed. Walter was still asleep after returning late the night before, as I prepared to sally forth into the highways and byways of Scarborough. My earlier independent sortie to get information from Old Simon at the Beehive, and incidentally from Miss Fitt at Tilly's Tea Room, had not been the great success I had hoped it would be, simply because the information I gathered was of little significance and Walter had obtained it at much less cost elsewhere. This time, however, I knew what I wanted to find out. I checked that my sketchbook, in which I had noted down the devastating words I had overheard in the churchyard, was still in my pocket, and set out for Lancelot's studio full of purpose and self-assurance, like a Templar knight going to the Crusades.

By the time I arrived at Church Stairs Street my purpose was intact but my self-assurance was in tatters. I was about to do nothing less than accuse an old friend of complicity in murder. How would he react? If he admitted his guilt, would our friendship save me, or would he stick a knife into me as well? But could he really be guilty? Lancelot, whom I had known since the days of art college; who, though eccentric, was as kind as any man I knew; who lived alone, he said, because he did not want to inflict himself on his fellow human beings – could this man be a killer? And what was his motive? Surely he would clear everything up, and I would go away with his laughter ringing in my ears, annoyed I had been so naive.

My knock on his door brought him clattering and swearing down the stairs. He was still Caravaggio, it seemed: dressed in his

Renaissance garb and with the sword swinging back and forth between his legs.

'Oh, it's you.'

It was not a good start. I had been hoping he had forgotten our last meeting, when Walter, in full Sherlock Holmes mode, had as good as said that Lancelot had wielded the knife that did for Thomas White.

'Yes, it's me. Can I come in?'

He looked at me doubtfully. 'If you must.' He led the way up to the studio.

Endymion and Selene had disappeared. Where to, I could not guess, unless it was among the ranks of canvases leaning against the walls, showing their graceless backs. In pride of place on the easel was Lancelot's latest piece: the modern-Caravaggesque pub brawl he had mentioned earlier. Where *Endymion and Selene* had been bursting with brilliant, vibrant colours, this picture seemed to suck light in rather than reflect it, leaving a mass of dark shapes out of which faces emerged here and there in unexpected positions. On, around and under a table charged with glasses of beer and wine, half a dozen ruffians, wearing Elizabethan outfits of doublet and hose, were grabbing, punching and clawing each other. Such was the confusion it was hard to tell which aggressive hand and which bloodied face belonged to which man. One of the brawlers was standing on his head; another seemed to have been turned inside out by the artist's deliberate distortions. The violence on display was extreme. This was nowhere more apparent than in the revolver – shining metal with a mother-of-pearl butt – which Lancelot, introducing his trademark touch of modernity, had placed in the right hand of the barmaid watching the scene. In her left hand she held a cloth, presumably to wipe up the mess. Call it self-suggestion, but I could not help seeing, in her painted face, the barmaid at the Beehive.

'Ah, the latest Pemberlow,' I said. 'What's the title?'

'*Pub Fight.*'

'It looks worse than that,' I said. 'That gun looks pretty deadly.'

He did not comment. We stood looking at one another for a while, each waiting for the other to speak. I gave in first.

'Aren't you going to offer me a port?'

'Should I?'

'Why ever not?'

'I'm not sure you've deserved it.'

'Not deserved it? What have I done?'

Lancelot's hands played with the hilt of his sword.

'Some policeman came to see me this morning,' he said.

'Really? Who was that?'

'The one who was at the funeral.'

'Funeral?'

'Your brother was talking to him.'

'Oh, yes.'

'Looked as though he'd been dragged through a hedge backwards.'

'That's Inspector Brasher. He's been to see us too.'

'He had my painting taken away.'

'Did he? Which one?'

'You know which one. My masterpiece. You told him all about it.'

'I don't recall ... I might have mentioned something to him. In passing, as it were. I'm sorry you feel so bad about it.'

'How do you expect me to feel? He as good as thinks I killed the poor fellow on the beach, since it was my knife sticking in him.'

'But didn't you tell him about the model?'

'Of course. But seeing as how nobody except Old Simon knows who the model is, the inspector didn't seem inclined to believe me.'

Neither was I inclined to believe Lancelot; not knowing what I knew. If I did not challenge him now, I could see myself leaving with nothing gained. I braced myself and looked him in the eyes.

'I'm not surprised he didn't believe you.'

His eyes narrowed as he tried to figure what my purpose might be. Then, abandoning the attempt, he walked over to the cabinet and poured out two small glasses of port. One he handed to me; the other he drank straight off before returning the glass to its place next to the decanter.

'Why don't you believe me, Sidney?' he said. 'Why do you of all people, one of my oldest friends, think I'm a murderer?'

'I don't.'

'Oh, I thought you –'

'But I think you know who the murderer is.'

There – I had said it. I sipped at my port. He stood looking at me, as a lion might stand looking before deciding to spring.

'What makes you say that?' he asked.

'A conversation you had in St Mary's churchyard this morning. With Mr Legard.'

'So, you've been talking to Mr Legard.'

'No. I overheard what you said to one another. I was behind one of the headstones.'

'You were hiding behind one of the –?'

'I was sitting sketching and it just so happened you came along and ... well ...'

'Well what?'

I brought out my sketchbook and opened it at the drawing of the church ruins. 'That nonsense with the knife,' I read out. 'Are you trying to get me arrested for murder?'

'You overheard that, did you?'

I nodded and continued: 'It would have been better if Old Simon had come.'

Lancelot smiled at this last remark. 'Yes, it would have been better. Though nothing would have changed.'

'I don't understand.'

'Why should you? It's none of your business.'

'It *is* my business – everyone's business – if you're shielding a murderer.'

'I do hope you're not going to be difficult about this, Sidney.'

'I'm going to do what's right. Unless you can give me a good reason why I shouldn't, I'm going to tell the inspector what I know.'

'Not a good idea.'

'No?'

'Another port?'

My glass was still half-full. 'No, thank you.'

Lancelot went to the cabinet. His sword lurched madly this way and that. Finally, calmly, he undid the belt and removed the offending weapon, dropping it on the floor. It seemed like some kind of surrender. He poured himself another port, then turned back to me.

'I've tried to protect you, Sidney. And Walter. I don't like seeing my friends get hurt.'

'That's a fine sentiment, but I don't see how you've protected us.'

'Accidents can be made to happen.'

'You?' I said. 'You're the well-wisher.'

'I can only do so much.'

'You can tell me what all this is about.'

He shook his head, then lapsed into thought, gazing at *Pub Fight*. After a minute or so, he heaved a deep sigh. 'If I assure you I've not killed anyone, and that if I'm silent about certain matters there is a good reason for my silence ...'

'I believe you,' I said. 'I've no reason not to. But it still isn't enough to stop me informing Inspector Brasher.'

He sighed again. 'Promise me you won't say anything just yet. Come here ... let's say the day after tomorrow, Wednesday, at midday.' He tossed off the port. 'By then I'll have worked out what I can tell you to make you understand.'

He had a defeated air about him, all energy gone. His Caravaggio garb – the costume of a rake and fugitive – hung limply on him, like a worn-out skin he was eager to shed. He was no longer a potential criminal but my friend from days of old.

I nodded. Then I handed him my glass, still not finished, descended the stairs and struck out for the centre of town.

As I approached the Grand, an ill-defined mass detached itself from the shadow of the entrance. It shuffled towards me, gradually resolving itself into the irregular but unmistakable contours of Inspector (Nathaniel? Algernon? Humphrey?) Brasher.

'Mr Paget,' he said, smiling and reaching for my hand, which he clasped and shook. 'They told me you'd gone out, so I decided the best thing to do was to await your return.'

'Well,' I said, wondering what had caused this almost miraculous transformation from curmudgeonliness to affability, 'here I am.'

He chuckled. 'Indeed you are. Now, what I'd like to propose is this. Would you join me for lunch tomorrow?'

'Tomorrow?'

'At my expense, of course.'

'Where?'

'I'll keep that secret for now, if you don't mind. But I'm told they do a very good meat pie. Shall we meet at the harbour at one o'clock?'

'Yes,' I said, unable to think up any other answer quickly enough.

'Till tomorrow then, Mr Paget.' He tipped his bowler to me, smiled again and stumbled off past the geranium beds.

I entered the Grand and made my way across the foyer, where I was soon to discover that the inspector was not the only one waiting for me. In the centre of the floor, just in front of the imposing staircase, there is a huge circular ceramic container for ferns and other greenery, the outside of which has been fashioned into seats with red velvet cushions. From one of these Miss Meakins rose.

'Mr Paget,' she said. 'I'm pleased to see you.'

'And I you, Miss Meakins.'

'Is your brother with you?'

'No. I've no idea where he is.'

'Then could I have a few minutes of your time?'

'Certainly.'

She gestured towards the plant container, and we sat down. A fern dangled overhead, threatening to obscure our view of one another, but Miss Meakins did not seem to notice.

Sitting so close to her, closer than I had ever been before, I became intensely aware of her attractiveness. Her skin was rosy and unblemished; her eyes a clear dark brown; her movements graceful and economical. I could scarcely blame Walter if he had indeed fallen for her. This was a lady who would not remain for long without a fiancé.

In her soft but precise voice she said: 'I want to ask your advice about this.' She pulled a folded piece of paper from her sleeve and handed it to me. 'It was found in Thomas's suitcase. He obviously intended me to have it, but I haven't the slightest idea what it could mean.'

The words 'For Julia' were pencilled on the outside. I unfolded the sheet and read the following, written in dark blue ink, in a beautiful copperplate:

> *When the sun shines and light rain begins*
> *to fall in town, you'll find there's room in*
> *the shelter for twenty people, and of these*
> *four will be required to collect money*
> *for tea and coffee served in a silver pot.*

Considering the strange events that had unfolded over the previous week, I would have been disappointed had the message been anything as straightforward as 'So-and-so is trying to kill me' or 'A motive for my violent end would be such and such'. All the same, I was not prepared for anything as bizarre as this. What on earth did it mean? It seemed to be in some sort of code. But why should Thomas White have left a coded message for his fiancée?

'Have you shown this to the police?'

'No. It might be nothing important after all. But it *is* curious.'

'Very.'

'Perhaps you could show it to your brother,' Miss Meakins said. The same thought was about to cross my mind, if I'm honest, but her obvious lack of confidence in me was galling. 'He might know what it means.'

'He might,' I said, 'or he might not.' I made a great show of examining the note, turning it this way and that, furrowing my brow and pursing my lips. I even held it up to the light to look for a watermark, simply because I imagined that is what Sherlock Holmes would have done. There was none, thank goodness; so no comment was required.

I asked: 'May I keep this for a few days?'

'Of course. I've made a copy of it.'

Not only attractive then, but sensible too.

'Now, Mr Paget, if you'll excuse me, I must go and meet my aunt.'

'Please give her my regards.'

'I will.'

We said our goodbyes. She rose, adjusted her hat, and glided towards the small patch of sunshine at the entrance, while I climbed the stairs. I was looking forward to an hour or two alone in my room, fathoming out the meaning of the peculiar words I held in my hand, then returning the decoded message – if message it was – to an appreciative Miss Meakins. I was halfway up the stairs when I heard a voice that made me stop and turn back. It was Walter.

'Julia, how pleasant to meet you.'

'Walter,' Miss Meakins said. Just one word, one name, but the way she said it made it clear that she had been waiting in the foyer for him, and had been content with me as second best. They immediately fell into an intimate, inaudible conversation, punctuated by glances and gestures in my direction.

Bowing to the inevitable, I went back down and surrendered the curious note to Walter. I left them to it. I went up to our room, where I sat gazing at the sea, my mind suddenly as empty as the cloudless sky.

I was jolted out of my reverie by Walter's storming into the room.

'Sidney,' he cried, 'this is more than we could have hoped for.'

'Is it?' I said, only half-alert. 'What is?'

He flourished Thomas White's note in the air like a victor's flag. 'We've had just about everything in this case up to now except a code to crack. And now we have it!'

I found myself wishing we had not had anything new at all, but had to acknowledge that I was deceiving myself. In my heart of hearts I did not merely want to rein in Walter, I wanted to surpass him. I would decode the message and solve the crime – not just to bring my brother down a peg or two, which it undoubtedly would do, but to become myself the man of the moment, the hero of the hour, a new and improved Brasher of the Yard.

'What do you make of it?' Walter asked.

'I've only seen it for a moment or two.'

'Here.' He dropped the note in my lap. 'I've memorized it.'

I folded it and stowed it away for later. I said: 'What have you been doing today?'

'I can ask you the same question.'

'You tell me first.'

Walter lay on his bed, his hands behind his head. 'I have been pursuing my theory concerning the murder.'

'Which is what?'

'Which is that a secret society of some sort is at the bottom of it. You remember the symbol the dear inspector told us was tattooed on Thomas White's hand?'

I nodded.

'Well, I did meet some men with that tattoo on their hand at the soirée. Many men. Very many. I found that if I removed my gloves and showed them my symbol, they were keen to remove their gloves and do the same. Mr Legard was one of them.'

'And what does that mean?'

'That Thomas White, Mr Legard and many others belong to a secret club or society. And judging by what we know and what we've seen, it is transparently clear what the nature of that club or society is.'

'Not to me.'

'Consider, Sidney.' Walter held up his hand. On his open palm was the symbol: a circle with a plus sign sitting on top of it, with an arrowhead on top of the plus sign.

'You haven't had a tattoo, have you?' I cried.

'Good heavens, no. It'll wipe off. I borrowed a stick of make-up from Julia.' I raised my eyebrows.

He continued: 'And I most definitely have not joined the club. Don't you recognize anything familiar about this symbol?'

I shook my head.

'Take away the bar across the arrow, rotate the circle clockwise a little ...'

'Of course,' I said. 'The sign for Mars, or male.'

'Male, I think, in this case. Put back the bar, which has the effect of deleting what is there ...'

'I see. Non-male. The lily brigade.'

'I wouldn't put it quite so facetiously. I'd say: all those who bear this symbol are pederasts.'

'If you like,' I said. 'But in any case it's illegal.'

'Indeed,' said Walter. 'Hence the need for secrecy.'

'And how does that tie in with the murder?'

'We are dealing here with Scarborough's deviant class. Thomas White had the symbol on him, so did Mr Legard, so did just about everybody at the Londesborough Lodge soirées. I dare say when we find the killer – who is surely the man that Old Simon found at the lodge and who modelled for Lancelot's painting before stealing the knife and using it on Mr White – when we find him I have no doubt he will also have the symbol tattooed on his hand. He is the impostor, the man who had his photograph taken instead of Thomas White. I have become more and more certain that Mr White disappeared of his own free will, lured away to Londesborough Lodge by the impostor, or possibly Mr Legard, in order to satisfy his sexual desires, which is what he and the impostor were doing on the beach just before he met his end.'

'But why should anyone want to kill him?'

'That we can only guess at just now. There are many possible motives: jealousy, blackmail avenged, necrophilia even. Once we have found the killer we shall find the motive.'

'Usually it's done the other way round.'

'This is an unusual case.'

'It's an interesting theory,' I said, 'and it helps to explain that symbol, but there's one thing that undermines it.'

'Yes?'

'Why, if Thomas White was that way inclined, did he get engaged to

Miss Meakins?'

'I admit that is a little difficulty at the moment. It's the one piece of the jigsaw that won't fit in.'

'Then perhaps the other pieces aren't fitted together properly.'

Walter let out a small cry of disdain.

I said: 'And how have you been pursuing this theory of yours?'

'I have been following Mr Legard.'

'Didn't he see you?'

'I was not myself. Nor Lord Dibblesdale. I was a street sweeper and totally unrecognizable.'

'You mean you hope you were.'

'I was totally unrecognizable. I caught up with him near Londesborough Lodge, then followed him at a discreet distance until he entered this hotel.'

'What did he want in here?'

'I don't know. I could hardly go in dressed as a street sweeper. But it's significant, I think, that he came in here for some reason. He left soon after, and led me here and there all over Scarborough as he approached various men, apparently at random. He finally went into the Beehive Inn, with which I believe you are familiar.'

'Haunt of Old Simon.'

'I waited for two hours for him to emerge, sweeping my little patch of street until it shone, but he stayed inside. I fear I shall have to go into the Beehive after all, and investigate Mr Legard's connection with it.'

'Don't expect much help from Old Simon.'

'In the meantime we have the coded message to occupy us.'

I took it out and looked at it again.

> *When the sun shines and light rain begins*
> *to fall in town, you'll find there's room in*
> *the shelter for twenty people, and of these*
> *four will be required to collect money*
> *for tea and coffee served in a silver pot.*

The words swam before my eyes. It made even less sense than it had done the first time I had seen it.

'Something about people sheltering from the rain and paying for refreshments,' I suggested.

'That would be a strange sort of note to write to anyone, don't you think?'

'I do. But what else could it mean?'

'We must ignore any apparent sense in the message as it stands. We must look for the key that will reveal its true meaning.'

'Where do we start?' The task seemed hopeless to me before we had even begun.

'There are many kinds of code,' Walter said.

'What do you know about codes?'

'A fair amount. I have studied them a little.'

'You've kept it quiet.'

'You may be my brother, but you can't know everything about me. As I was saying, there are many kinds of code. The simplest involves changing each letter to the letter following it in the alphabet – A becomes B, B becomes C, C becomes D, and so on – but here that would lead to a meaningless string of letters. Another technique is to take the first letter of each word and put them together.'

'Just a minute,' I said. 'That gives us WTSSALRBTF –'

'Or to take the second letter of each word.'

'HHUHNIAEO –'

'But, as I say, there are many types of code.'

14

A Pub Fight

According to our guidebook, there has been no shipbuilding in Scarborough for thirty years and more. Instead, the harbour is given over to the activities of sea fishing and holidaymaking. As I stood waiting for Inspector Brasher, I could see several brown-sailed yawls at their moorings, a steam trawler, and even a boat bearing the name 'Penzance', which told me it had made the long voyage from Cornwall, disbursing at Scarborough its silver treasure. Fishermen in sou'westers sat mending nets; ladies with parasols sauntered by – roughness cheek by jowl with elegance.

Winding his way between the ladies came the personification of *in*elegance, tipping his hat to them at every opportunity. He halted in front of me and waited for his clothes to settle before speaking.

'Another lovely day,' said the inspector, winking and tilting his head towards the ladies.

I ignored this crude invitation to camaraderie. 'Just the weather for sitting by a river, fishing rod in hand,' I suggested.

'Oh yes.' Brasher's eyes took on a dreamy, distant look. 'But business first. Or rather, a little lunch.' His eyes brightened up again and he set off walking. I followed.

'Here we are,' he said. 'Pie and pint, is it?' Without waiting for an answer he plunged into the dark interior of the public house to which he had brought me. I should have known: it was the Beehive. The place was as dusty and dingy as before, strongly lit in one area by the sun. The drinkers were half-hidden in shadow.

Brasher had stopped just inside the doorway, and now he whispered to me: 'Which one is Old Simon?' So that was it. The inspector was following up the information Lancelot had given him about the source of the model. I felt like telling him he was way behind Walter and me, but I did not think he would appreciate it.

I looked around. The barmaid was engaged as usual in wiping a glass. Whether through some trick of the light or the prompting of my confused brain, for a split second the glass turned into a revolver. Her eyes flashed recognition. I smiled in return. She gestured with her head towards one of the far corners of the room. My eyes had now become accustomed to the half-light, and I was able to make out Old Simon with his full head of white hair, moustache and beard.

At that moment, just as I was about to renew my acquaintance with the old fellow, I heard a familiar voice behind me. 'Allow me to buy a round.' It was Walter. Thankfully he was not dressed as a street sweeper but as his immaculate self, which at least made his munificence believable.

'What are you doing here?' I asked.

'The same as you, I suppose. Taking refreshment. Pints all round, is it?'

Inspector Brasher grunted. 'Pies as well,' he said.

'Certainly. Three pints of bitter and three of your best pies.'

The barmaid eyed him doubtfully.

Walter said: 'Where shall we sit?'

I had been too surprised at finding him there to decline a pint of bitter, but I had now collected myself enough to point to the corner where Old Simon was seated. As we sat down next to him he gave no sign that he was aware of our presence. He kept his head bowed over his glass. All we could see of him was his great head of hair. The barmaid brought our drinks.

'Hello,' I said to Old Simon. 'We meet again.' He glanced up briefly at me.

Inspector Brasher got straight to the matter. 'I've been having a chat with Lancelot Pemberlow. He tells me he asked you to find him a model for –'

'Just a minute,' said Walter. He reached across to Old Simon, seized him under the chin and jerked his head up. The old man glared, his eyes flicking rapidly between us. 'I thought so,' said

Walter.

What happened next I can only describe as Caravaggesque. Old Simon dived over the table in an attempt to escape. Our glasses of beer flew to the floor. Walter grabbed Old Simon, whose legs swung round, catching me and forcing me up against Brasher, who, reacting more swiftly to the turmoil than I would have thought possible, had stood up but now crashed over as I collided with him, landing on top of Walter and Old Simon. Then the table went over, and so did we. All in all, it was a fairly faithful reproduction of Lancelot's *Pub Fight*, and I was sorry he was not there to sketch the resulting melee.

The barmaid stood watching us, hands on hips and head thrown back. We all stood up, as though hypnotised by her. Old Simon slipped from Walter's grasp and ran out. Walter was after him, but the barmaid placed herself in his way.

'I don't keep a rowdy pub,' she said. 'You'll pay for the damage.'

Walter, ever the gentleman where the fair sex is concerned, charmed her with apologies and the immediate donation of a pound note. I set the table back on its four legs, and we left.

'Why did you provoke him?' Brasher asked. 'I was about to get some important information from him.'

'I very much doubt it,' said Walter.

'Yes, well I hope I can move as quickly when I'm his age. Old Simon indeed!' Shaking his head and smoothing down his clothes, which seemed to have been engaged in a fight of their own, the inspector took his leave.

As so often before, once alone with Walter I turned on him. 'What the blazes were you up to in there? And why have you been following me?'

'Why do you think so highly of yourself,' he said – which I thought was rich coming from him – 'that you imagine I'm following you. I came here to pursue my inquiries into Mr Legard and his activities. I left him inside the Beehive Inn yesterday, so I'm picking up the trail again. I told you all this. You're probably following me.'

'Nonsense. I had no idea where Brasher was going to bring me.'

'So you're working together with the Great Inspector, are you?'

On that matter I decided to let him writhe in ignorance. Instead I asked: 'Why did you try to grab Old Simon?'

'To find something out. And I have done – to my complete satisfaction. I don't think we'll be seeing Old Simon again.'

'What are you talking about?'

Whether Walter was intending to give me an answer I shall never know. He let out a cry and waved a hand. I followed his gaze. Miss Fitt was approaching beneath a new parasol. She beamed at us. 'A beautiful day, isn't it?'

'It is indeed,' I said.

Walter's mind was not on the weather (it rarely was). 'Did you see a man come running by? White hair. Beard. Shabby suit.'

'I'm afraid I didn't,' Miss Fitt replied. 'But then I've only just arrived.'

'Damn it!'

'Language!' I cried.

'It's quite all right,' she said. 'I understand enough of the world to know that sometimes our passions get the better of us' – she glanced in my direction – 'and we often express ourselves before we have properly had time to reflect. And if it is connected in some way with clearing up the terrible business of Mr White's death, then you are excused entirely, Mr Paget' – and she glanced in my brother's direction.

Walter made a small bow. 'I have not ceased working in your niece's interests since the day I arrived.'

It was Miss Fitt's turn to bow slightly. I was somewhat bemused by this mutual display of courtesy. The last I had heard they had been at loggerheads.

'Oh,' she cried, 'but you're both of you covered in cuts and scratches. Have you been fighting?'

'Just playing,' said Walter. 'Brotherly fun and games. We've always indulged in a bit of rough and tumble ever since we were young boys.'

'I see. How charming. And have you any news for us – or, rather, for Julia?'

'I hope to be able to explain the whole series of unusual events in a day or two,' Walter said. He did not notice my look of incredulity. He continued: 'I just need to dot the i's and cross the t's, so to speak.'

'Talking of which,' she said, 'have you been able to make any sense out of the note Mr White left for my niece?'

'What an extraordinary coincidence!' he cried. 'My brother and I were just about to take another look at it.' This was news to me. 'Sidney! The note!'

He had seen me put it in my pocket the evening before, after poring over it for hours in vain. I took it out and handed it to him.

'Let us sit down.' Walter walked towards a low wall at the edge of the beach, where a fisherman was sitting smoking his pipe. Miss Fitt and I followed. Seeing there was a dusting of sand and a few flecks of seaweed on the wall, Walter – not unlike his namesake Mr Raleigh, I could not help thinking – in one flowing movement removed his jacket and spread it out for her to sit on. We positioned ourselves on either side of her. Walter gave her the note to hold in the shade of the parasol, and we all three peered at it as if it were some strange sea creature we had just fished out of a rock pool.

To have been sitting together like this with Miss Meakins would have been positively scandalous, but with Miss Fitt, who had much of the matron about her, it did not seem so bad. Yet I could tell from the subdued excitement in her voice that the close proximity of two gentlemen was far from unwelcome.

She said: 'It really is most peculiar, don't you think?'

'Decidedly,' said Walter.

A long silence followed, while I waited for Walter to explain what we had, or rather had not, found out about the note, and he, presumably, waited for me to do the same. Fortunately, Miss Fitt fancied herself as a cryptologist.

'Have you tried substituting different letters?' she asked.

We assured her we had.

'Or taking the first letter of each word?'

Taking the first, second, third or what-have-you letter, we told her, resulted in nothing that could be recognized as English.

'How about giving each letter the number of its position in the alphabet – one for A, two for B, and so forth – then adding up the totals for each word and translating those totals back into letters?'

We admitted we had not thought of that, so we gave it a go there and then.

'The first word,' I said, 'is *when*, so that's, just a minute –'

'Twenty-three,' prompted Walter.

'Twenty-three for W, plus eight for H, plus five for E, plus fourteen for N, which makes –'

'Fifty,' said Walter.

'There are only twenty-six letters in the alphabet,' I said.

'Then deduct twenty-six or a multiple of twenty-six,' suggested Miss Fitt – rather impatiently, I thought.

'That leaves twenty-four.'

'The letter X,' said Walter. 'There are not many words beginning with X, unless the message is about a xylophone.'

We did the calculations on the second word, which was *the*, and arrived at the letter G.

'So we have XG,' said Walter. 'Not encouraging.'

'Perhaps the X means ten, as in Roman numerals.'

So we converted the next word, *sun*, and came up with B.

'XGB,' said Walter.

'That could mean Ten Great Britain, couldn't it?'

The next word was *shines*, which, consisting of six letters, took us a little while.

'V,' said Walter.

'Roman numerals again?' I suggested.

Miss Fitt summarized. 'Ten Great Britain Five – this is looking promising.'

'Do you think so?' said Walter. 'The next word is *and*, which gives us S, and the word after that is *light*, giving us D.'

'Ten Great Britain Five Shillings Pence …?' said Miss Fitt.

'Double Dutch.'

She had to agree.

We next read the whole sentence backwards, then each word backwards, then alternate words backwards and forwards, but from whatever angle we came at it, the note would not deliver up its coded message.

We had been sitting for some time, absorbed in our scrutiny of the mysterious text, when an idle wag with nothing better to do stopped behind us and peered over our shoulders. 'Got a love letter from both of you, has she?' he said in that broad flat accent endemic in the north, and burst into laughter.

Colour flooded into Miss Fitt's cheeks. I felt myself start to glow. Thank goodness the parasol was there to hide my embarrassment.

Walter proved himself equal to the situation. Laughing along with the fellow, he said: 'Still, better than having no love at all.'

This must have struck a chord with the man, who was dressed in the poorest of clothes and whose face was smeared with dirt. His expression switched in an instant from joyful to troubled. He wiped his nose on his sleeve and shambled off, muttering. I felt a surge of sympathy for him. How quickly and how brutally can ill-considered words infect our moods and blight our days!

Miss Fitt was standing up, a little flustered. 'We had better abandon our attempts for the moment. Please let me know if you make any progress. My niece and I would so like to know what Mr White wanted to say to her.' With a slight inclination of the head and a flicker of a smile she sailed off the way she had come.

'Curious, don't you think?' said Walter.

'Not only curious but impenetrable, I'm beginning to believe. I don't know that we'll ever crack it.'

'I didn't mean the note.'

'Oh?'

'I meant the intense interest Miss Fitt is taking in the contents of the note.'

'Where there's a mystery it's only natural to be eager for a solution.'

'I suppose so. But I wonder. I wonder.'

15

An Absence

The remainder of that day we spent resting in our room, gathering strength. The cuts and bumps resulting from the brawl in the Beehive were slight and hardly noticeable. We came up with an explanation for the bruises on our faces: we had tripped over the low wall at the beach.

The next day, Wednesday, the 12th of July, I headed for Lancelot's studio with a good deal of apprehension. Of course, I wanted to find out as much as I could about the murder – and Lancelot clearly had some vital piece or pieces of information – but I did not know how far into his confidence Lancelot would take me. At that very moment he might be preparing some subtle means of bumping me off and disposing of my body. Yet – ridiculous as it might sound – I believed our friendship, forged through several years of shared work and leisure at art college, would prevail. And was he not the well-wisher who had pushed that warning note under our door? Had he not said he was trying to protect my brother and me?

Seagulls screeched and laughed, sharp against the clear sky, as I made my way through the town, high above South Bay. The good citizens of Scarborough were going about their daily business – hoisting up washing, like sails, to catch the breeze; holystoning a doorstep; carrying crates of beer into the Ship Inn – unaware of the matters of life and death thronging my mind. Had it not been for these matters, I might have lingered, taken out my sketchbook and committed to paper these particulars of ordinary working lives. But the distant church clock showed a few minutes past midday, and for all his eccentricities Lancelot was a supremely punctual person, who expected others to be the same.

I quickened my pace. I had not taken this route before, and soon I was surprised to come to a short street with the delightful name of Paradise. Not Paradise Street or Paradise Road; simply Paradise. The street sign was an oblong of enamel let into a wall, bearing large blue letters on a white background. I gazed around to see what sort of Eden I had entered. It was then that I saw him.

Not a serpent, nor the devil, but a sailor, dressed in traditional navy blue suit and cap, with lanyard and white flash on the chest. His beard and moustache were dark and bushy. He was standing a good way behind me, leaning against a wall, lighting a cigarette – or pretending to light a cigarette, for he would glance up every few seconds as if to check I was still in sight. There was no one else around. He could only be interested in me.

In reaching Paradise I had gone too far. I needed to retrace my steps. As I did so, the sailor moved back, keeping the same distance between us. Clearly he did not want to be recognized. Who was it underneath the sailor suit and the facial hair? Could this be the elusive impostor who had killed Thomas White? I doubted that he could be a genuine sailor, since there was no naval base near Scarborough. With all this running through my mind, I darted down Church Stairs Street to Lancelot's house. I looked back. The sailor's head advanced briefly past the street corner, then disappeared. Once inside I would be safe. I knocked on the door.

A minute or so went by. I knocked again, glancing up the street every few seconds. Still he did not come to let me in. I knocked again. Something did not feel right. I realized what it was: the complete silence which hung like a dark cloud over the house. Lancelot would always start to shout and curse when someone interrupted his painting, or he would bang about in anger as he stomped down the stairs. But now: nothing. Silence. I glanced up the street again. No one.

'Nobody at home?'

I jumped in fright. The voice was behind me. Turning, I saw the sailor, staring at me with the most piercing eyes I think I have ever seen. He must have come round a different way and up Church

Stairs Street, but I had no time to consider that; something needed to be done. An image of Sherlock Holmes taking decisive action flashed across my mind, as I sprang at him and grabbed his lanyard. We both went down. I managed to force myself on top of him and, by pulling the lanyard hard to one side, threatened to choke him. His arms waved helplessly, pinioned beneath my knees.

'Why are you here?' I shouted. 'Who are you?'

His beard looked suddenly lopsided. I seized it with my free hand and it came away, together with the moustache. When I looked down, Walter was smiling up at me.

I released the lanyard. 'Thank you, Sidney,' he said, as though I had just done him some trifling favour. 'You don't really want to strangle your younger brother, do you?'

At that moment I really did want to strangle him; but the moment passed and I helped him to his feet.

'Why *are* you here?' I said.

'My disguise was obviously too good and you thought I was a common ruffian.'

I did not give him the pleasure of agreeing. I repeated my question.

'I'm here because I want to find out why you're here,' he said. 'I've a feeling you've been hiding things from me lately. Not taking me into your confidence like you used to.'

'That's good coming from you.'

'I don't know what you mean.'

Lancelot's house stood starkly white and silent in the intense sunlight. The silence was unusual. More than that – it was unheard-of. Something was wrong, of that I had no doubt. Now was not the time for recriminations.

'Lancelot won't open the door,' I said.

'Perhaps he's out.'

'He agreed to meet me here at midday exactly.' I pulled out my watch. 'It's just gone twelve.'

'Let me try.' Striding up to the door, he pounded on it as though he were a bailiff serving a writ. Even this brought no response from inside the house.

Walter said: 'We must break the door down,' and poised his shoulder for the run-up. This was typical of his devil-may-care attitude. I, on the other hand, always take my time to consider all available options.

'Wait.' I approached the door again and turned the knob. The door swung open. 'It wasn't locked.'

'Sidney, how intelligent of you.' He pushed past me. I followed him inside and closed the door.

If anything, the silence – the absence of Lancelot – was deeper than it had been outside. We climbed the stairs to the artist's studio. I feared the worst. Lancelot lying in a pool of blood, perhaps. Dressed as Caravaggio, with his sword through his heart. Each creak of the stairs was the groan of a dying man.

We entered the studio. I saw at once that *Pub Fight* had gone, leaving an empty easel. Walter swivelled round to face the wall behind the door, and let out a cry of amazement. The painting of the crowd round Prince Rupert in front of the Spa was still there, but it looked different. I soon realized what the difference was: it was finished. There were no ovals of bare canvas. Every body had a human face.

Walter examined the canvas closely before pointing to one face in particular. 'What did I tell you? There she is.'

It *was* her, or someone very like her. Miss Meakins was parading with a parasol beside the Spa.

We went over the rest of the house, but found no trace of Lancelot.

'It *is* a good disguise, isn't it?' Walter asked, picking up his beard and moustache from the roadside.

I could not deny it.

'I'm surprised you didn't recognize me, though.'

'How could I, with all that hair hiding your face?'

'It wasn't hiding my eyes. You do know what my eyes look like.'

I had to admit I did not.

'People can change the way they look, except for their eyes. Know the eyes, know the man. That's how I recognized Old Simon.'

'What?'

'I'll wager you don't know what colour eyes your wife has.'

'Of course I do. Edith's eyes are ...' I pictured her in my mind, but was shocked to find that her image was in black and white. 'Do *you* know what colour her eyes are?'

'Grey. Well, grey-green to be precise.'

'That's just what I was about to say.'

'Ha!'

He stuffed his beard and moustache in his pocket as we set out for the Grand.

'Where do you think Lancelot could have gone?'

I said: 'He might have suddenly gone to London with a painting, I suppose. He does sometimes. Though surely he would have told me. He definitely intended to meet me just now.'

'What about?'

'I don't know. He wouldn't say.'

'Something important?'

My reluctance to give an answer was answer enough.

'Let's do a deal,' said Walter. 'You tell me why you were at Lancelot's, and I'll tell you what I learnt this morning from the hotel staff.'

'Did you learn anything of importance?'

'Oh, yes.'

Walter knows that my curiosity will always get the better of me. We made the deal. I told him about the meeting between Lancelot and Mr Legard in the churchyard. I took out my sketchbook and related the conversation word for word:

> LANCELOT: ... *don't want you doing anything like that again.*
> LEGARD: *It was only a bit of fun.*
> LANCELOT: *Bit of fun? You've got them following you everywhere.*
> LEGARD: *I'm following them.*

LANCELOT: *And that nonsense with the knife. Are you trying to get me arrested for murder?*
LEGARD: *They can't prove anything.*
LANCELOT: *Why are you here today, anyway?*
LEGARD: *Why shouldn't I be?*
LANCELOT: *It would have been better if Old Simon had come.*

I said: 'I presume "You've got them following you everywhere" refers to us.'

'Very possibly.'

'It seems clear from what he says about the knife that Lancelot knows something about the murder.'

'I agree.'

'But I don't understand what he meant by "It would have been better if Old Simon had come." I asked him about it, and he said: "It would have been better. Though nothing would have changed."'

'He's quite right. Nothing would have changed. And yet it *was* different.'

'You're talking in riddles.'

'All will become clear.'

'It's obviously clear to you now, so why won't you tell me?'

'Because I'm not completely sure of my facts. As soon as I am, I will confide in you fully.'

How many times in the last few years have I heard him say that? And how many times did he confide in me eventually – when it was far too late to prevent him from making a fool of himself through nonsensical reasoning? Why should this 'adventure' in Scarborough be any different?

'At least,' I said, 'tell me what you found out from the hotel staff this morning.'

'I got nothing from the valets. Whether they were being discreet or truthful I couldn't fathom. But the chambermaids were more forthcoming – or, rather, one in particular was. I used my charm –'

It was my turn to cry 'Ha!'

'– and a little financial inducement and found out what I can only describe as a bombshell.'

He paused for a quite unnecessary length of time.

'Yes?'

'I found out,' he continued, 'that Miss Meakins and Miss Fitt did not hire the mourning clothes they wore at Thomas White's funeral.'

'So they bought them?'

'No. They brought them with them.'

'They did what?'

'They brought their mourning clothes in their luggage. In other words, they were expecting a funeral.'

'They were expecting Thomas White to die?'

'So it seems.'

'But that doesn't mean they killed him, does it?'

'No. It means they know more about the murder than they'd like us to know.'

We both fell silent. I have no idea what Walter was thinking (I never do), but I had a vision, a sort of daydream, in which the Misses Meakins and Fitt were walking towards me outside the Spa. They were dressed in their best – Miss Meakins in pure white, Miss Fitt in light blue – holding their parasols high, moving smoothly and gracefully. I inclined my head and smiled. In response, their faces contorted into the faces of wolves, their long muzzles opening to show their fangs. Miss Meakins's parasol was transformed into a scimitar, which the she-wolf whirled above her head, howling. Miss Fitt was holding a rifle, which she aimed straight at me. She cried like a hyena, mocking, hungry for blood.

'But I'm sure there's an innocent explanation,' said Walter. 'I can't believe Julia would deceive me.'

I could. Whether it comes from the deep concentration required to paint or draw a portrait, during which the sitter presents to you more of his character than he would think possible, or from my involvement with the Sherlock Holmes stories, nearly all of which turn on deceit and its uncovering, I have a healthy scepticism with regard to others, particularly strangers. All the same, I was reluctant to admit we had been outwitted by two scheming women. Perhaps they were extremely provident ladies, who always took mourning clothes with them on holiday so they would be prepared for every eventuality.

By now we were approaching the Grand. It was that time of day, mid afternoon, when carriages and carts came and went with great frequency, as the the hotel received a new influx of guests to replace those departing. The noise – of horses' hooves, drivers' shouts, the general babble of voices – was such that Walter had to speak close to my ear in order for me to hear him.

'You go on ahead. There's a little something I need to do.'

'What little something?' I asked.

'I'll tell you later. It has nothing to do with the case.'

As he walked towards the steps down to the seafront, he pulled the beard and moustache from his pocket and re-applied them, once more becoming the perfect specimen of a Royal Navy rating. How well the costume suited him; so well that I found myself wondering whether he should not join the navy, perhaps as some sort of official artist. It would be good for him. Or, rather, I confess, it would be good for me. Someone else would have to keep tabs on him, and I would be free, free, free ...

16

A Rest

The next day after breakfast, during which I wrote another postcard to Edith, my brother made a suggestion which fairly took my breath away.

'Sidney, let us relax today. It's time we had a holiday.'

'It's been time we had a holiday for over a week.'

'We can sit somewhere pleasant and mull over the facts of the case.' I should have known that his concept of relaxation involved intense activity of some kind.

The pleasant spot we decided upon was Valley Park, a little inland of the People's Palace and Aquarium and just below Londesborough Lodge. Grassy slopes were decked with flower beds and dotted with trees. One of the trees provided welcome shade as we settled ourselves on a bench beside the duck pond. A fountain was playing in the centre of the pond. From the aviary a little distance away we could hear the calls and twitters of more birds than we could ever identify. It was altogether a delightful place in which to spend a leisurely hour or so.

The leisure lasted for about ten minutes. Then the cogs in Walter's brain began to whirr again. I suspect he never truly stops thinking except when sleep interrupts him.

He said: 'His disappearance puts a new complexion on things, don't you think?'

'Whose disappearance?'

'Lancelot's. Why has he gone? That's the question.'

'And where?' I added.

'It certainly doesn't show Lancelot in a good light.'

I would have loved to disagree and support my old artist friend, but the facts didn't allow me to. On the point of revealing to me certain details about the murder, Lancelot had absented himself. The only conclusion to be drawn was that he had decided to keep the information to himself after all – information which must be too sensitive to disclose. He swore to me that he was not the murderer, but could I believe him? Why should I? Had he not just run off and left me high and dry?

'In fact,' Walter continued, 'by his actions he's pointing the finger of suspicion at himself.'

'But is it likely he did the murder?'

'Let's see, shall we?' He stretched out his legs, folded his arms and lowered his head in preparation for some hard thinking. 'We begin with the disappearance of Thomas White in the People's Palace and Aquarium. Since no one saw a man being dragged out against his will, I think we may safely say Mr White left of his own accord. Miss Meakins didn't see him leave, but he must have done. My guess is that he went out by some back door and immediately made his way to Londesborough Lodge, which is just over the road and can be reached by any of several paths leading through its gardens at the rear.'

'What would induce him to leave and cause so much misery to his fiancée?'

'I have a feeling he would have caused her misery in the long run whatever had happened. If my theory is correct – and I have no reason to doubt it – Thomas White was homosexual and would never have married. He didn't have the symbol with the circle and barred arrow on his hand when he arrived in Scarborough – I have asked Julia about that – but he did by the time he was murdered. The obvious explanation is that he joined the "secret" society of homosexuals who cavort at Londesborough Lodge. The impostor fellow was one of them. He lured Thomas White away from the People's Palace and Aquarium, although he didn't take much luring, and into the heady sexual whirl of the lodge.'

'But if he was homosexual, why did he court Miss Meakins?'

'It was the ideal way of concealing his perversion. Had anyone ever tried to accuse him or blackmail him he could point to his engagement, and presumably Julia would have vouched for him.'

'Why did the other chap, the impostor, have his photograph taken and pretend he was Thomas White?'

'I don't know. But it doesn't seem that important.'

Walter has a convenient way of deciding what is and what is not important so that it suits his thinking rather than fits the facts.

'Mr White,' he continued, 'is now part of the Londesborough Lodge society, as is the impostor fellow, as is Mr Legard.'

'As is Lancelot?'

'I doubt it very much. Don't you remember his carryings-on with the ladies of London when we were younger?'

I did. I blushed to think of them.

'Next we come to the manner of Thomas White's death. There can be no doubt that the knife that killed him belonged to Lancelot and appears in the painting of ... of ...'

'*Endymion and Selene*,' I prompted.

'Thank you, Sidney. The knife appears in that painting. Lancelot couldn't find the knife after the murder – no, because it was sticking in Mr White. Now, there are two possibilities. One: Lancelot painted the picture, and the model whom he hired stole the knife and later used it on Thomas White on the beach. In this version of events the painting preceded the murder. Two: Lancelot was on the beach, Thomas White was his model and they were making a preparatory study for the painting. Something went wrong and Lancelot stabbed Thomas. In this version of events the murder precedes the painting, which it could easily have done, since we only have Lancelot's word that the painting was done the day before, and not the day after. And what's more, we only have Lancelot's word that he used a model organized by Old Simon. Perhaps there was no model at all.'

'Bravo,' I said. I had to hand it to Walter: he had cut his way through the tangle of evidence with remarkable sharpness of mind. Nevertheless, there were a few sticking points. 'If Lancelot did commit the murder, surely he wouldn't then record it so exactly in his painting.'

'One would think not. But, assuming it's not some form of double bluff, you know as well as I do that once an artist has a concept for a work in his head it is hard to shift it until it is put down on paper or canvas. And one does not like to waste ideas.'

'Possibly,' I said. It seemed highly unlikely to me. Walter was clinging to his theory by his fingertips. 'And *why* would Lancelot kill Thomas White?'

Walter wriggled, sat up and bent forward, his elbows on his knees. He stared into the fountain as if one of the million drops of water might refract the answer to him. He sat like this for several minutes; just long enough for me to do a quick sketch of him. Then he jumped up and began to pace back and forth in front of the bench. At last he said: 'I don't know why.'

'Isn't motive the most important element in solving a crime?' I asked, imagining what Sherlock Holmes might have said had he been there.

'If Lancelot didn't do it,' Walter said, 'why has he now disappeared?'

'Perhaps he's been arrested.'

'There you are then.'

'That doesn't mean he's guilty.'

By now Walter was very agitated. 'Let's have *your* theory about what happened.' I hesitated for a few seconds while I gathered my thoughts. This was too much for my brother. 'Come on, let's have it!'

'Do sit down. You're making me nervous.'

'Ha!' He threw himself down on the far end of the bench, hunched, legs crossed.

'All I know,' I said, 'is that Lancelot knows.'

'What?'

'Lancelot knows who the murderer is.'

'He told you? As simple as that?'

'Well ... I said I thought he knew who the murderer was, and he didn't deny it.'

'Not quite the same thing, is it?'

'Well, no ... but ...'

'And did he say *who* the murderer was?'

'No.'

'So we've no means of checking if he knows or not.'

'I think he was going to tell me today.'

'But he wasn't at home. What a surprise. Really, Sidney, you're remarkably gullible.'

I did not rise to this provocation. Having established his superiority by saying it, Walter was now in a much better mood. His body relaxed and he breathed out audibly. He continued with his own analysis of the case.

'What I'm finding hard to fit into the overall picture is the fact – which I've mentioned before – that you and I were meant to find the body when and where we did.'

'Are you sure about that?'

'Surer than I am about anything else. The coincidence of our being on the beach at exactly the time of the murder is unlikely. And Thomas White had been dead some time when we found him. The screams that supposedly came from him must in fact have come from the killer.'

'But why? Why would a murderer actually want his crime to be discovered?'

'At the moment, your guess is as good as mine. Well, almost as good. The killer must have known where we were going that day and got there just before us.'

'Who could have known?'

'Perhaps you told Lancelot. You seem to have told him everything else.'

This was a gibe too far. I stood up. 'Let's walk on,' I said, 'and see where this path takes us.'

It took us, first of all, to the aviary. A cacophony of screeches, hoots and chirrups greeted our arrival. We wandered from cage to cage, gazing into the forlorn eyes of their prisoners. In one cage sat a group of zebra finches, so the information board told us – colourful, social little fellows; in another there was a rather drab bird called a bronze-winged mannikin, doing nothing at all; and in another a yellow-breasted chat was belting out his odd song of whistles, cackles and clucks. Apparently, in certain environments, the bright colour of the chat can, paradoxically, act as camouflage. This little bird put me in mind of Mr Legard with his yellow checked waistcoat. I pointed out the similarity to Walter.

'Although,' I added, 'Mr Legard's clothes always make him stand out. They could never hope to make him appear invisible.'

Walter said: 'Oh, but they can, you know.' I put this down as another of his gnomic utterances, and continued my examination of the birds.

'Your mentioning Mr Legard has reminded me of something. I won't be long – a matter of minutes.' And before I could ask him where he was going, he was gone.

In the event it was about fifteen minutes before he returned, carrying a copy of the *Scarborough Daily Post*, presumably the object of his little excursion.

'Since when,' I asked, 'have you been reading the local paper?'

'Since we came here. I've read it every day. There are some remarkable items contained within its pages, although most of it is dull enough.'

I was reminded of Sherlock Holmes, who often expressed himself in a similar manner with regard to the London daily press. If my brother had now started scanning the newspapers for crimes to solve, then my attempts at reforming him were failing – or, to look at the situation more positively, needed to be redoubled.

'You'll recall, Sidney, it was in the *Scarborough Daily Post* that I read the article about Thomas White's disappearance.'

'I wish I'd never bought it for you. It was supposed to distract you, take your mind off things. Instead of which, we've spent I don't know how many days –'

'Nine.'

'– nine days tangled up in a murder case which, when all's said and done, is not our concern.'

'Justice is the concern of everyone.' With a shake of his arms, Walter opened out the paper, folded it in half a few times, and handed it to me.

'What am I supposed to be looking at?'

'The obituaries.'

'More dead people!'

'Don't be so cynical, Sidney. Glance through them and see if one of them catches your eye.'

I did as he asked, and read the following.

> BROWN, Arthur – *Suddenly, on Friday last, aged 78. Loved by many, missed by all.* – Loving wife Winifred.
> LEWIS, Emily – *Aged 45, late of Whitby. Will remain in our hearts for ever.* – Her sorrowing sisters.
> SIMON – *The bees will leave the hive at two o'clock.* – Mary.

'This is an odd one,' I said.

'Which is that?'

'Simon.'

'Well done! Simon – or Old Simon.'

'Do you think so?'

'What's the name of the hostelry he drinks at?'

'The Beehive.'

'There you have it.'

'What does it mean, "the bees will leave the hive at two o'clock"?'

'A rather fanciful way of putting it, I feel, but it means he will die at two o'clock today.'

'Old Simon'll be murdered?'

'No, no.'

'Then what? He'll drop down dead of his own accord?'

'More or less. And I think we should be there when he does. I want to see what other bees are buzzing around.'

Walter's words made as little sense as they often do. All the same, I was intrigued by the possibility of such a strange event as a death foretold – assuming Walter's deduction to be correct, that is.

'Who is Mary?' I asked.

'We shall meet her at two o'clock.'

The mynah bird shrieked with laughter, evidently amused by my perplexity. I threw it a threatening glance and it fell silent.

'What time is it?' Walter asked.

'Nearly twelve.'

'Then I suggest we spend the next two hours enjoying ourselves.'

I could only assume that so confident was Walter of his deductions that he now had the time and mental energy for something other than deep thinking. It is true that his idea of enjoyment can sometimes be my idea of hard labour, but on this occasion it seemed he really was ready to relax – or at least try to.

'There is,' he said, 'one place mentioned in the guidebook I would love to visit, on account of its historical connections. I believe you are also a great enough lover of England's past to derive pleasure from such a visit.'

'What place is this?'

'King Richard III's house, down by the harbour.'

'He had a house here?'

'At any rate he stayed here on several occasions, when he brought his fleet to Scarborough.'

'I should be very interested in seeing it.'

'Then follow me.'

We found ourselves standing in front of a plain three-storey building which presented nothing out of the ordinary to the eye except for a sign announcing 'King Richard III House, Admission 1d'. It seemed inconceivable to me that Richard should have put up here rather than at the nearby castle, and I said as much to Walter.

'I agree with you,' he replied, 'but you must remember he was made Admiral of the Sea when he was only nine. Sailing and ships were in his blood. So it's not at all unlikely he should choose to lodge within easy reach of his fleet.'

Hoping for something more interesting on the inside, we paid our pennies and entered. The lower room, dominated by huge oak beams supporting the ceiling, contained various items of furniture from past centuries, although none of these laid claim to any royal association. Upstairs, a tester bed might have been the one in which Richard rested his noble head, or it might not. The ceiling, also of dark carved wood like the bed, was covered with representations of animals, strikingly executed. I was so taken by an image of three hares (which had two ears each but only three ears between them) that I made a drawing of it.

'Very instructive,' said Walter. 'What you see is not always what is there. And vice versa.'

We left without having encountered Richard III's ghost, or even the ghost of a connection with him.

Walter led the way, up towards the castle. 'Let's go and see Mary now,' he said. 'We've just got enough time. And we can drop in on Lancelot, if he's in – which I doubt.' By now I had ceased trying to make sense of what Walter was saying. I followed meekly, trusting there would be some degree of enlightenment at the end of the road.

A few minutes later we were climbing Church Stairs Street. Walter knocked on Lancelot's door. The silence was as heavy and as dead as a stone. Walter said: 'Perhaps he's visiting Mary, like the others.'

My brother was showing definite signs, I thought, of being crazy. Had his amorous interest in Miss Meakins turned his mind? As we approached Paradise I kept a very close watch on him, ready to intervene and maintain public order should the need arise.

At the top of the hill we walked a little farther. I took out my watch. It was one minute past two o'clock. Walter stopped, flung out an arm and said: 'Sidney, let me introduce you to Mary. Mary, this is Sidney.'

And there she was.

17

Another Funeral

I cursed my stupidity, but not out loud. 'I knew what you meant,' I said.

'Ha!'

'I just didn't want to spoil your joke.'

There she was. Mary. St Mary's church. SIMON – *The bees will leave the hive at two o'clock.* – Mary. So here we were: two o'clock at St Mary's. Where were the bees?

'Look,' whispered Walter, pointing. We were standing beside a high wall, over which we could just manage to see the churchyard a little way up the hill. Imagine my surprise when I discovered Miss Meakins and Miss Fitt, in full mourning dress, and Mr Legard, resplendent in his yellow waistcoat, gathered round a grave next to the resting place of Thomas White. A coffin lay on the ground at their feet. The vicar was coming towards them, prayer book in hand.

'What are the ladies doing here?' I said. 'They didn't know Old Simon, did they?'

'It seems they must have done, though I must say I didn't expect them to be here. Legard certainly. He was very close to the deceased.'

'Do we join them?'

'I think not. We don't have a good reason to, do we?'

'What's *their* reason?'

'That we shall have to find out. But where on earth is Lancelot? I did think he might turn up. He did last time.'

'He still might. At least Inspector Brasher's not here.'

'Thank goodness for that.'

At Walter's suggestion we moved into the shade of a nearby tree, whose overhanging foliage hid us from view as we peered over the wall. From there we watched the same ceremony unfold that we had witnessed on Sunday. The vicar's lips moved. His two assistants appeared and, using their ropes, heaved the coffin into the grave. This time it was Mr Legard who stepped forward. He scooped up a handful of earth and flung it, rather than dropped it, onto the coffin lid. I thought I saw him smile as he did so. As soon as the rest of the earth had been shovelled in, the three mourners – if they could rightly be called that – drifted away, the assistants stowed their spades and ropes in a wooden bin against the church wall, and the vicar, gathering his robes, picked his way over the grass back to the vicarage.

'I'm glad you didn't leap over the wall and manhandle the coffin.'

'No, I thought it would be better to do that later – under cover of darkness.'

When the clocks struck twelve on the night following Old Simon's burial, you might have seen two disreputable-looking characters, dressed in dark clothes, loitering behind a gravestone in St Mary's churchyard. These two characters were Walter and I. We were making sure the coast was clear before we set about our dubious task.

Midnight usually finds me tucked up in bed or nodding over a novel. But on this occasion the events I had observed in the churchyard, with the Misses Meakins and Fitt apparently mourning a tramp they had never met, disposed me to listen to Walter's theories. That afternoon, in our room, I had given him free rein.

'Do you remember my saying that eyes are very distinctive, indeed individual, in their colouring?'

'I do,' I said.

'That was what led me to my discovery.'

'What discovery?'

'That Old Simon never existed.'

'He did. Unless that was a ghost you grappled with in the Beehive Inn.'

'He became a ghost as soon as I looked into his eyes.'

He was talking in riddles again.

'Can't you be a bit clearer?'

Walter waved his hand in a gesture of impatience. He fetched his deerstalker, put it on and began to pace up and down.

'When I danced with Mr Legard at the soirée I was able to study his eyes closely. He stared into mine with the intensity of a lover. In fact, I do believe he was falling for me.'

'I trust you didn't encourage him.'

'You may rest assured, dear brother, that I did not. The iris of his eyes – that's the coloured part –'

'Yes, yes, I do know.'

'The iris was an unusual shade of green. Somewhere between Paris green and emerald. And in his right eye there were two black flecks: one positioned at three o'clock and one at nine. Now, when I saw Old Simon in the Beehive I caught a glimpse of his eyes. They were green. They therefore merited further inspection. I forced him to raise his head. He glared at me in anger, which is exactly what I wanted him to do. I got a clear view of his eyes. They were exactly the same shade of green as Legard's, and the right eye had two flecks in exactly the same place.'

'So, you're saying ...'

'Old Simon was Arthur Legard in disguise. As soon as Legard realized I'd rumbled him, the game was up. You know what happened next. After he'd made his getaway, I imagine Legard licked his wounds for a while, then decided to kill Old Simon off.'

'I'd never have thought the two men were the same.'

'That's because you don't look closely enough.'

'Tell me,' I said, stung by his criticism, 'does wearing that hat make you more intelligent? Or are you just trying to annoy me?'

'It's scarcely my place to judge, but it does seem to increase my intellectual powers.'

'All right then, Mr Clever Dick,' I said, 'answer me this. If Old Simon didn't exist, why should he need to be given a burial?'

'That's precisely what we're going to find out.'

And that is why we were standing huddled together behind a gravestone at midnight, peering into the darkness beyond the ruins of the earlier church. Somewhere beyond that lay the path between the current church and the vicarage, and beyond that the corner where Thomas White and the ghost of Old Simon took their rest. A solitary lamp in Paradise cast a feeble glow into the night.

'I can't see anyone,' said Walter.

'Nor can I.'

'Are you ready?' He lit the candle in the lantern he had brought, hidden beneath his coat.

'I feel like Burke and Hare – or one of them at any rate.'

'Are you ready?'

I nodded. Walter had given me my instructions hours before. While he went off straight ahead to locate the grave, I veered to the right and followed the wall of the church round to the wooden bin in which the spades were kept. When I opened the flap and lifted them out, their blades rattled together, so that to any drunk or highly strung passer-by a skeleton might have been heard dancing amongst the tombs.

Walter shushed me; far too loudly, I thought. Taking a spade in each hand, I crossed the path to where he was standing, pointing down at a slightly elevated mound of earth, at one end of which he had set down the lantern. He snatched one of the spades and began shovelling for all he was worth, like a treasure-seeker digging for a chest of gold. I did my best to keep up with him. Every now and then I would stop, look and listen, but no one was watching us. I marvelled at Walter's energy, fuelled by his determination to get at the truth. I spent so long watching him dig that I was later able, with a curious mixture of shame and professional pride, to sketch the scene I had imprinted on my brain.

'No slacking, Sidney.'

We were not used to manual labour of any kind, let alone serious digging. All the same, the urgency of our task and curiosity as to its outcome spurred us on. As Walter had said earlier: if Old Simon's body was not in the coffin, what was? It was surely far-fetched to suppose an empty coffin had been buried there. What would be the point?

At last our spades scraped the wooden lid. Bending down as best we could in the confined space, we cleared the earth away from the edges of the coffin.

'And now?' I asked.

'We use this.' Walter reached over the heap of soil we had created and held up a crowbar. The light from the lantern, which I had lowered onto the coffin lid, threw a giant shadow of him onto the mound behind. For a flickering moment or two he became a Greek hero going into battle brandishing a spear.

'Where did you get that?'

'I borrowed it from a cubbyhole at the Grand. I've had it under my coat.'

I could have queried the word 'borrowed', but it did not seem like the time and place. We had come so far already that a little light larceny would hardly make any difference. And I had no doubt that Walter would return the crowbar – if he could.

As Walter had predicted, the coffin was a simple, cheap affair made of planks nailed together, entirely without finish or decoration. He got to work with the crowbar quickly, prising up the corners one by one, then worrying away at the nails along the sides, until with a great groan the lid toppled off. I held the lantern so its light fell fully on whatever was inside.

How I stopped myself from dropping the lantern in shock I'll never know. I suppose something within me knew that we had to bear witness to what we saw.

Lying in the coffin was Lancelot. He wore some dirty old painting clothes. His head was turned to the left, exposing the spot on his right temple where the bullet had gone in. His right hand was gripping a revolver with a mother-of-pearl butt.

'Oh no,' I said, 'it's the gun.'

'What gun?'

'I'll explain later.'

I would have had no time to explain had I wanted to. At that moment several loud cracks sounded over our heads, followed by dull bangs. I held up the lantern. There was another crack, and a patch in the middle of a nearby gravestone turned to dust.

'Somebody's shooting at us,' I cried.

'So they are.'

'Shall we run for it?'

'I think we'll be safer here.'

'But we're trapped like rabbits in a hole.'

'Put your lantern up there.'

'Why?'

'Just do it.'

I reached up and settled the lantern on top of the mound of earth. It was the only bright thing in all that silent darkness. But not for long. It exploded in a shower of glass and everything went black.

'That I think is that,' Walter said, as though he had just finished some menial task. 'There'll be no more shooting.'

We waited for a while until the faint glow of the moon allowed us to manoeuvre the lid back onto the coffin and shovel the soil back into the grave. Terrified, and only half believing I was not going to be shot dead, I replaced the spades in the bin. Walter came towards me, carrying the crowbar.

'Over there,' he said, and pointed towards a narrow lane that skirted the hill on which the castle stood. 'Do you see?'

It was the figure of a woman, or at least of someone dressed like a woman. The face was in shadow.

'That's where the shots came from,' Walter said, 'although it wasn't necessarily her doing the shooting. She might have someone else with her.'

'She's not very good at keeping out of sight.'

'Oh, she wants us to see her.'

And as if on cue, now it had been seen, the figure turned down the lane and disappeared.

I said: 'Shouldn't we go after her?'

'I think not. We were in no danger of being killed, but we might be if we push matters too hard just at the moment.'

'In no danger of being killed? I suppose they weren't bullets that were whizzing past us!'

'Whizzing past us – precisely. If they had wanted to kill us, don't you think they would have walked up to where we were digging, shot us accurately at point-blank range, dumped our bodies next to Lancelot's and filled the grave in again?'

'Well, yes, but –'

'There's no but about it. They were deliberately missing us. It was a warning, just like the falling candelabra.'

'Then it was a pretty deadly warning.'

'Yes, it did have something final about it.'

'So what do we do?'

'We carry on. And we take extra care.'

Our exertions had wearied us beyond belief. We hurried back to the Grand as fast as our tired limbs could carry us and collapsed into bed.

An hour or so later, we were still awake, turning over in our minds the events of the evening.

'Lancelot couldn't have committed suicide, could he?'

'Why ever not? He was an artist. Artists are eccentric and unpredictable.'

'*Some* artists are,' I said, not wanting to be included in their number. I have always tried to live a life governed by reason and reasonableness. 'But what I mean is: if Lancelot had intended to kill himself he would have done it with his usual panache. He would have dressed as Vincent Van Gogh, an artist who did shoot himself.'

'Ideally, yes. But what if the suicidal urge overcame him so suddenly he had no time to dress up?'

'It's possible, I suppose.'

'And remember that he would have had a very good motive.'

'Motive?'

'If he had indeed been the killer of Thomas White.'

'But why would someone bury him secretly if he'd killed himself?'

'To hush it up. Suicide is a crime, after all. Perhaps some family members ...'

'He didn't have any family.'

'We don't know that for certain.'

'There were none at the funeral. Anyway, how would anyone know he'd killed himself?'

'He might have sent off a letter before doing it.'

'*Where* did he kill himself?'

'We don't know.'

'No.'

A strip of moonlight, slipping between the curtains, had run across my bed and onto Walter's. It was as if we were held down, fettered in a huge silver band.

Walter said: 'What did you mean earlier when you said "It's the gun"?'

The image of Lancelot lying in the coffin floated before my inward eye once more. His right hand was holding the revolver, his right temple had received the bullet. Why could he not have committed suicide? I was unable to say, yet I was convinced it was out of the question.

But it was the revolver all right. The revolver that appeared in the barmaid's hand in Lancelot's painting *Pub Fight*. I explained it all to Walter.

'So,' he said, 'we have Thomas White killed by the knife in one of Lancelot's paintings, and we have Lancelot himself killed by the gun in another. I never realized art could have such deadly consequences.'

Of course, it had nothing to do with art. What has art to do with murder? It was not his paintings that had led to Lancelot's death, even though he portrayed the murder weapons in them. But what was his connection with the death of Thomas White? He had wanted to tell me something about it, and he had been silenced; of that I was sure.

'It would be a simple matter,' I said, 'to shoot Lancelot with his own gun and put it in his hand afterwards.'

'Assuming it *is* a real gun, and not just a prop he used for his pictures.'

'How can we find that out?'

'We can't. Unless we dig up the evidence again. And I, for one, have no inclination to do so.'

'Me neither,' I said.

18

Accused

Inspector Brasher arrived the following morning.

'I'm glad to find you gentlemen in residence,' he began in his usual polite way. 'I have something of the utmost seriousness to communicate to you.'

Walter invited him to sit down, which he did with a sigh, his crumpled suit crumpling up even more.

'Always ready to be of assistance,' said Walter, which was not quite the truth but near enough, no doubt, for the purpose of a clear conscience.

Brasher grunted several times as he settled into the chair, making little circular movements like a porker bedding down in hay. Then he sat a few moments dandling his bowler in his lap while he collected his thoughts.

'I've been hearing some unfortunate things about you two gentlemen.'

Straightway I thought of the female figure watching us as we dug in the churchyard. Whatever had possessed me to agree to Walter's suggestion? Was it the same spirit of intellectual curiosity that Walter claimed was his? In any case, he had been proved right: Old Simon was not in his coffin. He had vanished, probably killed off by Legard, the man who had given him birth. But how could we explain this to Brasher?

'Some very unfortunate things,' he said, 'which may or may not be true. I thought it only right to lay these accusations at your door, so to speak, before deciding whether to act on them.'

Into my mind came a vision, a nightmare. I was sitting in a prison cell with Walter, with nothing to do with my time but make pencil sketches of him. He would not keep still. He was walking about laughing, enjoying himself. Through the grille in the cell door a hand reached in. The hand belonged to Edith. All this, she said, was my fault for not looking after my little brother like I had done at Cromer.

I looked Brasher full in the face. 'Whatever we did we did for the best.'

'It's surprising how many people say that.' He heaved himself up and sat leaning forward, more alert than I had ever seen him. 'Even the most hardened criminals.'

Walter said: 'Surely you're not suggesting –'

'I'm not suggesting anything. Merely repeating what I've heard.'

Maybe we could brazen it out. It's one person's word against ours, I thought. Deny everything. Mistaken identity. Or perhaps admit we were in the churchyard, but doing something else. Such as what? What does one do in a churchyard at midnight except dig up a dead body?

'You were seen.'

'Seen?' said Walter. 'By whom?'

'A young lady who stood observing you for some time.'

'And what did she say she saw us doing?'

'She saw you with the dead man.'

What would Walter say now? Perhaps: what dead man? Or: we can't have been there because we were in bed? Or even: it's a fair cop, Inspector? I thought I had better inject some truthfulness into the proceedings before they spun out into a great web of lies, with Brasher the spider at the centre and Walter and I caught like flies.

I said: 'I think I'd better explain about Lancelot.'

'Lancelot? Oh, Mr Pemberlow. Yes, do you know he's disappeared?'

Walter jumped in. 'Has he really? Well, well. But tell me, Inspector, when did the young lady say she saw us?'

'Why, the day of the murder, of course.'

'And where?'

'On the beach itself, where he was found. She was taking a walk when she heard voices.'

So it was *that* dead man; not Lancelot. Brasher knew nothing of our midnight exploits, and I had nearly given the game away.

'She peered over the edge of the cliff and saw two gentlemen struggling with a naked man. One of the gentlemen was holding a knife with an ivory handle.'

'And what did she do?' Walter asked.

'I beg your pardon, I don't understand.'

'Did she raise the alarm, scream, throw a rock at them?'

'She was so afraid she did nothing.'

'Nothing? We sent for the police – hardly the action of criminals.'

'She did nothing, that is, until just recently, when she realized who the two gentlemen were.'

'Just one moment,' I said, eager to make my intelligence felt. 'How does she know it was us she saw?'

'How?'

'Had she been introduced to us before, so that she was able to identify us?'

'I see. No, she saw you later and realized then she'd seen you on the beach.'

'And who, if one may ask,' said Walter, 'is this observant female?'

'I don't think there's any need for sarcasm, Mr Paget. The witness made a good impression on me. Her name is Amy Tranter.'

'Never heard of her,' I said.

'You've seen her. She's the barmaid – well, the landlady actually – of the Beehive Inn. After that little fracas with Old Simon she sought me out and told me you were the two men she had seen.'

'I'd been in the inn before,' I said, 'on my own. She spoke to me. Why didn't she recognize me then and report me to the police?'

'I did mention that to her. She said she wasn't sure it was you. But when she saw the two of you together, she was in no doubt.'

'Well, she must be,' I said. 'Or, more likely, she's lying.'

'As I say, she made a good impression.'

'Yes,' said Walter, 'she does have certain charms and isn't hesitant about putting them on display.'

'I can assure you that years of police work have hardened me in that regard. I am immune.'

'If you say so.'

'I do.'

Brasher glanced down at the collar of his suit jacket and, spotting an errant hair, removed it between two fingernails with the precision of an entomologist examining a rare specimen. Then he rubbed it into a little ball and poked it into his waistcoat pocket. Yes, I thought, a Nathaniel.

Walter asked: 'How do you intend to act on the information you have received from Miss Tranter, Inspector?'

'At the moment I don't intend to act at all. That is, not unless you admit your guilt.'

Walter burst out laughing and carried on laughing well past the point of embarrassment.

'We certainly don't admit anything,' I said. 'We are innocent.'

'Perhaps you are, perhaps you aren't,' said Brasher, brushing his waistcoat with the back of his fingers. 'We shall see, shan't we?'

'What about the impostor?' I said. 'I thought you were going after him.'

'I was. But perhaps that was just some sort of prank, designed to distract us from the real culprit. I'm pretty well convinced we need look no further than your friend Mr Pemberlow. Everything points to his having committed the murder with his knife, although the motive is still somewhat obscure. As to whether you were his accomplices, I have an open mind.'

'The best sort,' said Walter.

'When we find him, perhaps he will enlighten us as to exactly who was involved and why. But for now ...' He pushed himself up out of the chair and turned to me. 'You were going to tell me something about Mr Pemberlow, weren't you?'

I was so alarmed by this question that all I could say was: 'Was I?'

'You were. Perhaps you were going to reveal where he has disappeared to.'

'Where he has – no, no – how on earth should I know where he is?'

Brasher eyed me with suspicion, then smiled. 'But you'll let me know if you hear anything?'

'Of course,' I said.

He turned to Walter. 'And the same goes for you, Mr Paget.'

Walter bowed, strode to the door and held it open while the inspector shuffled out, nodding his head vigorously, as if everything in the puzzle had finally fallen into place – which, since he did not know about Lancelot and his whereabouts, was impossible.

'That was a close thing,' I said, collapsing onto my bed.

'You should only volunteer information in answer to a direct question. Otherwise you give yourself away.'

I had to acknowledge how right he was. 'Here's a direct question,' I said. 'What do we do now?'

'We can't do much about poor Lancelot until we discover whether he killed himself or was murdered.'

'How do we find that out?'

'I've no idea. Not for the present at least.'

'We could ask Miss Meakins or her aunt why they were at Old Simon's or, rather, Lancelot's funeral.'

'Their attendance does seem mysterious, although the explanation may turn out to be a disappointment. Perhaps they are inveterate funeral-goers.'

'What?'

'Oh, there are such people. Just as there are people who love standing outside churches and watching complete strangers emerge as man and wife. They even bring their own confetti.'

'Well, that might be why the two ladies had mourning clothes in their luggage.'

'It might. But in reply to your question "what do we do now?", I suggest we have another crack at that dratted coded message – if that's what it is.'

Several hours later we were sitting staring ahead of us, hypnotized by the five lines of the message, which we now knew forwards, backwards and sideways.

'Let's ring for some drinks,' said Walter. 'They might help to stimulate our jaded brains.'

'I've got it!' I cried.

'What?'

'Of course.'

'What's the first word?'

'No, I don't mean the message.' I slapped the note down on the table and began to pace up and down. 'You know how you can sometimes be racking your brains trying to think of something, then you give up and do something else, and while you're doing that, the thing you were originally trying to think of pops into your head? Well, I know now that Lancelot must have been murdered.'

'Great Scott!'

'You remember how we found him in the coffin?'

'I shall never forget it.'

'And you remember how he nearly drew his sword on you when you angered him that time – when he was dressed as Caravaggio?'

'I shall never forget that either.'

'Compare the two images.'

Walter closed his eyes.

19

The End of Mr Legard

About ten seconds later he opened them. 'No, I can't see what you're driving at.'

'Lancelot went for his sword with his left hand. I've never thought of it before, but he was left-handed. So he would never shoot himself with a gun held in his right hand.'

'If I didn't know you as well as I do, Sidney, I'd call you a genius.' This was as close to a compliment as I could hope for from Walter. He added: 'Rather obvious, really.'

For the rest of the morning we went about in a subdued mood as we brooded on the significance of Lancelot's murder. Gone was any attempt to keep my knowledge or thoughts to myself. We were both now threatened by the outrageous accusation from the barmaid, who must have been somehow mixed up in the murder of Thomas White. We might be arrested if Brasher's investigations ran into the ground, as they very well might, seeing that he had firmly taken hold of the wrong end of the stick. It was time for Walter and me to pull together, as brothers should.

I finally told him, in as much detail as I could remember, everything about my visit to Lancelot and his promise to divulge to me what he could about the murder if I returned later. The one thing he did tell me was that he was not the murderer, and I believed him.

'What made you believe him?' asked Walter.

'Nothing in particular. Just that he seemed to be telling the truth.'

'That wouldn't stand up in a court of law.'

'It won't have to, since Lancelot himself won't be standing up in one. But surely it makes sense to suppose that the real murderer of

Thomas White killed Lancelot to prevent him from revealing anything to me.'

'And who might the real murderer be?'

'I don't know.'

'Honestly, Sidney! It stands out a mile. The most obvious suspect is the man who killed off his alter ego Old Simon and then used the empty coffin to get rid of Lancelot, which he nearly did but for our sterling work.'

'Mr Legard?'

'Mr Legard, who had that revealing conversation with Lancelot in the churchyard, in which Lancelot berated him for some "nonsense with the knife" which might lead to "arrest for murder". The first time I met Legard I knew there was something not quite right about him.'

'You thought he was Thomas White.'

'Did I?'

'In which case he would have murdered himself.'

'Well, I might have been wrong in that small detail, but he's a very slippery character, as I found out nearly to my cost at the soirée.'

'Too slippery to catch out, you think?'

'By no means. In fact, I think our next task should be to pick up his trail. If we keep tabs on him for a while, the chances are he'll make some mistake that'll land him in trouble.'

'Or us in trouble.'

'Have faith in yourself, dear brother. Come, let's to the chase!'

He snatched up the deerstalker and we hurried from the room. Too impatient to wait for the lift, Walter bounded down the stairs, three at a time. He was soon out of sight, way ahead of me. Then suddenly he was there again, walking back up. I stopped.

'There's one small snag,' he said.

'What's that?'

'We don't know where to find Legard.'

In his enthusiasm Walter had started the chase without the quarry, and I, in my enthusiasm, had blindly followed. As a pair of investigators we left a great deal to be desired.

'He could be anywhere,' I said.

'In which case,' said Walter, 'we'd better stay put.'

We walked back up to our floor, both of us downcast, the prospect of an inactive afternoon stretching out ahead of us.

'I know,' I said. 'We could ask Miss Meakins and her aunt a few questions.'

'A capital idea.'

We continued up the stairs to the tenth floor. Walter knocked on the door to room 281 and tidied up his appearance while waiting for a response. But there was none. The ladies were apparently elsewhere.

'What do we do now?' I said. 'We don't know where they are either.'

'We can make a good guess though. Today is overcast and a little breezy, quite unlike the recent glorious weather, and doesn't tempt one to venture too far afield. Let us see if they are perhaps in the hotel tea room.'

We went down the stairs, taking our time.

'Miss Meakins. Miss Fitt. How fortunate to find you here,' said Walter with a little bow.

'We're waiting for the sun to show itself again,' said Miss Meakins. 'It's been a very disappointing day.'

'I fear we've been spoilt of late,' I said.

'We have,' said Miss Fitt, favouring me with a smile. 'Won't you join us?'

We drew up two basket chairs to their table and ordered tea and rock cakes.

Miss Meakins laughed. 'We were just talking about you.'

'Favourably, I trust,' said Walter.

'Neither favourably nor unfavourably. We were wondering whether you'd made any sense of that note from Thomas.'

Walter assured her we were making progress. We were, of course, making none.

I decided to ask Miss Meakins a question about something that had been puzzling me for some time. 'Why do you think your fiancé left you that note?'

'I've asked myself that a thousand times, Mr Paget, without finding an answer. Thomas often did strange things – like visiting me in a different resort every year. Do you think the note is meaningless?'

'Certainly not,' said Walter. 'Everything has a meaning. We just have to find it. And we will.'

I cursed him under my breath. His eagerness to please had got the better of him again, and here he was, raising hopes where there were none to be raised.

'Until then,' Walter added, 'it must remain a mystery.'

'I hope you solve it soon,' said Miss Meakins. 'Our holiday ends in two days' time.'

'Then I shall give it my utmost attention.'

Miss Meakins inclined her head to indicate her gratitude.

'There is another mystery,' Walter said, 'that you may be able to illuminate. My brother and I happened to be passing St Mary's church yesterday and we noticed you and your aunt present at a funeral. I sincerely hope another of your acquaintances hasn't passed away unexpectedly. That would be very bad luck.'

'Thank you for your concern, but it is quite unnecessary. We were asked to be at the ceremony by a gentleman named Mr Legard. An old friend of his had died, who – being somewhat of a recluse – had very few to mourn him. My aunt and I were happy to oblige and add a certain dignity to the proceedings.'

'You are to be commended.'

'May I ask you ladies a question?' I said.

'Please feel free,' said Miss Fitt.

'I noticed that you were wearing very fine mourning dresses at the funeral. Now, I shall in all probability have to attend a funeral soon – a dear friend is very ill ...' – this elicited from the ladies the expressions of commiseration I had expected – '... and I shall need to wear appropriate clothes. Could you tell me where in Scarborough you obtained your outfits, so that I may pay a visit to the same shop?'

'Oh,' said Miss Meakins, 'I'm afraid that's impossible.'

'Why?'

'We brought the dresses with us.'

'You brought them with you?' I tried to sound as surprised as I could.

'Yes. Once we were on holiday and an uncle with whom we were staying passed away suddenly, and we had to hire dresses. Since then we have always come prepared.'

'A very wise precaution,' Walter said. 'It meant you were able to help out Mr Legard without extra fuss and expense.'

'Indeed.'

'How long have you known him?'

'Do you know him too?'

'I have that honour.'

'We fell into conversation one day outside the Spa. He has shown himself to be a gentleman of impeccable breeding and sensitivity.'

'Exactly the words I would use myself,' said Walter. 'I've had many an instructive conversation with him about various interests that we share. In fact ...' – he paused, as an actor might pause for effect – '... I have a small favour to ask of him. Do you know where he is staying?'

'I'm afraid I don't.'

'I do.' Miss Fitt beamed as she took up the baton, so to speak. 'I saw him one morning as he emerged from a hotel.'

'You didn't tell me that, aunt.'

'I thought it better not to.' Miss Meakins blushed and turned her head aside.

'Do you remember which hotel it was?' I asked.

Miss Fitt looked me full in the eyes. 'I don't mind telling you, Mr Paget.' She leaned over and whispered in my ear.

'Thank you,' I said.

'My pleasure,' she said, simpering like a young girl. 'My pleasure entirely.'

A wave of embarrassment flowed freely around the table,

washing over every one of us. We took refuge in our tea and cakes.

'Absolutely delicious,' said Walter.

Miss Meakins said: 'I do believe they are the best rock cakes in Scarborough.'

'I must disagree with you there, Julia. I am certain, and I'm sure Mr Paget will concur ...' – Miss Fitt cast a glance in my direction – '... that the best rock cakes are to be had in Tilly's Tea Room. Wouldn't you agree, Mr Paget, that it is a delightful place for a little talk over tea?'

I pushed back my chair and rose. 'If you will excuse me, ladies, I have a few urgent matters to which I must attend.'

'Oh, what a shame,' said Miss Fitt.

'I keep telling him we're on holiday,' said Walter, 'but he is simply too conscientious. Ladies ...' He, too, rose and we made our escape.

'That was a clever way of asking about their mourning clothes, Sidney. Well done.'

'Thank you.'

'I'm not sure I believe their answer though.'

'No.'

'Still, we've done very well. We now know, probably, where Mr Legard is staying.'

'Correction,' I said. '*I* know.'

Despite the pained expression on Walter's face, I was not about to reveal the little I knew. That would have meant straggling behind him as he hared off to intercept the suspect. Knowledge is power, somebody famous once said, and I intended to use my power wisely.

'I'll lead the way.'

'Really, Sidney!'

I walked calmly back to our room, where I changed my shoes, put on another tie and picked up my boater. All the time Walter was chafing at my heels like a retriever. I ignored him until I was ready to sally forth.

I opened the door. 'Follow me.'

He followed.

Our destination was a fair jaunt away, in Queens Parade overlooking North Bay. This suited me very well. I was determined to get there at my own speed, a saunter, and was looking forward to the first truly leisurely stroll since our arrival in Scarborough. And leisurely it would have been but for Walter's remonstrances, expressed in a loud voice at almost every step. It was quite comical to see him straining at the leash, having to slow down to match his pace to mine, fuming and fulminating, unable to do a thing about it. I was nearly tempted to stop, take out my sketchbook and do a drawing of him.

'You do realize that Legard is probably hundreds of miles away by now!'

I refused to rise to the bait. Serene and grateful for the light breeze accompanying the return of the sun, I meandered this way and that, down one alley and up another, crossing a street then crossing back almost at once, and back again. How Walter cursed! At every corner he wanted to know: 'Aren't we there yet?' I said nothing. After a while, seeing he had no alternative, he calmed down a little.

Eventually we passed the castle and came in sight of the sea; or, rather, we came in sight of some of the sea. Blocking our view on the right was the Warwick Revolving Tower. This was the first time we had seen it, but Walter recognized it immediately from the drawing in the guidebook and reeled off all the information he had read there.

'It was designed by the London engineer Thomas Warwick and consists of a circular passenger platform around a central tower. Powered by steam engine, the platform rotates on tracks as it is pulled up the tower by steel cables, balanced by counterweights. Two hundred passengers can be accommodated on the revolving platform, and these are offered stupendous marine views from a height of 155 feet.'

As we watched, the platform was indeed moving up to its maximum height, and we could hear the excited voices of those inside as Scarborough and the sea revealed themselves.

Walter continued: 'There are similar revolving towers in Great Yarmouth and Morecambe.'

'Thank you for that,' I said, strolling off to the left along Queens Parade, a stately elevated promenade which follows the long curve of North Bay and overlooks the Clarence Gardens.

After a hundred yards or so I halted.

'Here?' Walter asked.

'Near here. We'd better hide behind this wall.' We positioned ourselves behind a building on the corner and, peering round, looked along the row of hotels and superior residences bending away in front of us.

'Third one along,' I said. 'The Blenheim Hotel.'

'Ah, yes.' Walter's overloaded mind again whirred into action. 'Position unequalled. Full sea view. Close to golf links, tennis and cricket grounds, castle and all entertainments. Terms from 4/- to 5/6 per day.'

'Very interesting,' I said, facing him and letting my annoyance show, 'but the only piece of information we need now is whether Mr Legard is inside the Blenheim Hotel.'

'He isn't.'

'How do you know?'

'Because he's just come out.'

I turned and there he was on the hotel steps: morning coat, top hat and yellow checked waistcoat, as usual. In addition he was carrying a small brown suitcase.

'Trying to make his getaway,' I said. 'Well, he won't with us on his tail.'

After a few moments of sniffing the air, Legard strode off northwards. I expected Walter to be after him like a shot, but he had other ideas.

'Keep him in sight, Sidney. I won't be long.' He dashed into the Blenheim, leaving me on my own, uncertain how to go about 'shadowing' someone, as I believe it is called.

Legard walked straight ahead, full of purpose and speed. I did my best to keep up, pulling down the brim of my boater in case he should turn round and recognize me. A few minutes' walking brought him to the end of the promenade. I heard the sound of steps and turned to see Walter running towards me, a little out of breath.

'Where is he?' he said.

'Just ahead. There, by —' Only he was not. Legard had vanished.

'Come on,' cried Walter, racing past me. I caught up with him where I had last seen our quarry. Walter was surveying the grassy slope below the promenade that fell away to the North Sands and was criss-crossed with narrow footpaths. Holidaymakers of all varieties were progressing up and down them, as if taking part in a giant game of snakes and ladders.

'There,' said Walter, pointing at a figure already near the bottom. We shot off down the slope with little regard for such niceties as footpaths which would have required that we zigzag to, rather than make a beeline for, our destination. On our precipitous downward journey we received many a surprised comment — none, I think, complimentary.

Legard was on the upper edge of the beach now, tramping along unsteadily behind the bathing machines that were not in use. We followed at a distance.

'He seems to be making things as awkward for us as he can,' said Walter, lurching sideways as his feet slipped in the sand. 'I'll get the wretched stuff in my new shoes.'

'Surely,' I said, 'your shoes are of no importance when there's a crime to be solved.'

Walter grunted.

We battled on in the sand, as did Legard. Fortunately he did not look back. He pushed on purposefully, his suitcase swinging in his hand. Soon he came to Scalby Mills, where Walter and I had drunk beer just over a week ago, shortly before discovering Thomas White's body. Legard did not stop for refreshment. He climbed up onto the cliff-top path.

'History appears to be repeating itself,' said Walter, as we took the same path we had taken the week before, skirting fields and gorse bushes, accompanied by the insistent cries of gulls. Rising, dipping and curving, the path took Legard out of sight every now and then, but he was always still visible once we had crested the hill or rounded the bend. We passed the cove where we had watched the puffins and, after walking for what must have been over an hour, found ourselves approaching the cove known as Cloughton Wyke. It was here that our previous ramble had ended in murder. I wondered if the same thing could possibly happen again.

By the time we had reached the top of the cove, Legard was already sliding and slithering over the rocks by the headland.

'What's going on?' I said. 'He's going to the scene of the murder.'

'So it would seem.'

Walter made to go after him. I stretched out a hand and held him back. 'Do you think it's safe? Goodness knows what he's got in that suitcase.'

'My dear Sidney, there are two of us, and only one of him.'

In no way did that satisfy me, but Walter was off down the path and towards the headland like a dog after a rabbit. I followed. I had no choice.

We stumbled over the wet rocks. However ridiculous it might sound, I was truly afraid I would be confronted with another murder scene, perhaps even an identical one, with a naked man, dead, sprawled on the platform of rock.

What we actually found was the opposite. Lying on the large, flat rock was not a naked man but a pile of clothes, with the yellow checked waistcoat on top. The wearer was nowhere to be seen.

'Our Mr Legard has a sense of humour,' said Walter.

'Here!' I cried, for I had noticed a set of footprints leading down to the water's edge. 'Do you think he's swum out to sea?'

'I'm sure that's what he wants us to think. Look at this.' He held up the suitcase. Where have we seen this before?'

Inside the lid were the initials TW, printed in gold in a flurry of curlicues. The case was empty.

'Room ...,' I began before my memory gave out.

'That's right, room 320.'

'But why should Legard have it?'

'I think he's giving us a sporting chance by leaving us a clue.'

'What?'

'Well, Legard's not, since he is now, to all intents and purposes, deceased.'

'What are you talking about?'

'At last I understand, and I admit I should have worked it out earlier. In fact, I nearly did – when I first met Legard and thought he was Thomas White in disguise.'

'But he couldn't have been, because Thomas White was killed.'

'That's right. The man calling himself Arthur Legard was actually the impostor who pretended to be Thomas White – or rather, the impostor has been pretending to be Legard and Old Simon all along. Now those two have been killed off, the impostor is once more himself again.'

'Who is he?'

'That is what we have to find out.'

'Why did he bring an empty suitcase with him?'

'Oh, I've no doubt it had something in it – like a change of clothes. Our impostor is probably well on his way back to Scarborough by now. My God, we've been taken for fools, Sidney!'

My first impulse was to respond with 'speak for yourself', but when I had heard Walter's account, convincing as it was, I had to acknowledge that I too had not covered myself in glory.

'You're probably wondering why I dashed into the Blenheim Hotel before we started to follow Legard.'

'It did cross my mind.'

'I found out that Legard was *not* staying there. He had simply been hanging around, waiting for one of the guests – or so he said – before he abruptly left as soon as we'd arrived.'

'Yes, the timing was very odd.'

'Not really. Not when he'd been waiting for us.'

'What?'

'Ever since we took an interest in the disappearance of Mr White, someone has been taking an interest in us. While we've been watching them, they've been watching us. They've tried to predict our every move, and have fairly well succeeded.

'The murder of Thomas White was carried out where it was solely in order for us to discover it. Similarly, today we were intended to follow Legard to the same place and conclude that he had walked into the sea in a sudden fit of self-destruction. We've been led by the nose like imbeciles, Sidney. Lancelot knew what was going on, and seems to have been involved in it. He reprimanded our impostor, dressed as Legard, for killing Thomas White with his knife, instead of in the presumably simpler way that had been agreed on. Lancelot was silenced before he could divulge anything to you.'

'But what's the motive? All for the death of an ordinary holidaymaker.'

'We deduce from that that Thomas White *can't* have been an ordinary holidaymaker.'

'Then what was he?'

'Your guess is as good as mine, at present. Clearly not just the fiancé of Miss Meakins.'

'No,' I agreed. 'Just a minute! If Legard wasn't staying at the Blenheim –'

'I assure you he wasn't.'

'Then Miss Fitt, when she said she'd seen him come out of the Blenheim ...'

'Yes?'

'She must have been lying.'

'Of course she was.'

'I wonder why.'

'We shall have to ask her. But first I would like to find our impostor. It's a pity we gave the only photograph to Brasher, although I don't think it would have helped us much.'

'Why not?'

'Photographs are black and white, Sidney.'

'So?'

'The eyes – think of the eyes.'

20

Pablo Goes Dancing

'The best place to look for him,' said Walter, 'would be Londesborough Lodge or the Beehive Inn. He frequented both in the form of Legard and Old Simon. The Beehive is more difficult, since the landlady appears to be implicated in the crime, or she wouldn't have lied in an attempt to get us arrested.'

'Perhaps she was just offered money to do it,' I said, remembering the shilling she had managed to prise out of me.

'Perhaps.'

We were sitting in a train from Cloughton to Scarborough, returning from our pursuit of Legard. Considering he had slipped through our clutches, Walter was in a remarkably sanguine mood. His legs were crossed, and now and then he hummed a tune to himself.

'When we get back,' he said, 'we'll find out if there's another soirée at Londesborough Lodge any time soon. It's easy to look someone in the eyes when you're dancing with them.'

He smiled and settled down for a brief doze.

As luck would have it, there was a soirée arranged for that very night. I had no intention of becoming Reginald Smithers again and having to limp all evening. Happily, Walter fell in with my wishes. When the time came to get ready, he presented me with what looked like a small pile of colourful fabrics.

'What's this?' I asked.

'Tonight's soirée is fancy dress, which means you can be whoever you like and no one will ask who you really are.'

I unfolded the various items he had given me. On top of the pile was a buttonless open-necked shirt in bright blue satin with yellow puffed sleeves. Next was a broad red sash, presumably to be worn round the waist, and a pair of baggy trousers in an unpleasant shade of green. Last was a black bandana with white dots. As I was trying to make sense of these, Walter handed me two more items.

'I nearly forgot. You'll need to wear these.'

They were huge black leather boots with cuffs. They were so big I could have got both feet into just one of them.

'And this.' He dropped a large metal hoop on the dressing table.

'What's that?'

'Your earring.'

'Earring?'

'Every gypsy wears an earring.'

'I'm not going as a gypsy.'

'Pablo would be a good name for you.'

'And what are you going as?'

'I'll show you. Close your eyes.'

This was the sort of thing we had done as children, and was hardly appropriate for our more advanced time of life, but I said nothing. We would get to the point more quickly if I humoured him. I closed my eyes. After a minute or two Walter gave me permission to open them.

'You can't possibly go like that!' I cried.

'Why ever not?'

'You know why not.'

'It's fancy dress. One can wear what one likes.'

He stood before me in frock coat, ulster and deerstalker. In his right hand he held a clay pipe.

'The game's afoot,' he said, flourishing the pipe. 'Come along, Sidney, we're late already. I'll give you ten minutes to transform yourself into Pablo.'

Another large tip gained us entry to the soirée. In the ballroom there was as thick a crush of bodies as before. Most of them were swirling about in time to the music from the band, or stumbling, the worse for drink, from table to table. I observed a host of Beau Brummells, complete with top hats, curly hair and white stocks; several examples of Charles I, thankfully in his pre-execution state; and the usual assortment of vaguely historical characters in vaguely historical costumes. I was surprised to see, in one corner of the room, Queen Elizabeth holding court while stroking her beard.

The broken candelabra had been removed, leaving a ragged hole in the plaster ceiling. Nor was Lord Dibblesdale there to remind anyone of our previous visit. Walter was no longer the attraction he had been. It seemed that the relative plainness of Sherlock Holmes made him a less appealing prospect to the more flamboyantly inclined who comprised the greater part of the guests. No one rushed up to ask him to dance. I was beginning to suspect, from the looks I was attracting, that a colourful gypsy was more to their taste.

'Show me your hand,' said Walter, and I held out my right hand, palm up. The symbol, which Walter had marked in make-up, was still intact. 'Remember: green eyes, with two flecks in the right eye. Good luck.' He plunged into the mass of dancers, like a swimmer into the sea, and was swallowed up.

I stood on the edge, hesitating. How had it come to this? To be on the verge of waltzing with a string of strange men – strange in both senses of the word – while dressed as a gypsy and sporting an earring! If Edith could have seen me, what might her reaction have been? She would probably have repeated what she said when I first hinted at my plan to take Walter to Scarborough: 'You're wasting your time. You'll never change him. All that'll happen is he'll lead you astray and you'll end up embarrassing yourself.' Well, here was embarrassment in full measure.

I must have looked like a startled rabbit. Unfortunately, this was not deterrent enough. One of the Beau Brummells cast a glance my way, then followed it, asking: 'Would you like to shake your maracas with me?' I regret to say I blushed, which only served to increase his interest. He took me by the wrist, turned my hand over to check for the symbol, showed me the symbol on his hand, and led me onto the dance floor.

I'm not much of a dancer. Edith complains I kick her in the shins when I'm not walking all over her feet. So imagine how much less of a dancer I was at Londesborough Lodge that evening! Locked in an intimate embrace, not with a demure specimen of the fairer sex, but with a lustful dandy with pomade in his hair and make-up on his face. I shuffled about in my oversized boots as best I could, unsure whether we were dancing a waltz or a mazurka.

'Isn't this lovely?' my partner asked. I remained silent for fear of encouraging conversation. On and on the music went. Round and round we whirled, Beau Brumell laughing gaily – at my discomfiture, I had little doubt. I decided to take decisive action. I raised my head, which I had kept lowered for most of the time under the pretence of concentrating on my footwork, and looked him straight in the eyes.

I saw his face light up, as he misinterpreted my gesture. In an instant I had stopped and disengaged myself from his arms. I mumbled: 'Thank you.'

'Rejected so soon?' he wailed.

I cannot now remember what colour his eyes were. I do know they were not green, and that was all that mattered.

I pushed my way out of the melee of dancers, half aware of Walter's deerstalker bobbing about above the heads around me, and flung myself onto a chair like an exhausted seal making landfall. I hardly had time to get my breath back before a man with thick whiskers and wearing a crown hoisted me up, checked for the symbol on my hand with practised ease, and dragged me back into the heavy swell of bodies. With his long robes he bore a passing resemblance to a medieval king, perhaps Edward the Confessor. Before we could start dancing, the music came to a stop, leaving a babble of high-pitched voices.

'Thank you,' I said and tried to flee. He held me by the arm.

'We haven't danced yet.'

'I can't,' I said.

'Why not?'

'I've got a limp.'

'No, you haven't.'

'Reginald Smithers has.'

'Who?'

I let my gaze pass over my partner's face. Eyes not green. Enough! Go!

I broke away. At that moment the band started up again, playing a wild polka. Back and forth the dancers rushed, knocking me this way and that like a shuttle on a loom. I backed into someone, who spun me round and whisked me off at frightening speed to the edge of the dance floor then back to the other side without making the slightest allowance for anyone who happened to be in the way. He was dressed as a buccaneer, as well he might be.

Suddenly, and fortunately, the music switched to a slow waltz, and I finally had my chance to look into my partner's eyes – or, I should say, eye, for his pirate's patch was hiding one of them. I lifted my head. This small movement was enough to dislodge my bandana, which had been working itself loose during my enforced exertions in the polka, and which now dropped over my face, rendering me blind. My partner laughed. He turned over my hand, presumably to check for the symbol, then pulled me closer to him, trying to whisper in my ear.

'May I?' Someone else had taken hold of me, and the buccaneer sailed away in search of other booty. 'You do look rather ridiculous,' my new partner said.

'Probably no more ridiculous than you look,' I spat out, by now tired of the whole business. Whatever had possessed me to fall in with Walter's plan? It had seemed quite sensible in the quiet of our hotel room, but I had to admit I had not thought it through and foreseen the practical problems it would involve. I was dressed as a gypsy, about to begin a slow dance with a man I could not see and cursing my brother inwardly for all I was worth.

'Are you enjoying yourself, Sidney?'

I tore off the bandana. Walter was standing before me in all his Holmesian splendour, his deerstalker only a little awry.

'What do you think?' I said. 'The idea was mad from the first.'

'No, because we've learnt one thing.'

'Really? What's that?'

'That the man we're looking for isn't here tonight. There are no green eyes anywhere in the room.'

'You can't have danced with everyone.'

'Of course I haven't. I've simply kept my eyes open and looked into as many faces as possible during my peregrinations around the dance floor. I think I've covered everybody. It's a pity he's not here, but we'll find him.'

'How can you be so sure? You can't go up to every man in Scarborough to check the colour of his eyes.'

'Nor would I want to. The man we're after has already killed one person, perhaps two if Lancelot fell victim to him. He knows we're on his trail – witness the charade on the beach today. So he might feel cornered and strike out. We must be very careful.'

As a result of Walter's warning I became suspicious of just about every man who crossed my path. Was the newspaper seller outside the hotel the killer? Or perhaps the man who had moved into the room next to ours? Or how about the waiter bringing our coffee the following morning? He seemed to be evading my gaze ...

'What's the matter?' asked Walter.

'What do you mean?'

'You look like a thief afraid of getting caught.'

'Hardly.' I explained my nervous state.

'Relax,' he said. 'The killer isn't likely to come looking for us, is he? He'll be lying low.'

'I suppose so.' All the same, I decided not to drink my coffee that morning. Poison is usually the method of choice of female criminals, but there can always be an exception.

Back in our room, we gave the remainder of the morning over to yet another perusal of the coded message that seemed so vital to the two ladies. As before, we struggled and made no progress. At twelve o'clock I left Walter to it and, donning my boater, took a stroll through the centre of town, as much to convince myself I was not afraid as to stretch my legs.

The sun was on full display once more, agreeably tempered by a light breeze. Had it not been for the knowledge that one of the passers-by could be the killer of Thomas White, and possibly of me, I would have rejoiced to be alive on such a morning. As it was, I could muster nothing more than a moderate glow of pleasure.

I passed the handsome Elizabethan mansion that was now the Town Hall, and turned right and down the hill towards the harbour. Judging by the masses of people ascending and descending, the shops and bars lining both sides of the street were doing brisk business. About halfway down I came across the premises of an antiquarian bookseller, who had laid out some of his wares on a trestle table in front of the shop. These were, I was disappointed to discover, cheap editions of popular novels at knockdown prices, well within the price range of the ordinary holidaymaker. Peering through the grimy window I spotted several bound volumes of the *Strand*. Pride got the better of me and, removing my boater, I entered the shop.

To my surprise and delight, the person keeping shop was not a wizened, bespectacled septuagenarian but an attractive brunette in a rather close-fitting golden dress.

'Good morning,' she trilled. 'Are you looking for anything in particular?'

'I'd like to take a look at one of the *Strand* volumes you have in the window, if I may.'

'Of course. Which one?'

'Volume five, I think it is.'

'I'll get it for you.' She smiled, reached across a table and into the window space. 'Here we are.' Her delicate ringless fingers held out the book. How I would have preferred to clasp those hands in mine at yesterday's soirée!

'Thank you.' I laid my boater on a row of encyclopedias, took the proffered book and looked at the familiar cover: a view along the Strand towards the church of St Mary-le-Strand, picked out in black on light blue cloth.

'Let me know if you need me,' said the vision in gold. She drifted to the back of the shop while I mused on the possible interpretations of her words.

I opened the book at the index. There they were, at the top of the list, printed in capitals: ADVENTURES OF SHERLOCK HOLMES by A. CONAN DOYLE (*Illustrations* by SIDNEY PAGET). My name in a slightly smaller font than that of Doyle, but that's only right. I turned to the story I had come in to look at: XVII – THE ADVENTURE OF THE 'GLORIA SCOTT'. Directly opposite this title, on the next page, was what I considered, and still consider, to be my most successful representation of the Great Detective.

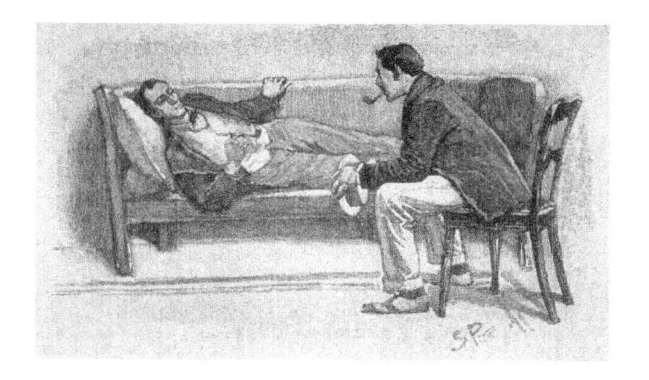

Holmes is stretched out on a couch, resting his ankle, which has been bitten by a friend's bull-terrier. The friend is sitting next to him, cleverly hiding the damaged ankle (thereby saving me a considerable amount of tricky drawing). What I think I have caught so well in this picture is the combination of languidness and alertness so peculiar to Holmes. Although he is obviously relaxing, with a pipe in his right hand, his left hand is gripping the back of the couch, ready to pull him up and launch him into action if the occasion demands it. Also, the crease in the friend's trousers is very well done, I think.

Still musing on the felicity with which I had discharged my commission, I let my gaze wander to the text of the story.

Somewhere near the beginning I read: 'He had picked from a drawer a little tarnished cylinder, and, undoing the tape, he handed me a short note scrawled upon a half sheet of slate-grey paper. "The supply of game for London is going steadily up," it ran ...'

'My God!' I cried.

'Are you all right?' The dear thing had dropped what she was doing – literally, for I heard the thud of books hitting the floor – and rushed to my aid.

'Thank you,' I said. 'I couldn't be righter. I do apologize for my outburst.' I seized my boater and headed for the door.

'What about the book?'

'Book?' I echoed, not understanding.

'The book in your hand. Volume five of the *Strand*.'

I laughed. 'Of course. I'm so sorry. How much is it?'

'Seventeen shillings and sixpence, I'm afraid.'

'It's a bargain.' I fished out a one-pound note and pressed it into her snow-white hand.

'I'll get your change.'

'No. I don't want any. Good day.'

Leaving the shop, I ran uphill.

21

Decoded

Walter was stretched out on his bed in room 185, either dozing or reflecting; I could not tell which. I tossed the *Strand* volume towards him. It landed on his legs, jerking him up into a sitting position as if he were an animated wooden toy.

'What the devil!'

'It's only me, your intelligent older brother. Take a look at that book.'

'What?'

'Where I've marked it.' I had kept a finger between the pages all the way back to the hotel, then replaced it with one of the business cards the management leave lying around so liberally.

Walter opened the book. 'That's right,' he said, 'rub my nose in it.'

I could not make sense of what he was saying and told him as much.

'You sketched me when I was asleep', he said. 'Without my permission.'

'I'm not bothered about the picture.'

'But I am. I would have made a much better job of it.'

'Don't you remember the story? *The Adventure of the "Gloria Scott"*.'

'No, because I've never read it.'

'Why not?'

'I've got better things to do than waste my time with detective stories.'

This was rich, coming from a man who devoured yellowbacks as if they were the one thing that kept him alive. I snatched the book from him. 'Listen. "The supply of game for London is going steadily up. Head-keeper Hudson, we believe, has been now told to receive all orders for fly-paper, and for preservation of your hen pheasant's life."'

I saw the expression on Walter's face and chuckled.

'What in heaven's name is all that about?'

'It's a code,' I said. 'A very simple code. We've been racking our brains to find some complicated code to fit Thomas White's note, when all along it's been as easy as this.'

He eased himself into a more comfortable position, sitting with his legs over the edge of the bed. 'Go on.'

'As Holmes explains later in the story, you get the message by taking the first word and then every third word after that. So what I've just read out becomes: "The game is up. Hudson has told all. Fly for your life."'

'If you apply that to Thomas White's note,' he said, thinking at top speed, 'you get "When shines rainfall you'll room shelter people these be collect tea served silver". Where's the sense in that?'

'There's none. But if you take every fifth word –'

'Why every fifth word? Why not every fourth word?'

'Because the message is spread out over five lines. That's the key. If you take every fifth word ...'

'By Jove, yes!' He sprang up and paced about. 'When light in room twenty-four collect coffee pot.'

'Precisely.'

'Well done, Sidney.'

'Thank you.'

We smiled at each other, and for a moment I had something approaching a feeling of brotherly love. Then, just as suddenly, our smiles faded.

'It makes some sort of sense,' Walter said, 'but what does it mean?'

'I ... I don't know. But it must mean something to someone.'

'Of course it does.' He strode over to the writing table, sat and picked up his pen. 'What was it again?' He wrote the words in capitals on a sheet of hotel notepaper, repeating them after me. 'WHEN – LIGHT – IN – ROOM – TWENTY-FOUR – COLLECT – COFFEE – POT.' We must tell our two mysterious ladies we have solved the puzzle.'

'And then?'

'We wait to see what they do as a result of receiving the message.'

Our proposed visit to room 281 had to be postponed, however. No sooner had we prepared ourselves – mentally, emotionally and sartorially – for the encounter than the timorous knock heralding Inspector Brasher was heard on our door. He entered with his usual deference and lowered himself gently into the armchair.

'Good afternoon, gentlemen. I hope I've caught you at a convenient time.'

He had not, of course, but we assured him he had.

'I'm pleased,' he said, looking as if he had lost a shilling and found sixpence. He was holding his bowler like a new-born baby, caressing it and muttering little sounds of affection. Then, with a start, he recalled the purpose of his visit.

'What I have to say is of the utmost importance and urgency. I would ask you to pay attention.'

I told him we were all ears. We even leaned forward as we sat on our beds, the better to catch his words at the exact moment of their utterance.

'Earlier today I received this.' He relocated his hat to his lap and dipped into an inside pocket, from where he extracted what looked like a telegram. 'It comes from –' He stopped himself and jumped up out of his chair with a speed and agility of which I would never have thought him capable.

'Please rise, gentlemen.' We rose, somewhat bewildered. 'It comes from Her Majesty.' Having paid due reverence, we sat down.

'I realise artists are unconventional in their attitudes, but I trust they are loyal subjects of –' He got up again. 'Loyal subjects of Her Majesty.' He sat down again.

I glanced at Walter. He was stifling his laughter as much as I was. Brasher's behaviour reminded me of some parlour game in which every time a certain word was mentioned everyone had to perform an action. I do not think Walter or myself would have had a very good chance of winning against a formidable player like the inspector.

'Do you really mean to say,' said Walter, 'that it came from …' He hesitated. Brasher had his arms up, ready to haul himself out of the chair. 'From the Palace?'

'Well, not exactly. It would be more accurate to say it came from the Home Office.'

I was getting a little tired of beating about this particular bush. I asked: 'What does the telegram say?'

'I was coming to that,' said Brasher in a tone of reproach. He shook out the slip of paper and cleared his throat. 'Stop investigation stop repeat stop stop …' He ground to a halt and sighed. 'I do beg your pardon – I seem to have lost my way. I've left my glasses in my other suit, you see, and …' (Other suit? Perhaps he has two, I thought, that are equally shabby.) He handed the telegram to me. After a quick perusal I handed it to Walter.

> STOP INVESTIGATION STOP REPEAT
> STOP STOP RETURN LONDON STOP
> STOP OTHERS INVESTIGATING STOP

Primed by our recent analysis of Thomas White's coded message, I had no difficulty in filleting the meaning of the telegram. Neither did Walter. 'Stop investigation. Repeat: stop. Return London. Stop others investigating.'

'That's about the long and the short of it,' said Brasher.

'By others I presume they mean me and my brother.'

'I fancy so.' The inspector allowed himself a broad grin.

I asked: 'Why are you being asked to stop?'

'I wouldn't know.'

'Don't you want to know?'

'I follow orders. I shall return to Kent, where I hope to find some time to do a bit of fishing. That will be enough for me. Are either of you gentlemen interested in fishing?'

'I fear not,' said Walter. 'We are artists.'

'What does that have to do with it?'

'We are sensitive beings. We don't like to see animals hurt.'

'But you don't mind eating them, eh?'

Walter laughed. 'Touché, Inspector. Touché.'

Now beaming all over his face, Brasher stood up. 'Then I'll bid you gentlemen good day. Enjoy the rest of your stay in Scarborough.' He began his shuffle towards the door, only to be halted by Walter's speaking.

'Inspector,' he said, 'how exactly are you going to stop us from investigating?'

He looked at us as though we were mad. 'I expect you to follow orders too, gentlemen. Considering where they come from.'

'We are free citizens, and are not doing anything illegal.'

'No, but ...' His features hardened. He tilted back his head. 'Remember I can have you arrested if I so choose.'

'Can you?' said Walter. 'On what grounds?'

'On the grounds that you were seen by Miss Tranter of the Beehive Inn, struggling on the beach with Thomas White.'

'A pack of lies. You know it is.'

'Anyway,' I said, suddenly inspired, 'you can't arrest us.'

'Oh no? And why not?'

'Because you've been ordered to withdraw from the case.'

Brasher's face fell. He shot his cuffs and stared at them for a moment, comparing one against the other. Then he gripped the handle of the door.

'Good day, gentlemen.'

'One more thing, Inspector.' Walter held out his hand. 'Can you give me back my photograph?'

'Photograph?'

'Of the impostor.'

'Yours, is it?'

'I paid for it, so yes, I suppose it is.'

Brasher searched all his pockets before bringing out the photograph, which had taken on all the creases and wrinkles peculiar to its temporary owner.

'I trust it was of use,' said Walter, taking it.

'No blooming use at all. Like looking for a needle in a ruddy haystack.' And with that expert summing-up of the case, the inspector bowed his head to us and departed.

'Our suspect is looking a bit dog-eared,' Walter said, flourishing the battered photograph, 'but I'm sure he's still recognizable.'

'Recognizable as whom?'

'That, my dear Sidney, is the question we must answer.' He scrutinized the image, holding it close to his face in order to concentrate on one detail after another. 'I'm sure I've seen him before.'

'You've seen him dressed up as Legard and Old Simon, of course.'

'And here he's claiming to be Thomas White. But who is he when he's being himself, damn it?'

In a fit of frustration he threw the photograph towards me. I picked it up from the floor and examined it.

Again I was struck by the insolence of the man's expression, challenging and mocking us. He wore a self-satisfied grin, and his eyes, which might have been any colour under the sun, were bright with intelligence. His dark, wavy hair was brushed back off his forehead. His moustache was small and trim, and perhaps, of course, not genuine. The creases that Brasher had made in the photograph gave the impostor two large scars, one across the brow and the other from ear to chin.

I spent some minutes staring at his unattractive face, at the end of which time I was certain I had *never* seen him before.

'Shall we give up?' I said. 'Like the inspector asked us to.'

'Do you want to? You'd still have a day and a bit left for your holiday.'

'If you think we've a chance of catching the killer, then no, I don't want to stop.'

'Good man, Sidney. I knew I could rely on you.'

He knew nothing of the sort, because I had only that moment come to realize I had to see the whole affair through to the end, come what may. The fact that I would rather be lazing in a deckchair listening to the Spa orchestra was neither here nor there.

'Very well, then.' Walter slipped the photograph into his pocket and picked up the decoded message. 'Let's see what the ladies make of this.'

Miss Meakins's furrowed brow disturbed the serene beauty of her face as she scrutinized the sheet of hotel notepaper Walter had given her.

'There is some sort of sense in it,' she said, 'but what does it mean?'

'We were hoping you might be able to tell us that.'

'It seems to be an instruction to a servant about some coffee.'

'Why would Mr White write you such a message?' I asked.

'I've no idea.'

Miss Fitt, who had been hovering impatiently behind Miss Meakins, leaned forward and snatched the piece of paper from her niece's hand. Miss Meakins let out a small cry of surprise and looked extremely anxious – not angry or annoyed, as might have been expected, but definitely anxious, which struck me as curious. Within seconds she had regained her composure.

'What do you think, aunt?'

'I think someone is trying to make a fool of you.' She looked up and caught my eye.

'Not me,' I said, 'I assure you. Or my brother.'

She softened immediately. 'No, I didn't mean to imply ... I'm very grateful for your help, Mr Paget.' She turned to Walter and nodded. 'Mr Paget.'

'Miss Fitt.'

'I'm only sorry it should have turned out to be so unsatisfactory.'

'Unsatisfactory?'

'With the murderer of poor Mr White still at large and this

decoded message being so ridiculous.'

'There's still time to catch the killer,' said Walter.

'Oh, but you've done more than enough,' said Miss Meakins. 'I wouldn't dream of imposing on you any further.'

'It's no imposition. When do you leave for home?'

'The day after tomorrow.'

'Then I wish you sunshine for the rest of your stay. Good day, ladies.'

As soon as we were out in the corridor we began a sort of frenzied whispered conversation.

'Something not quite right there,' I said.

'Everything wrong, I'd say.'

'Do you think the message is nonsense?'

'Miss Fitt certainly doesn't think so.'

'The way she grabbed it means it must be something important.'

'We'll have to keep our eyes on those two.'

Back in our room, Walter went over to the window and started to sea-gaze again, just as he had done when we first arrived in Scarborough.

'Looking for inspiration?' I asked.

'Of course.'

'Have you any idea at all what that message means?'

'Oh yes.'

'Then tell me.'

'It's just an inkling at present. Have you got that guidebook I was reading in the train?'

I dug it out from the little pile of books on my bedside table.

'Thank you,' said Walter. 'Let's hope I'm right.'

He flicked through the guide, one way then the other, sighing in frustration.

'What are you looking for?'

'Please, don't distract me!'

Murmuring to himself, he flapped the pages back and forth. Then, with a cry fit to rival that of Archimedes in his bath, he found what he was searching for. 'Yes, by Jove!'

'What is it?'

He clapped the book shut. 'All in good time. Thank you, Sidney.' He handed the guidebook back to me.

'What do we do now?' I said.

'You *have* become eager for the chase, haven't you?'

I could not deny it.

'Now,' said Walter, 'we go down and get ourselves some tea. I'm parched.'

22

The Tower Revolves

Over the next hour or so, Walter's spirits sank so low that even Earl Grey and a plate of chocolate cakes could not revive them. The trigger for this reversal of mood was a visit we paid to room 24 on our way down. I do not know what my brother was expecting, but I can say I was totally dumbfounded when, in answer to Walter's peremptory knock, the door opened to reveal a bishop in full pontifical vestments, mitre and all.

'Good afternoon,' he said, stroking his bright red chasuble and not at all put out. 'Can I be of assistance?'

Walter and I stood open-mouthed.

'I'm just trying on my new outfit,' he continued. 'I haven't turned my room into a place of worship. Not yet, anyway.'

Walter stammered: 'I ... I ...', and I managed to get out: 'Do you drink coffee?', at once ashamed of such an inane question.

'I'm afraid I can't stand the stuff,' he said. 'But you're welcome to come in and I can ring for some tea.'

'Well,' I began, 'that would be –'

'Thank you,' said Walter. 'Goodbye.'

'Goodbye,' I echoed.

'Goodbye. Nice to have met you.' He closed the door as if our encounter had been the most natural way in the world to get to know people.

Now, in the hotel tea room, his refreshments untouched, Walter sat wallowing in gloom. His arms were folded, his chin was lowered onto his chest and he stared at the floor, wrapping himself in silence. For all his impassivity, I knew from past experience that a turbulent battle was going on within, stirring up feelings of inadequacy that might threaten to unbalance him at any moment. It was like watching a volcano, waiting for it to erupt.

I was feeling bad. I had brought Walter to Scarborough with the intention of providing physical and mental relaxation. Instead of that, his inquiring mind and circumstances had conspired to entangle him in a murder case. Far from doing everything in my power to divert him from his investigations, I had allowed myself to get slowly sucked into them, to the extent that I was now as desperate as Walter to hit upon the solution. We seemed to be so close to it – or at least Walter did – that to fail now was unthinkable. But if room 24 had no role to play in the mystery, what did the coded message mean?

'Perhaps,' I said, 'he wasn't a real bishop.'

'Ha! And he really loves coffee?'

'I ... I don't know.'

'Then keep quiet.'

Walter was still morose and moody when I finally convinced him we should go up to our room to rest and perhaps have a stimulating drink or two. We stretched out on our beds, side by side, staring at the ceiling. This was exactly what we had done as children when we had some exciting news to talk about – the nightmare one of us had had the night before; why the maid had been dismissed; when our tadpoles might turn into frogs. The difference now was that Walter would not talk at all, despite my various promptings. Several hours passed in this manner.

Had it all been a disastrous waste of time? Perhaps we should have stayed in London after all, even though the likelihood of stumbling across criminals was much greater in the metropolis than on the Yorkshire coast. Yet what our so-called holiday in Scarborough had taught us was that nowhere in the country was completely free from evil. At least we were coming to grief in beautiful surroundings.

There was a knock at the door and Bert came in with the drinks I had ordered: a Scotch for Walter and a cognac for me.

'Put them on our bedside tables, if you please,' I said, still fixing my gaze on the ceiling.

'Certainly, sir.' He moved silently from bed to bed, and I was aware only of two light clunks as the glasses came to rest beside us.

'Will that be all, sir?'

'Yes, thank you, Bert,' I said.

'The gentlemen do not require any supper?'

'No.'

'If you would like to eat in town, I can recommend a very good restaurant.'

'We aren't hungry, but thank you.'

Bert withdrew, closing the door with the quietest of clicks.

I reached out for my drink without sitting up. It was not easy. My arm would not –

'My God!' Walter had leapt up. 'What perfect idiots we've been!'

'What's the matter?' I sat up, seized the glass of cognac and gulped down the contents.

All he said was: 'Follow me!'

'What about your drink?' I said, but he grabbed his deerstalker and was out of the door before I had stood up. As soon as I had, I followed him. What else could I do?

Walter flew off down the stairs, again too impatient to take the lift. By the time I had caught up with him, seven floors lower, he was standing in the centre of the foyer, scanning the faces in the crowd of guests coming and going like busy insects.

'What is it?' I wanted to know.

'No time for explanations. There!' He pointed to the entrance, where a figure stood with his back to us. Walter ran towards him. The man turned. Now I understood. The impostor. The killer.

When he saw us coming for him, he fled down the steps and out into the half-light of St Nicholas Cliff, where he zigzagged between lamp posts, horses and promenaders in an attempt to shake us off.

'We mustn't lose sight of him, Sidney,' Walter shouted to me – rather unnecessarily, I thought.

The evening was now fairly well advanced. The lamps were lit, lending their indistinct glow to the darkening streets through which we ran, Walter ahead of me, turning now and then to shout instructions in case I could not keep up with him.

'He's going past the Town Hall.'

Of course, Walter had more or less memorized the guidebook, and so was acquainted with the notable buildings of Scarborough and their locations, whereas I was becoming aware of most of them for the first time. The Town Hall, however, was known to me.

'Up here,' he cried, turning left.

By the time I had rounded the corner, he was already well up the hill, sprinting and dodging among holidaymakers out for a pleasant evening stroll, just as our quarry was sprinting and dodging a little way in front of him.

'On to the post office,' Walter shouted before vanishing from view.

I marvelled that he could run so fast. I was puffing and labouring like a locomotive running out of steam. But I forced myself on, arriving at the point where I had last seen him, and looked around. Fortunately I caught sight of him just before he careered into the tangle of side streets behind the post office – or, at any rate, the building I took to be the post office.

Running through these streets, which were narrow and unlit, was like being in the sort of nightmare where you are lost without any point of reference. There was still a little daylight, but only enough to make visible the general shape of things. So although I was able to avoid running into buildings, carts and the like, I had not the first idea where I was running to. Walter's voice had become a distant echo. I was exhausted. I stopped.

Even as I stopped, a shadow flashed by me and I set off in pursuit without thinking. It was our man. His height was that of Legard; his bulk belonged to Old Simon. But now he was running for his life – his own.

Somewhere behind me I heard Walter calling out directions: 'Left, right, right again ...', unaware that, with all the twists and turns of the streets, I had ended up ahead of him. I pushed on.

Our man broke out into the halo of a street lamp near the church. He halted, turned to look at me and smiled. It was the smile in the photograph, the smile of the impostor pretending to be Thomas White. Walter came running up at that moment. All three of us stood for a moment gazing at one another, then the chase resumed as Walter dashed suddenly forward.

'The castle!'

Again I was quickly left behind. The man did not run up the path to the castle – which is extremely steep – but skirted the mound, heading for North Bay. I came in sight of the sea to find Walter was waiting for me. So, it seemed, was our man, who stood a hundred yards or so away with arms akimbo. He was behaving as if we were playing a children's game of tag.

Off we flew once more. He sped towards the Revolving Tower, with my brother and me close on his heels. The revolving platform was at ground level, the last in the queue of passengers had just climbed in, and it was beginning to turn slowly. The impostor flung open the door and jumped in at the last moment.

'Don't worry,' said Walter. 'He can't go far.'

We waited. The door came round again and we sprang aboard.

'You go that way,' I said, 'and I'll go this.' No sooner had Walter nodded than I realised I had given my younger brother an order which he had, perhaps for the first time in his adult life, implicitly obeyed. But I had no time just then to wallow in the achievement.

The revolve began to rise, turning the while. I pushed past seated passengers who, not unreasonably considering they had paid for it, cursed me for blocking their view of Scarborough by twilight. Apologizing and stumbling over legs, I saw him just ahead of me, sitting calmly, pretending to be a simple holidaymaker.

There was no pretending any more. I lunged for him. He shot up like a jack-in-the-box. Outside, the darkening sea in South Bay swung in and out of vision. Inside, Walter was fast approaching from the other direction. Our man was trapped.

He smiled, then spoke. 'All right,' he said, 'the game's over now.' Visibly relaxing, he straightened his clothes and started to make his way towards Walter.

I'll never know the reason for what happened next. Whether he lost his balance, or whether it was some demented attempt to escape, he fell against the door by which we had entered. It gave way.

Walter threw himself forward. I could only watch aghast. The suspect, the impostor, the killer – call him what you will – had eluded our grasp after all. The revolve had reached the top of the tower, and he fell 155 feet onto the hard ground below.

Having witnessed events, the operator of the Revolving Tower brought us all safely back to earth as quickly as he could. A small group of passers-by had already gathered round the dead man, who was lying face down. Hurrying towards us came a policeman. At first I didn't recognize him in the gathering dusk, but his features and his shape soon resolved themselves into those of Constable Brightman.

'What's going on here?' he demanded. 'Oh, it's you again, is it?'

I said: 'This gentleman fell from the tower.'

He considered my words carefully, as if uncertain of their meaning. 'Did he?' He pushed up his helmet and looked askance at me.

'It was a horrible accident.'

'You were chasing him,' said one of our fellow passengers.

What could I say? I could hardly launch into a long explanation about murder and disguises that would convince no one, least of all Constable Brightman.

Walter came to the rescue. 'Allow me to explain.' He stepped forward. 'My brother and I were indeed chasing him – because he had stolen my watch.'

Only he had not, of course. But then I looked at Walter's waistcoat and noticed that his watch chain was missing. Bending down, he reached into the dead man's jacket pocket and drew out the 'stolen' watch, dangling and spinning at the end of its chain. He performed the trick so naturally that nobody, not even myself, saw him palm it.

From the murmured comments of those around us I could tell

that we were no longer villains but victims, ill used by the scoundrel lying on the ground, who had got what was coming to him. Constable Brightman moved everyone along except my brother and me. Then he took out his whistle and blew it. A minute or so later Constable Rudge came running up, his shiny buttons announcing his arrival long before his face was visible.

Constable Brightman bent down and turned over the corpse. 'Do you recognize him?' The head was badly injured, bleeding, yet still recognizable.

'As I have said, constable, he is a common thief,' said Walter, 'so, no, we don't know him.'

The dead man's outstretched right hand lay open, the symbol visible. I looked at the battered face. The features undoubtedly resembled those of Thomas White, Arthur Legard and Old Simon. But even in the dim light, whether it was his true identity or not, the man on the ground was clearly Bert, our valet at the Grand.

By the time we had made our statements at the police station it was almost midnight. Our walk back to the Grand was the first opportunity we had had that evening to discuss the extraordinary events in which we had become embroiled.

'So,' I said, as soon as we had stepped out through the police station door, 'the impostor and killer was Bert all along.'

'I can't believe how foolish I've been.'

'Don't be too hard on yourself.'

'I've been a complete idiot, Sidney, and you've been even worse.'

'Well now, I don't –'

'The solution was right under our noses – literally.'

'That's often the one place you forget to look.'

'What did I accuse you of, when I came down in the lift that first day dressed as a fine gentleman?'

'If I remember rightly –'

'Don't interrupt. I said you looked but you didn't see. And what have I been doing these past two weeks? Precisely that. Looking but not seeing.'

'But you got there in the end.'

'Tell that to Lancelot!'

The death of our fellow artist was weighing on his conscience – I had not known how heavily until that moment. He sighed and lapsed into silence.

'What was it that gave you the clue?' I asked, in an attempt to focus on his success.

'Something Bert said tonight when he brought up our drinks. He said he could recommend a restaurant.'

'So?'

'It set up an echo in my mind. At first I couldn't think why, and then it came to me. I recalled him recommending something else.'

'What?'

'The coastal walk to Cloughton Wyke, where we found Thomas White's body.'

'Of course. He'd have known where we were going.'

'He'd be the only one who would have known. He was able to lure Thomas White there and kill him at just the right moment for us to discover his body.'

'I still don't understand why he should have wanted us to discover it.'

'Perhaps not just him. We mustn't forget Lancelot. Or the landlady of the Beehive. Where do they come into the equation?'

'*Do* they come into the equation?'

'I'm not sure.'

I tried to order my thoughts but failed. 'You know what? I've done enough thinking for one night.'

Walter agreed that a period of mental rest was called for, so we walked on in silence through the warm, dark streets, with the occasional street lamp lighting our way. It was not until we had passed the Town Hall that I noticed it – or, rather, its absence.

'I say, where's your hat?'

'What?'

'Your deerstalker.'

Walter searched all his pockets.

'Did I give it to you?' he asked.

'Certainly not.'

He became as distraught as a small child who has lost his favourite toy.

'I should have it somewhere.' And he continued to rummage in his pockets.

'You've lost the wretched thing, which may turn out to be a godsend.'

Walter grunted. 'I'll buy another.'

It was well after midnight before we got to bed. I knew I would not be able to fall asleep straight away, for questions were buzzing round in my head like flies in a jar. We might have discovered the identity of Thomas White's killer, but who had murdered Lancelot? And what about motive? Why had Thomas White and Lancelot been killed? What part did the coded message play in the whole affair? Why did the Misses Meakins and Fitt seem so concerned to make sense of it? Their behaviour was a little strange, but was it criminal?

I wondered if Walter's mind was similarly afflicted.

'What's puzzling me in particular,' he said, thereby giving me my answer, 'is that business about room 24.'

'And the rest of the message.'

'No, that's quite clear.'

'That stuff about the coffee pot?'

'If only I could ... room 24 ...'

'I suppose it does refer to the Grand Hotel,' I said. 'I mean, it could be a room in another hotel entirely, in which case –'

'No! That's it! How could I have overlooked that?'

'What?'

'Ha!'

'Do you know what the message means?'

'I do.'

'Does it have any significance?'

'Great significance.'

A long pause followed, during which I could hear Walter turning onto his side and settling down to sleep.

I said: 'Aren't you going to tell me?'

'It can wait. If it's already happened, there's nothing we can do about it. But with any luck we'll have some illuminating answers, and possibly some adventure, tomorrow.'

'What are you talking about? If *what* has already happened?'

'Good night.'

'Walter!'

But his mind had now been freed from its self-critical torture, he was already preparing for the next day, and the only reply I received was a deep and hurtful snore.

23

A Day Off

When I woke the next morning after a few hours' sleep, the first thing I decided – even before getting out of bed – was that I would never again trust a servant. It was a sad conclusion to come to, especially since the staff in my household in London were, and are, possessed of the highest virtue – or, at least, I think they are – but Bert's deceitful activities had severely undermined my confidence.

Of course, it was our fault as much as his. Had Walter and I not taken Bert for granted, had we not regarded him simply as someone to fetch and carry for us but had looked him in the face and seen the colour of his eyes, the case could have been closed much earlier. Then we would have had a week or so at our disposal to enjoy a holiday, which was after all the original plan. Now we had only one day left before we returned home, and this, according to my brother, was to be filled with yet more intrigue.

Imagine my surprise when Walter, after taking a leisurely breakfast, announced that the day was ours to do with as we chose.

'You mean a day of relaxation?'

'If you wish.'

'I do wish. But what about the decoded message, adventure and the rest of it?'

'That will come later. I'll explain once we're settled in our deckchairs.'

Oh, the bliss of it! To rest one's limbs for a while and watch the world go by.

The world on this occasion was Scarborough's South Sands, whose temporary inhabitants were busy escaping the everyday:

sitting and catching the sun, like Walter and me; running and shouting for the sheer joy of it; wading into the sea from the bathing machines. So invigorating was the activity around us that several times I roused myself from the pleasant torpor into which I had sunk and took out my sketchbook and pencil. Just a few swift lines and a little shading are generally sufficient to capture a variety of postures for use in future illustrations.

What with sketching and dozing in the blissful heat, I had nearly forgotten about the murder case and the coded message.

Walter had not. 'You see,' he said, 'there *is* no room 24.'

It took a moment or two for my mind to latch onto what he was talking about.

'There is,' I said. 'There's a bishop in it.'

'In the message, I mean.'

'What?'

'It was your mentioning the Grand that made me see the light. The floors and rooms of the hotel are arranged according to the calendar. Now what does the number 24 conjure up in that context?'

'Twenty-four ... hours in the day.'

'Exactly. The message is giving a time – 24 hours or midnight.'

'Then which room is it?'

'Whichever room is occupied by the recipient of the message, of course. It doesn't need to be specified. I suspect it's room 320.'

'Room 320?'

'Where we found the suitcase and clothes, you remember. So, if I'm right – and I think this time I definitely am – we simply have to be in the vicinity of room 320 at midnight.'

I have never been happy with my brother's use of the word 'simply'. Very few of his suggestions have turned out to be simple.

'But what's all that about the coffee pot? Who's collecting it?'

'No one. I'll explain all that tonight. Time now for a little snooze.'

He stretched out his legs, digging his heels into the sand, and interlocked his fingers over his chest. It seemed like a good idea, so I did the same.

With my eyes closed, sounds were more intense. Seagulls shrieking – children laughing and screaming – parents calling them back lest they run into the sea – the sea sighing and pulsing, far off but getting closer – ever closer – and Walter, a boy again, shouting for sheer joy at the prospect of a day on the sands building castles and moats.

Looking back, I think I must have been deceiving myself to imagine that I, let alone Walter, could spend a whole day in a state of calm relaxation when a midnight deadline was hanging over it like the sword of Damocles. I felt both excited and terrified. If Walter was right, we would at last be able to make sense of the extraordinary events of the past two weeks, but at the same time there would surely be those who would rather we did not make sense of them, and would not be averse to employing forceful methods to achieve that end. The fact that those involved might include the Misses Meakins and Fitt in some way made the situation even more fraught.

Still, we did our best. We strolled up and down the Esplanade in the South Cliff quarter. We sat and listened to the Spa band play its complete repertoire several times through, while I dashed off the final postcard to Edith. We even climbed up the steep paths to the castle and endeavoured to interest ourselves in its turbulent history. But our hearts, and our minds, were not in it.

It is remarkable how nervous anticipation can ruin one's appetite. In the hotel restaurant that evening we left so much food on our plates we were afraid the chef might be offended. We pleaded indisposition from the heat and dragged ourselves upstairs to our room.

During the course of the day I had asked Walter repeatedly to explain what he thought was going to happen at midnight. Each time he had refused. I asked him again.

'What does the message mean? You must tell me if you want me to take part in whatever it is we're to take part in.'

I was seated in the armchair, feeling tired and crumpled in a

Brasher-like way. Walter was lying on his bed, ankles crossed and hands behind his head.

'Very well, Sidney. I think the time is now ripe.'

I sat up, casting off my fatigue.

'In order to tell someone about an event,' he continued, 'three pieces of information are necessary: the place of the event, the time of the event, and the nature of the event – in other words, what the event is. Are you following me so far?'

'Yes.'

'In the decoded message the place is the room where a light is to be placed – presumably a lamp at the window, in time-honoured fashion – the time is 24 hours, or midnight, and the event itself is described in the words "collect coffee pot".'

'It doesn't seem much of an event, does it? Collecting a pot of coffee.'

'As ever, your mind is working too literally. Here.' He picked up the guidebook to Scarborough and District from his bedside table and tossed it to me.

'Page 55.'

I turned to the page in question and found a section of a map of Scarborough, showing the coastal area round the promontory on which the castle stands.

Walter said: 'Look in the top right-hand corner and tell me what you see.'

'Coffee pot,' I said.

'Bravo! The Coffee Pot is the local name for the shelf of rock jutting out into the sea below the castle.'

'Why is it called that?'

'Next page. I've marked it.'

I turned to page 56 and read out the sentence that Walter had underlined in pencil. 'The name comes from a limestone rock with a profile like a coffee pot which rises from the sea at low water.'

'So no one is going to be collecting a coffee pot,' said Walter. 'Rather, someone is going to be collected at the Coffee Pot. By boat, I presume.'

'But who?'
'Who was the note addressed to?'
'Julia. I mean Miss Meakins. But who's going to collect her, and why?'
'Who was the note from?'
'Thomas White. But he's dead.'
'Is he?'
'Of course.'
'Thomas White was photographed upon a whim, and now that's all that's left of him. Come,' he said, leaping up from the bed, 'it's time for action.'

When the mystery of the coffee pot had been explained to me, my first reaction was not one of wonder and gratitude – though I did congratulate my brother on his deductions – but one of dismay. Were we going to be crouching on some cold, damp rocky headland at midnight in order to see who was collecting whom? Was this really necessary? Could Walter not manage it alone? But I had misjudged him, as perhaps I had misjudged him several times before.

'Don't worry,' he said. 'We're not going to be stationed at the Coffee Pot. I want to see what happens in the room with the lamp in the window.'

'Room 320?'

'I fancy so. It has a sea view, so it's ideal for signalling to passing ships.'

I began to understand. The decoded message read: 'When light in room twenty-four collect coffee pot', but its full sense was: 'If you put a light in the window of your room at midnight, then we will collect you from the Coffee Pot' – 'we' being a ship that would send out a rowing boat to the shore. Why Thomas White should have this message on him, however, or why it should be intended for Miss Meakins, was beyond me. I said as much to Walter.

He asked: 'How do we know it was intended for Miss Meakins?'

'Her name was written on it.'

'Anyone could have done that at any time. Didn't you notice her name was written in pencil, while the message itself was written in blue ink?'

I had to admit it had escaped my attention at the time.

'So perhaps,' he continued, 'Thomas White was the recipient of the note, and the words "For Julia" were added after his death.'

'I suppose so,' I said, not following him at all.

We were standing at the end of the corridor on floor eleven, hidden in a niche that had contained a small sofa, which we had moved to make room for us. By risking a glance every now and then, we could see what was happening in the corridor and, more particularly, outside room 320. We had only been in position for a few minutes – my watch showed a quarter to midnight – when I heard hurried footsteps at the other end of the corridor, then voices.

'Have you got the matches?'

'Of course.'

I took a quick look, enough to see Miss Fitt carrying a lamp and Miss Meakins turning the key to room 320. I drew back. As soon as we heard the door click shut, we stepped out into the corridor.

I thought we might stand outside the room and listen, but without any warning Walter knocked on the door loud and long enough to waken the dead, had they been sleeping in the adjoining rooms. He continued to knock until the door was opened by Miss Fitt. Her eyes flashed surprise and anger. Before she could speak, Walter had pushed his way inside. I squeezed in after him. The door slammed to.

The room was dimly lit by moonlight. By the window, beyond the end of the bed, stood Miss Meakins. Her hand was on the chimney of the lamp, which she had set down on the table between the open curtains. A box of matches lay beside the lamp. All this I saw in an instant, as if I had taken a photograph of the scene. It is no doubt because I am a practising artist that I can observe things so quickly, but even I am not quite sure what happened next, and in what order. My recollection, however, is as follows.

I believe Walter was the first to speak. 'How delightful,' he said, 'to see you again, Julia, before you leave for home.'

Miss Meakins's face hardened into a mask, as unlike her soft feminine features as imaginable. It was just as this thought came to me that I pitched forward and fell against the lady, almost upsetting the lamp. Someone had pushed me from behind. When I had regained my balance and apologized, I turned to find the door open and Walter gone. We have discussed this many times since. Walter maintains he did nothing except escape during the distraction caused by my unexpected movement, and that it must have been Miss Fitt who pushed me – though why she would wish to do so is not at all clear to me.

Whatever the truth of the matter, Miss Fitt now closed the door and directed upon me the glare of a gorgon. I attempted to look at her with something approaching the tenderness she had hoped for when we had eaten cakes together in Tilly's Tea Room, but with little success.

'What are you doing here?' she barked.

'I ... we ...' What could I say?

'I thought,' Miss Meakins said – a little uncharitably, in my opinion – 'we'd seen the last of you two.'

'I'm afraid not,' I said with a light laugh. 'You see, we saw you come into this room, which we know isn't your room, and we said to ourselves, let's say goodbye to the ladies before they –'

'Poppycock!' cried Miss Meakins. 'Tell us what you know.'

'Know? I don't know what you mean. We don't know anything.'

'Lock the door.'

I watched her aunt, still with her eyes fixed on me, turn the key in the lock. When I turned back, Miss Meakins had a pistol trained on me.

It was as if the Mona Lisa had suddenly sprouted a moustache. Nothing could have seemed so out of place as that weapon in that woman's hand. I was only sorry Walter was not there: it would surely have expunged from his mind any romantic notions he still had about her.

I was so shocked I could not keep my eyes off the gun.

I heard Miss Fitt say, 'Don't hurt him.'

'Oh yes,' Miss Meakins said, 'you've got a soft spot for him, haven't you?'

Her aunt gave a snort. 'No softer than the spot you've got for his brother.'

'That nincompoop?' If only Walter could have been there! He would not believe me, of course, if I reported her exact words to him.

Miss Fitt sprang to his defence. 'That nincompoop, as you call him, decoded the message. If he hadn't done that –'

'Actually,' I butted in, 'it was I who decoded the message.'

Miss Fitt smiled at me. 'Then we are extremely grateful to you.'

'You see,' Miss Meakins said, 'the other one *is* a nincompoop.'

'No, no,' I said, fired up with the brotherly sympathy that was sometimes aroused in me despite myself, 'he may behave a little eccentrically at times, but he has a good brain.'

'But not good enough. I hope he is not going to ruin things tonight with another of his mad ideas.'

'Why,' I asked, trying to sound as naive as I could, 'what are you planning?'

'You know perfectly well,' Miss Meakins said, still pointing her pistol at me, 'or you wouldn't be here.'

'All we know is –' I had gone too far, but it was too late to go back.

'What do you know?'

'Only that you're going to be signalling with that lamp in the window.'

'What else?'

'Nothing else.'

'Why are we signalling?'

'I've no idea.'

'If you've worked out the first part of the message you'll have worked out the second part too.' Miss Meakins smiled at her own astuteness and, most likely, at my stupidity.

'Well ... something about being collected at the Coffee Pot.'

'Yes,' said Miss Fitt, 'but tonight it is we who are going to do the collecting.'

'Don't say too much!' snapped Miss Meakins.

'It'll do no harm. Mr Paget is going to stay here with us while the operation takes place.'

'He is.' Miss Meakins gestured with the gun. 'Sit on the bed and keep quiet.'

I did as I was told.

'And let's hope your fool of a brother doesn't make things difficult for us.'

I silently agreed. Miss Meakins tossed the pistol to her aunt, who caught and held it as though she had been brought up to do so. With her finger on the trigger, she lowered herself into a chair and kept watch over me while Miss Meakins busied herself with the lamp. I noticed that Miss Fitt did not, however, train the gun on me, but held it in her lap. She also gave the briefest of smiles whenever my eyes met hers.

Miss Meakins struck a match, lit the wick of the lamp, adjusted it and replaced the chimney. Soon a strong glow filled the dark space between the curtains, brightly visible to any craft at sea. Miss Meakins dropped the spent match into a small dish on the table.

'We've done all we have to do,' she said. 'Now we wait.'

'How long?' I asked.

'Until the others come.'

'What others?'

'You're far too inquisitive.'

'I'd just like to know what's going on.'

'Unfortunately, we're not in a position to tell you.'

'I see.'

I must have looked severely bewildered or disappointed, because Miss Fitt decided to offer me some consolation. She said: 'You may rest assured, Mr Paget, that your contribution has not been in vain. You have helped to protect the sovereignty of this glorious country of ours.'

'My contribution?'

'That's enough, Sarah,' said Miss Meakins.

Sarah? Was her name not Euphemia?

'I'm sorry,' said Miss Fitt. 'I simply wanted to tell Mr Paget how –'

'Enough! Why does everybody talk so much?' Miss Meakins began to pace up and down between the bed and the window, every now and again casting a glance into the dark outside.

I thought of Edith. What would she say, what would she do if she could see me now: alone in a locked hotel room at midnight with two women and a gun? My imagination ran riot for a few moments before the sound of someone crying ... It was Miss Fitt, obviously upset at the harsh way her niece had spoken to her.

Miss Meakins was quickly at her side. She bent down and kissed her on the cheek, a gesture which Miss Fitt reciprocated. Miss Meakins then placed a hand on her aunt's breast – which I thought was going a little far – and Miss Fitt responded in a similar way, until the two of them were fondling each other intensely, writhing and emitting low sounds of pleasure. They seemed to have forgotten about me.

They stopped as abruptly as they had begun. Miss Meakins went back to the window, and Miss Fitt picked up the pistol which she had laid in her lap during their brief interaction. But she did not point it in my direction, nor did she look at me after that – out of a sense of shame, I like to think.

By now I was completely disabused of any notions I had had regarding the Misses Meakins and Fitt. Two elegant parasol-twirling ladies had metamorphosed before my eyes into a pair of lewd gun-toting crooks. What were they now waiting for? What was going on at the Coffee Pot? If Euphemia was really Sarah, who was Julia?

In the confusion of my thoughts I sank back onto the bed and must have fallen asleep almost at once. When, returning to consciousness, I looked at my watch by the window, it was nearly two o'clock. There was no one else in the room. The lamp had gone. Everything was back to how it had been before – only, of course, it was not. Something had happened in those two hours. But what?

Walter and I had agreed that if for any reason we became

separated that night, we would meet outside the People's Palace and Aquarium as soon as possible thereafter. I rose, brushed myself down, assured myself with relief that the door was not locked, and left room 320 and the Grand Hotel to its habitual state of nocturnal silence.

24

Secrets

Walter was waiting for me outside the entrance to the People's Palace and Aquarium. The short walk from the Grand in the coolness of the night had helped to clear my head, and by the time I arrived at our rendezvous my thoughts were in a much calmer state.

I realized with a shock that this was the place where the whole case had its origin: the disappearance of Thomas White. Now we were there again, nearly two weeks later, hoping to lay to rest our confusion as he had been laid to rest in St Mary's churchyard. In the meantime Walter had narrowly avoided death by falling candelabra, our friend Lancelot had been murdered, and we had been falsely accused by a barmaid. Our temporary valet Bert had turned out to be the killer, at least of Thomas White, and the owner of two extra, alternative identities: Arthur Legard and Old Simon. This much I knew, but how it all hung together was still something of a mystery. If Walter could explain what had been going on that night while I was asleep in room 320 ...

'Where've you been?' he asked.

'You know where I've been.'

'You should have been able to escape, surely. But never mind that now. Let's go for a walk.'

Walter began his narrative as we strode towards Valley Park. 'When you fell against Julia –'

'I was pushed.'

'Or was pushed by her aunt, I took advantage of the situation to make my getaway. As soon as I saw the lamp in the window I knew I was on the right track and they were going to signal to some boat or other. So I hotfooted it down to the harbour, then edged my way into a position from where I could watch any comings and goings at the Coffee Pot.'

Walter paused, making me aware of how quiet the night was. The fountain in Valley Park had been silenced.

I said: 'What happened at the Coffee Pot?'

'It was a dark and stormy night. The waves battered the tiny boat as it struggled to make headway in –'

'Cut the melodrama,' I said. 'Give me the facts. Anyway, the sea was as calm as a millpond.'

'So it was. I was able to crouch behind a large rock and still have a good view. At sea I could make out a ship of some kind with all its lights extinguished. After a few minutes a smaller dark shape came floating towards the shore. The moon gave just enough light for me to see a rowing boat touch the sand in front of the Coffee Pot and a figure jump out and drag the boat up. Another figure stayed seated between the oars.

'What happened next happened at dizzying speed and was over in less than a minute. From nowhere there appeared half a dozen men, who leapt like mountain goats over the rocks towards the boat. They seized the man who was standing on the shore. The man in the boat got out and tried to push it back into the water, but he was soon overpowered.

'During all of this, our old friends Constables Brightman and Rudge were watching from a distance. They didn't intervene, of course. They knew exactly what was going on.'

'Espionage,' I said.

'Excellent, Sidney. What's your evidence?'

'Well, first of all there's the coded message – the sort spies send to one another. And then there's something Miss Fitt said.'

'I don't recall anything.'

'You weren't there. She let it slip tonight while I was being held hostage. It was rather indiscreet of her, but I think she wanted me to know they weren't crooks and that we'd helped to preserve national security.'

'Yes, we've done rather well.'

'Do you know Miss Meakins has a gun?'

'It doesn't surprise me.'

'I was shocked.'

'Someone was shooting in the churchyard that night.'

'And you think it was ...'

'Why ever not? Our two ladies may be on the side of good in the long run, but that doesn't stop them from using violence to achieve their ends.'

'I meant I was shocked a lady was holding a gun.'

'You lead a very sheltered existence, Sidney.'

We had now reached the aviary. The occupants of the cages were all silent, probably asleep. Even the yellow-breasted chat had nothing to say.

'So who was Thomas White exactly?' I asked.

'Possibly a spy working for a foreign government.'

'Who happened to be Miss Meakins's fiancé?'

'I admit that is rather strange.'

'And why did he disappear? Why didn't she just shoot him?'

'Perhaps she did.'

'He was stabbed. On the beach.'

'Was he?'

'You know he was. We were there.'

'It's just an idea I'm getting.'

'Then let me have it too,' I said.

'I'll have to think it through first. But it might explain everything. Time, I think, for some shut-eye.'

We bade farewell to our feathered friends and made our way back to the Grand.

The next morning was our last in Scarborough. We were due to return to London by the early evening train, almost exactly two weeks after we had arrived. At the time of our arrival, I had been looking forward to a restful holiday which would lighten my burdened mind, and I was hoping for the same for Walter. Instead, a paragraph in a local newspaper, catching my brother's eye, had thrust us into the centre of a criminal investigation that had spread like a dark stain over the whole fortnight and taxed our brains to the utmost.

Now, as we stood packing our bags – having lost the services of Bert – I felt myself yearning for some compensation in the form of clarification of the whole affair. We could learn nothing more from the Misses Meakins and Fitt. They had not come down for breakfast, and upon our inquiring after them we were informed they had already departed by a very early train.

For all his masquerading as the Great Detective, Walter was the most likely source of enlightenment. I could not deny he had used what intellectual abilities he possessed to good effect, even if he had not yet penetrated the full mystery of the case. I like to think I had contributed to the solution, such as we had it, but I was baffled as far as the exact details were concerned.

I folded another shirt as best I could (Edith would have been horrified to see it). 'Well,' I said, 'have you had that idea you were getting yesterday?'

'Which one?'

'Something about Thomas White not being stabbed on the beach after all.'

'Oh, that. Yes, it's still forming in my mind. I'm not quite there yet.'

'Tell me when you are, won't you?'

'Of course, my dear fellow.'

As it happened, answers came from a different quarter. There was a tremulous knock on our door, and I admitted Inspector Brasher.

'Good morning, Inspector,' said Walter. 'I'm pleased to see you. I thought you were already knee-deep in the waters of Kent, torturing our scaly brethren.'

'You artists have a very imaginative way of putting things. No, I'm very much still here, as you can see. But you're about to leave, are you?'

Walter beamed at him. 'How very perceptive of you, Inspector. I can see why you have such a reputation.'

'You will have your little joke. May I sit down?'

'Of course.' I shifted a heap of socks from his usual armchair, and he substituted himself for them.

'I've been asked by ...' He paused, clearly wondering whether, having just sat down, he had the strength to stand up again quite so soon, even for his sovereign. He had not. 'I've been asked by the Home Office to communicate with you two gentlemen.'

'That's very good of them,' said Walter, all charm and flattery.

'Goodness doesn't come into it, I'm afraid. Before I say another word I must ask you both to bear in mind the Official Secrets Act.'

'I've never heard of it,' I said.

'Me neither,' said Walter.

'Not many people have. That's why I'm going to tell you about it. The Official Secrets Act 1889 makes it an offence to disclose information which might endanger national security.'

'Good heavens,' said Walter, 'why would we want to endanger national security? And, in any case, what information do we have that could do that?'

'Oh, you have plenty. Though you may not know it.'

'We certainly don't.'

'It appears you've been a little too clever for our country's secret service. The local constabulary haven't been clever enough, but you've gone too far in the opposite direction.'

Walter settled himself on the bed, leaning forward in pleasurable anticipation. 'How do you mean, too clever?'

'All will become clear, Mr Paget. Whatever I say to you now must go no further than these four walls. Is that understood?'

'Fully,' said Walter.

I nodded.

'After all,' Brasher added, 'we don't want a scandal in Scarborough, do we?' He stretched his legs and brushed down his waistcoat with the back of his hand. Slipping the same hand inside his jacket, he withdrew a scrap of paper, to which he referred now and again as he unburdened himself of what he had been briefed to say.

'It was discovered,' he began, '– although in what manner and at what time I am unable to tell you, and even if I were able I would be prevented by the aforementioned Official Secrets Act – it was discovered that an enemy nation – which nation it was I am unable to tell you, and even if –'

'Inspector,' Walter broke in, 'perhaps you could just give us the information you do know and that you are allowed to tell us. We do have a train to catch.'

'My apologies, gentlemen. When does your train depart?'

'In about six hours' time.'

Brasher chuckled. 'Another of your little jokes. But I take your point. Let me see ... where was I?'

'You had just begun to tell us about an enemy nation,' I said.

'Ah yes. It was discovered a little while ago that an enemy nation was receiving highly accurate secret intelligence about the British navy. The exact nature of that intelligence is not our concern, but suffice it to say that the knowledge of it in the wrong hands could have seriously compromised the defence of our coast.

'Our secret service, which of course doesn't officially exist, swung into action. The source of the intelligence reaching the enemy nation was traced to Scarborough, and so several senior operatives were sent here.'

'Miss Meakins and Miss Fitt,' I volunteered.

'I couldn't say,' said the inspector, 'but you may be right. Also the operative who was detailed to eliminate the spy.'

'One Bert, or Albert, Barnes,' said Walter.

'My, you *are* well informed.' Brasher allowed himself a brief nod of admiration before continuing. 'They joined up with several operatives already stationed here.'

'Miss Amy Tranter,' said Walter, 'the barmaid at the Beehive.'

Brasher made no reply to this suggestion, but I noticed he reddened a little.

Walter added: 'And our old friend Lancelot Pemberlow.'

'What!' I cried. 'Lancelot working for the Secret Service?'

'You said yourself he knew all about the murder of Thomas

White. And what do you think he lived on when he hardly sold a painting from one year to the next? His trips to London were not to art dealers but to his handlers. I'm right, aren't I, Inspector?'

'I really couldn't comment. You understand: the Official Secrets –'

'Yes, yes.' Walter sighed and fell back on the bed into his usual relaxed state. 'Please, carry on with your narrative.'

Brasher sniffed, coughed and carried on. 'The spy working for the enemy nation was an Englishman –'

'The swine!' It came out before I could stop myself.

'Your reaction does you credit, Mr Paget. He was indeed a swine, a treacherous swine. It seems he would receive instructions in code through the post and then signal his answers in the Morse alphabet to a ship, using a lamp at his window in the Grand.'

'Room 320, I think,' said Walter.

Brasher made no reply. 'His foreign paymasters realized his cover was blown. They made arrangements to pick him up by boat at night, and sent him a message to that effect. Unfortunately for him, but fortunately for us, the letter with the message inside was intercepted here, at the hotel, and never reached him. All the same, it was thought advisable to eliminate the fellow – to prevent him from causing any more trouble and, it must be said, as a punishment for his treachery.'

'Quite right,' said Walter.

'He was eliminated as you saw – stabbed in the heart on the beach at Cloughton Wyke. Apparently Barnes was ordered to knock the swine unconscious and fling him over the cliff, so it would look like an accident, but some of these Secret Service types get carried away, you know. Think they're acting in a melodrama.'

I said: 'That explains why Lancelot was so angry with Barnes, disguised as Legard, in the churchyard that time. Because Barnes used Lancelot's knife when he shouldn't have, and created a murder scene identical to the one in Lancelot's painting when he didn't need to.'

'But the important thing,' Brasher went on, 'was that you two gentlemen should find the body.'

'Of course!' cried Walter, standing up. He began to pace around. 'How could I have missed it? That's why we were given the photograph.'

'I don't follow,' I said.

'You will. I'll explain later.'

'You seem to have a good understanding of the case,' said Brasher. 'Which makes my task easier.' He straightened a wrinkle in his trousers. 'Barnes was able to lure the spy to the beach with the promise of ... well, whatever it is that two men do that a man and woman normally do, if you take my meaning.'

'Perfectly,' Walter said.

'The spy happened to be that way inclined, so Barnes invented Legard to entice the spy, at Londesborough Lodge and elsewhere. I have a feeling that Barnes was that way inclined too –'

'Oh, I'm sure he was,' Walter added. 'That must be why he was chosen for the assignment.'

'Meanwhile, the secret message was proving difficult. No one in Scarborough could decode it. It was sent to London, where the so-called experts at that sort of thing couldn't make head nor tail of it either. In desperation, the message was given to you.'

'Why?' I asked.

'Well, I'm only reporting what I've been told, but it appears they were impressed by your tenacity. You were supposed to find the spy's body on the beach and then carry on with your holiday, instead of which you decided to investigate the irregularities that cropped up. They thought that if you could solve the murder, as you seemed to be doing, perhaps you could also solve the problem of the coded message.'

'And we did,' said Walter.

'Yes, we did,' I agreed. It would have been churlish to correct him, and I was pleased to see him in good spirits.

'As you found out, the coded message contained details of the arrangements for collecting the spy.'

'Why do you keep calling him the "spy"?' I asked. 'We're talking about Thomas White, aren't we?'

'Who?' said Brasher.

The look of blank amazement on his face rendered me silent, as did the mocking laugh issuing from my brother. Before I could recover and tackle him on the matter, Brasher had hauled himself up and waddled to the door, where he stood a moment with his hand on the knob.

'I think I've said enough.' He returned the scrap of paper to his inside pocket. 'I bid you gentlemen good day.'

'Goodbye, Inspector,' Walter said. 'It's been a pleasure.'

'Goodbye, Inspector,' I echoed.

A smile crept over Brasher's face. 'Call me Bill.' And he was gone.

For a short while we continued packing in silence. I knew Walter would explain things in his own good time, and that time had not yet come. But one question he could perhaps answer.

'Why on earth did Brasher tell us all this if it's supposed to be secret?'

'Precisely for that reason.'

'What?'

'The Secret Service people are aware we know a lot already. By giving us fuller information they hope we will no longer feel the need to investigate, and by citing the Official Secrets Act they effectively stop us from passing our information on to anyone else.'

'Yes, of course.'

'There!' Walter threw the last of his handkerchiefs into his case and pressed down the lid. 'I won't be long.'

'Where are you going?'

'I'd rather not say. Not just yet anyway.'

Left on my own to my confused thoughts, I made slow progress with my packing. Why had the inspector reacted in such a strange way to my mention of Thomas White? He knew who I meant. But why was Miss Meakins – or whatever her real name was – walking out with a spy? I shook my head and removed the hotel antimacassar that had somehow found its way into my case.

Then I too went out.

The headstone was now in place.

THOMAS WHITE
Was Photographed upon a Whim,
And Now That's All That's Left of Him.

A cruel joke to play on a dead man, even if he was a spy. Yet surely there must be something more remaining of him than a photograph, now creased and crumpled in one of Walter's pockets. Memories shared by relatives and friends? Repercussions of his actions? Emotions stirred in those who knew him or who crossed his path?

Here, in any case, lay Thomas White. Had he really been Miss Meakins's fiancé although she knew him to be a foreign spy? She had paid for his funeral, which was to her credit, but she had also paid for this sardonic epitaph, which was not.

And here, next to him, lay Lancelot, with a headstone declaring him to be Old Simon – just that: the name. No epitaph, no dates. I suppose it made no difference to Lancelot in the place where he found himself, but what a sudden and sorry end he had met. His name was now wiped out as completely as he was.

As I turned away from the churchyard and made my way for the last time past Paradise, the gulls on the rooftops set up a shrill keening that accompanied me all the way back to the Grand.

Walter was sitting in room 185, waiting for me.
'Where have you been?' he asked.
I did not feel like talking, and told him so.

25

Departure

It was not until about half an hour into our journey towards King's Cross that Walter, casting aside the yellowback he was reading, decided to divulge his thoughts on recent events in Scarborough.

'So, dear brother, what is it you don't understand?'

Not wanting a lengthy lecture, I started off with a specific question. 'Where does Old Simon fit into it all?'

'Old Simon was one of the incarnations of the operative known as Albert Barnes, apart from Legard and the hotel valet Bert. I take my hat off to him. He was almost my equal as a master of disguise. I fancy he used Old Simon simply as a means of observing people and following events. Of course, Lancelot was angry that Barnes had used Lancelot's dagger to kill the spy, so he got his own back by making things difficult for Barnes: he dragged an unwilling Old Simon into the affair by telling us he was the source of the model. And he *was*, in that Old Simon and the model were the same man. I imagine our barmaid, Miss Tranter, was in on Lancelot's little bit of revenge, and played along with it.'

'The irony,' I said, 'is that Lancelot ended up in Old Simon's grave, so Barnes got the last laugh.'

'He did.'

'I'm sure Lancelot was killed to stop him telling me too much, but who do you suppose killed him?'

'Well, we know Julia had a gun.'

I was dismayed he was still using her Christian name, but I let it go. 'Do you really think that she ...?'

'Why ever not?' I could see from the gleam in Walter's eyes that the idea excited him. I have long thought his taste for sensationalist literature, such as can be purchased at any railway station, is having a deleterious effect on his moral outlook, and this was surely proof of it. He seemed to be taking pride in his acquaintance with a woman who had probably killed in cold blood one of our oldest friends.

I explained that I had gone to the graves in St Mary's churchyard that afternoon and spent some time musing on mortality. 'It's sad,' I said, 'that Lancelot has to lie in another man's grave.'

'At least *we* know where he is. The slops think he's done a runner. Anyway, he's in good company. His grave is next to Thomas White's.'

'So?'

'With another misnamed headstone.'

'What do you mean?'

'Exactly what I say.'

'But Thomas White's in there. You said yourself there was a body in the coffin when you helped to lower it.'

'Oh, there is. Only it's not Thomas White's body.'

For a moment or two I could not speak. The clatter of the train's wheels obliterated everything in my mind before I was able to get out: 'Then whose body is it?'

'I don't know his first name, but his surname is Smith. Or, at least, that was the name he was going by when he was murdered at Cloughton Wyke.'

I admit, rather ashamedly now, that I could make no sense out of what Walter was saying. My face must have betrayed as much.

'You looked bemused, Sidney. Whereas everything is as plain as day. Mr Smith was the spy. He was staying in room 320, remember? His name was in the hotel register. You pretended to faint so that –'

'Yes, yes.'

'Barnes, or Mr Legard, was able to use room 320 as often as he wanted once he had established friendly relations, shall we say, with Smith. That's why there were so many clothes in it.'

'Well if Smith is the spy, where is Thomas White?'

'Nowhere.'

'What? How can he be nowhere?'

'He is nowhere because he doesn't exist, and never has done. A whim is all that's left of him.'

My whole body ran cold as I listened to my brother. It was as though I was being made, very much against my will, to turn into a complete stranger with different ideas from my own.

'Things have not been what they seemed,' Walter continued. 'People too. It's shameful that we – artists – who are supposed to see things clearly, should have let our vision become clouded. We did not look for ourselves and we did not look closely enough. We accepted what we were told without question. But had either of us seen Thomas White before he disappeared? Had anyone? Is there the slightest sliver of evidence that Julia ever knew anyone of that name?'

'But she said ... and Miss Fitt said ...'

'Precisely.' He clasped his hands together and leaned back slightly, like a vicar about to deliver a sermon. 'We've been led on a pretty goose chase ever since we got here, Sidney. They needed someone to search for the non-existent Thomas White who had supposedly disappeared from the People's Palace and Aquarium, and we turned up. The trap is then sprung. Barnes, who has been chosen for the job in Scarborough because he bears more than a passing resemblance to the spy, makes himself look even more like Smith and has his photograph taken. I have no reason to believe that Mr McNair was anything other than an innocent bystander. The police, who would have been the ideal choice, show little interest in the case, so when we appear on the scene the two ladies – secret service operatives from London, remember – are delighted. We are their witnesses. We take our walk along the coastal path at the suggestion of Barnes, who gets ahead of us and kills Smith. When we find the body we naturally take out the photograph and, since the dead man's features closely resemble those in the photograph we assume he is Thomas White and make no complaint when he is identified as such by the ladies. Altogether a very clever plan, showing great knowledge of human nature. What they didn't reckon on, unfortunately for them, was *our* nature. We didn't relinquish the case, as we were supposed to do, but kept on getting in their way.'

'If we *had* stopped after finding the body on the beach, and had a holiday instead, Lancelot would still be alive.'

'True. But we also wouldn't have decoded the message and helped protect our country. Perhaps we have saved many lives.'

I had to admit the truth of this. It went a long way towards soothing my conscience. I lay back and closed my eyes, allowing all the pieces of the puzzle to fall into their respective places. It took a while, but at last I was able to relax a little and enjoy the passing landscape in all its sun-dappled brightness: the shining river, the patchwork colours of the fields, the trees like huge sticks of charcoal as they flashed by. Yet there was one thing more I wanted explained to me.

I asked: 'Where did you go this afternoon?'

'Oh, nowhere special.'

'I've told you where I went.'

'Very well. I went to get this.' He brought out a photograph and handed it to me. I found myself looking at a smiling Miss Meakins, who was gazing straight back at me and looking lovelier than ever.

'Mr McNair is an astute businessman,' Walter said. 'He knew the picture's worth and insisted I pay it.'

I turned the photograph over. The name Miss J. Meakins was written in pencil. It struck me that we had been here before. Miss Meakins was no more her name than Thomas White's had been that of Albert Barnes. Another person pretending to be someone they were not.

'McNair took it for that painting Lancelot did of all those promenaders outside the Spa.'

Walter's face had taken on a wistful but not unhappy look. I decided not to tell him about the woman-to-woman intimacies I had witnessed in room 320. The likelihood was that he would never see Miss Meakins again, so to dispel his fantasies would have been nothing short of cruel, and I am not a cruel person, whatever else might be said about me.

I handed back the photograph. 'Can I have the one of Thomas

White – I mean Albert Barnes?'

'Of course. We have no further use for it now.' He gave me what had become a torn and crumpled mess, with patches missing from the poor man's face.

'May I?' I asked.

'Feel free.'

I ripped in two the photograph that had given us so much trouble, then in two again, and again, and again. Stretching up and pulling open the tiny window, I released the pieces into the air, where they tumbled briefly like injured birds before being borne away on the smoke from the engine. Then I settled back to indulge in a light doze for the rest of the journey.

I was jolted awake by a thought which had started as a nagging at the edge of a dream before exploding into full consciousness.

'Just a minute,' I said.

'Yes?' Walter was wide awake.

'Why should the Secret Service go to all that trouble of pretending that first Barnes and then Smith were Thomas White? Why not just bump Smith off?'

'Because Thomas White is the best hiding place imaginable. No one will ever find Smith now, certainly not his paymasters. You see, Sidney, when you take on another's identity you eradicate all trace of your former self.'

And with that he reached into the bag beside him. 'When I was out this afternoon I bought this. I hope you approve.'

He placed the brand new deerstalker on his head and sank back into his seat with a sigh.

What could I say? What could I do?

I took out my sketchbook and pencil.

Epilogue

We resumed our artistic lives in London. Edith was delighted to see me again, and I her. My tanned skin, together with the series of postcards I had sent, told of the wonderfully relaxing holiday I had spent on the coast. About the events in which we had become entangled I breathed not a word.

When my wife asked after Walter, I was able to say he was a little better. For he *was* better, at least for a few weeks after our return. He was almost serene, so pleasant was he in manner and conversation, although I could detect a rumble of dissatisfaction beneath the surface. He was undoubtedly buoyed up by his successful investigation of the case. At the same time, what bothered him, as it bothered me, must have been the death of Lancelot. On top of this, I caught him several times mooning over the photograph of the deadly Miss Meakins.

History must judge whether, in taking Walter to Scarborough that summer of 1899, I exacerbated tendencies already visible in him. I can only say that my intentions were good, and that if chance had not thrown the Thomas White business in our way, then I believe my brother would have recovered a sense of normality. Should I have discouraged him from getting involved in the case more than I did? Would my discouragement have had any effect? Did I set a bad example by allowing myself to be drawn in? These are questions to which I have no answers. I leave it to the reader to supply his or her own.

In the meantime, Walter lives out an artist's existence which, as far as I can tell, is relatively blameless. Of course, I am not his keeper, but I will always try to use my experience as an older brother to guide and advise him, to the best of my ability. I saved him from the sea at Cromer many years ago, and go on saving him I must, if necessary, in all the years to come.

This narrative is closely based on real events. I am mindful of the Official Secrets Act, and have made small changes to preserve national security. In particular I have changed all names apart from those of Walter and myself. Whether the powers that be consider this to be enough to avoid identification, I cannot at present say. If you are reading this, then presumably they do; or at least they have not thought it wise, for whatever reason, to attempt to prevent publication.

In real life Lancelot had an even more outlandish name. Now the poor fellow has none but Old Simon – itself not the actual alias used by Barnes, who was not in reality called Barnes. The Misses Meakins and Fitt exist, but not under those names or anything like them. Not Inspector Brasher, but another inspector, can be found fishing the rivers of Kent. In other words, the people we encountered during our eventful fortnight in Scarborough are all real; only their names are not.

Sherlock Holmes, of course, is entirely imaginary.

Printed in Great Britain
by Amazon